"The story of these women touched the deep places in my heart. The threads of God's grace are evident in this story, weaving together women of strength and devotion who, above all, need the gift of grace. An exceptional read and one that will live with me long after I close the book."

—*Jaime Jo Wright*, best-selling author of *The House on Foster Hill* and *The Reckoning at Gossamer Pond*

"*Swimming in the Deep End* is a heart-touching tale of four women who have each suffered the wrenching loss of a child. With a rare warmth and Christlike attitude, Nelson unfolds their personal tragedies and taps into our souls as unbridled emotions and past wounds spill out of these characters' lives into our own. They must work together to surmount impossible challenges, and their inspiring selflessness is all for the good of an innocent child. A moving read guaranteed to evoke sad as well as happy tears, you won't soon forget this book!"

—*Marilyn Rhoads*, president of Oregon Christian Writers

PRAISE FOR CHRISTINA SUZANN NELSON

"If you love discovering new authors with a lyrical, literary voice, then you're in for a treat. If you like those voices to also deliver a powerful, engaging story with true emotional depth, then you're in for a feast. Highly recommended."

—*James L. Rubart*, best-selling author of *The Five Times I Met Myself* and *The Long Journey to Jake Palmer*

"A tension-filled tour de force of suspense and human emotions."

—*Library Journal*, starred review

"Nelson skillfully draws readers into character emotions in a way that sets us up for what lies ahead. . . . [Her] storytelling is a gift to her readers."

—*Cynthia Ruchti*, author of twenty-two books, including *A Fragile Hope*

"Christina writes with an unpretentious poetry and finesse that charmed me from the first page to the last. . . . Beautifully raw. Elegantly real. Simply stunning."

—*Camille Eide,* award-winning author of
The Memoir of Johnny Devine

"Christina Suzann Nelson is a writer to watch!"

—*Deborah Raney,* author of Christy Award finalist
Home to Chicory Lane

CHRISTINA SUZANN NELSON

Swimming in the Deep End

Kregel
Publications

Printed in the United States of America
18 19 20 21 22 23 24 25 26 27 / 5 4 3 2 1

This book is dedicated to the women
who chose to mother me,
and to the women
who chose me to be a mother.

Chapter 1

JILLIAN CLINE

FRIDAY, MARCH 9

The air in the spectator area of Brownsburg High's swimming pool is nothing short of heavy, but there's a safety in the thickness. An illusion in the midst of the humidity lulls me into a belief that my daughter is safe, protected from the evil in the world. Maybe that's why I push her to compete. Maybe that's why I can breathe in the moisture-rich environment other mothers dread.

Izzy stands on the dive block, her toes curled over the edge, her arms wrapped around her middle as if she's cold. The horn blows and with a fraction of hesitation, she dives.

And the race begins.

The first in weeks, a postseason meet, and for some reason veiled to me, she didn't want to participate.

Five rows of girls stretch, skimming through the water toward the wall to make their final turn. A swimmer in the lane closest to me botches her flip, a beginner's mistake. Water splashes me, tickling through my hair and down my scalp. It's the kind of flaw Izzy conquered in elementary school. At the flash of memory, an ache settles over my heart. Where has my little girl gone? In a little more than a year, she'll be off to college.

I can't help it. My legs lift me from the bench, and I lean toward the bar separating the fans from the racers.

After ten laps, they're all tired, but this is the point my daughter is famous for, the moment Izzy stands out above the other athletes. Any second she'll burst forward with an explosion of power like a dolphin racing a school of tuna, and she'll leave the competition in her wake.

But Izzy doesn't make her move.

"Come on." I lean farther over the rail, my words echoing around my head.

One swimmer, then another, slip ahead of my daughter, the reigning state champion and future Olympian. A hand slaps the wall, and a second, then Izzy's.

Third.

Stepping back, I extend my fingers now aching from the tense way I've gripped the bar. I'd been a fool to think this bug Izzy's been fighting would run its course. I should have taken her to see Dr. Wheaton weeks ago. What if something is seriously wrong? A girl in the middle school has leukemia, and another child was recently diagnosed with diabetes. The blanket of muggy air can't push away the cold shiver that comes with a mother's worried heart.

Izzy bobs in the water as the other swimmers hop out of the pool and chatter with teammates. Her pain is mine. A possession I can't give away even if I want to.

I collect my jacket, phone, and the romance novel I've been reading during every event my daughter didn't race. The book fits perfectly into the pocket along the side of my purse. With everything collected, and the strap flung over my shoulder, I wipe at the moisture on my forehead and move toward the door alongside fifty other parents.

"Can't win them all, I guess."

I don't have to look to recognize Jasmine Monk's screeching voice.

A knot tightens in my stomach, pressing up against my diaphragm. No, Izzy can't win them all, but she didn't have to lose against certain people's daughters. I paste on a smile, force my shoulders into a non-defensive position, and twist to meet my rival face-to-face. "I suppose you can't. Joanna swam well today. It's good to see her improving."

"Improving?" Jasmine plants one bony hand on her hip. "She beat Izzy.

That's a first. No offense, but Izzy probably needed a loss more than a win anyhow. We wouldn't want her thinking she's perfect." Her serpent's tongue sticks on the last word.

Why do so many people preface insults with phrases like *no offense?* My cheeks burn with the effort required to maintain a pleasant exterior. "No one ever said Izzy was perfect." I bite down hard on the inside of my cheek to stop the next words from pushing their way free. There's no sense irritating Jasmine. It's not like she's someone who can be ignored. Not only do we have daughters the same age, but Jasmine's son is one of my son Zachary's best friends. Jasmine may lack compassion and tact, but she does a wonderful job managing the women's ministry at church.

Reasoning my way through all the consequences of giving Jasmine the tongue-lashing I long to give her isn't enough to settle my heart rate. "I'm afraid I've got to run. There's dinner to get on the table as soon as Izzy's ready to go." I turn, pointing my mouth safely away from her.

"I'll be at the church in the morning. I assume you have those flyers all printed."

My spine shoots ramrod straight. Without looking, I can imagine Jasmine's right eyebrow cocking up in the way it does when she feels she has me under her thumb. I swallow another line of ill-chosen words. No way I'll fess up to not having Jasmine's request completed.

Cold slams me as I swing open the door and step into the crisp wind. Winter held on for an encore this year. I duck my head and walk the ten steps to the school's back door.

A group of swimmers dressed in warm clothes, their hair still hanging in wet mats, come from the locker room.

Echoing clicks accompany my heels along the blue and yellow linoleum tiles, a tacky choice even if they are the school colors. I hesitate at the display cases filled with trophies and plaques, some of which are engraved with my daughter's name, Isabella Cline. My gaze drifts along the metallic shine of past victories and lands on a framed newspaper article. Only a junior and Izzy has won the state championship in not just one, but *three* events. She's in line to be valedictorian next year, and she's been given the opportunity to train with an Olympic-level coach for the summer. Maybe she isn't perfect, but my daughter is close.

I lean against the wall, my lower back aching for the day to be over and my mind begging for just one more chapter. Parents greet athletes with congratulatory hugs or sympathetic pats on the back. One of Izzy's classmates, a new driver, twirls a key ring around her finger.

The baseball team bursts through the steel doors at the end of the hall. Chunks of sloppy mud fling free from caked cleats and splatter the tiles. The pungent scent of wet earth mixed with teenage boy takes the pleasant feel from the moment and replaces it with dread.

There in the middle of the group, strutting as though he is more than he ever could be, is Travis—star baseball player with more than just a few problems at home. He flicks his head, throwing his almost black hair away from dark eyes. For a girl with such great grades, Izzy isn't too smart when it comes to choosing boys. While I admit he's a great deal better than his parents, he's still not the hero in my Izzy's story.

Familiar tension squeezes my muscles. When will she listen to me?

I tug the cell phone from my pocket and check the time. Four more swimmers exit the building as the baseball team disappears into the boy's locker room, their smell lingering behind.

The hallway transforms in the silence, leaving my skin chilled. I run my arms into my coat sleeves and shove my cell phone into the pocket on the outside of my purse. Could Izzy have gone by while I was lost in my imagination?

I push the locker-room door open and walk between institutional rows of stacked yellow lockers. The stench from the fusion of chlorine and industrial cleaners burns my nose, as water trickles across the cement floor toward the lowest point and a metal drain.

Izzy sits on a bench in the center row, head in her hands, elbows pressed into her towel-covered thighs. Her shoulder blades stand out at sharp angles and her dark brown hair hangs in a clump of wet curls. She seems thinner, fragile.

My mother's heart melts. Sinking onto the bench, I slip my arm around my daughter.

Izzy's body flinches. Her chin shoots up, and she pulls the towel tight around her chest.

"I'm sorry, Iz. I didn't mean to startle you." I run my fingers through her wet hair, untangling a wad of curls. "It's one silly race. Nothing to worry about. There will be others."

Eyebrows pressed together, Izzy opens her mouth as if to speak, but remains silent. Her eyes are red at the rims, circles from her goggles still etched into her tender, fair skin. After a pause, she nods. "Sure. No big deal."

"Let's get home and have a yummy dinner. There's Italian chicken in the Crock-Pot, your favorite."

Color drains from Izzy's face. She turns away.

"What's the matter?" I lean forward, arms crossed on my knees. "Are you feeling okay?"

"Just tired." She stands and pulls her clothes from the locker then threads her feet into sweatpants.

"Aren't you going to take off that wet suit?"

Izzy shakes her head. At that moment, the towel slips from her grip and cascades to the wet floor. Izzy lunges for her sweatshirt.

Cold, like ice water, washes through my veins and sends a chill down my arms that leaves my fingers numb. I look away. I can't help it. Maybe it was the angle, or maybe . . . I can't even finish the thought.

No.

I must be wrong.

The change, so slight only a mother would notice.

Izzy can't be pregnant.

*　　*　　*

The Crock-Pot insert slips from my soapy hands, the first realization that I've forgotten to put on the purple latex gloves I always wear when washing dishes. It thunks into the side of the porcelain sink then settles to the bottom, and a faint break of glass is muffled by water.

Moments tick by as I procrastinate, rolling my head back and forth against the death grip my neck muscles hold on my spine. So much like what I'm doing with my daughter who picked at her dinner and now hides behind the barricade of her bedroom door. Maybe it would be better not to know what's shattered below the surface.

Zachary brushes past me and swings the refrigerator door open.

"What are you searching for?"

He doesn't look up. "I'm starved. What do we have to eat?"

Crumbs decorate the dining room table, evidence of a task I haven't yet checked off my post-dinner list. "We just ate."

He straightens, one hand on the open door, and shrugs. "I'm hungry."

"Here." I break a banana from its bunch and place it in his hand.

Lines furrow his forehead. He's disappointed in his bounty.

He complains that he's shorter than his friends, but I can see the growth spurt has begun. Soon he'll be tall and broad like his father. Too soon. Already Zachary's boyish face is transforming with the sharper features of a man.

A cold shiver freezes my blood and stops my breathing. What have I done to my children? Are they about to come face-to-face with the consequence of my sin? Why had I ever pretended I could outrun my past?

"What?" He's caught me staring.

"Have you finished your homework?"

The corner of his lip lifts into a snarl. "Math is killing my creative spirit." He sighs with a depth that reminds me of a Shakespearean play, then walks away toward the family room.

I nod and turn back to the sink. It's time to face whatever is fractured under the cloud of bubbles.

Sliding my hand through the water, I pull the plug and the soapy surface slides down the sink wall, revealing the shattered edge of my favorite teacup. I don't even remember putting this prized possession into the suds.

A tear slips down my cheek, and I swallow back sobs. An overreaction, but emotion knows no rationale. I pile the broken shards on my palm. Their ragged edges mirror the condition of my heart.

Behind me, her breathing gives her away. It's the kind of slow, purposeful breaths that tell me she doesn't want me to know she's there. As if traveling a moment behind her, the coconut scent of her shampoo floats over me, but I still don't turn. Now isn't the time to face my daughter. Not with the tears cascading over my cheeks and the brokenness of my past so raw and in the open.

Her soft steps round the corner and the door to her room swishes over the carpet.

I breathe again.

Taking one last look at the hand-painted rose and gold-lined rim, I tip my palm and let the pieces drop away like dreams into the trash.

The last connection to my mother is gone. The only beautiful reminder of life before our ugly ending, destroyed. If I had it to do over again, what would I change?

Probably nothing.

◆ ◆ ◆

Light reflects off the wet blades of grass sparkling in the glow of the streetlamp. Swaying forward and back, the hem of my purple, ankle-length robe, the one Izzy bought for me with her own money a couple Christmases ago, rubs across the tops of my feet like the edges of grabbing ocean waves. My gaze drifts away from the place where the porch light brings the night into focus and out into the darkness.

I've seen him out there before, a figure masked by darkness, sneaking to my daughter's window. And I didn't stop him because I was afraid of how our different feelings about Travis were tearing our relationship apart. I was afraid I would be alone again, without a mother or a daughter.

Instead of dealing with the issue directly, I gave them a few minutes, then made noises in the hall. He always disappeared.

Anger licks my cheeks and lights a bonfire in my chest.

I should have slashed his tires, smashed his precious windows.

I choke on a sob and my regret.

Can't Izzy's situation be just another one of my nightmares?

These memories have been packed away and hidden in the basement of my mind. It's where I put them to rest, and where they were supposed to stay. But, like it was yesterday, the moment from twenty-three years earlier crawls out of its box and attacks.

My pain is true and real, but now, through the heart of a mother, it burns deeper, spreads wider, takes over every cell in my body. It's too late. The carefully covered wound is torn open, and my shredded heart is vulnerable to the flames.

There's no way out.

No escape.

My mother told me I had a choice, but it was a choice she made for me. It wasn't a moment of empowerment but of handing over my independence. She did this to me, and I can never forgive her.

I can tell myself lies all night, but they won't blur the pictures that scald my mind every time my eyes close. Izzy's thin figure didn't cover the telltale rounding in her abdomen, the slight curve over the tips of her hip bones. How have I missed the signs?

We taught her better than this, but what can we expect from a boy like Travis Owens, son of a drunken father, brother of a crook. And a mighty fine actor.

Biting my lower lip, I scold myself for falling for his show. I'd believed he cared for my daughter, believed he might be different.

How could he do this to my Izzy?

The light switches on behind me. Grabbing my robe, I pull it tighter around my chest.

"There you are. I'm about packed. You ready for bed?" Garrett's duffel bag drops by the front door with an all too common thud.

Turning, I glare at the camo sack and military boots. Another of his monthly Guard weekends. They creep up and attack at the worst times.

"I know." He pulls me into a hug, the warm scent of Irish Spring clinging to his body. "It's only two nights, then I'll be back. At least I'm not deployed." His chin taps the top of my head as he nods. "Could be worse."

I pull back. Could it really? My mouth opens and I try, really try, to tell him everything, to unload years of lies and the new sorrows, but the gentle curve of his mouth, that look of a proud father who hasn't yet been shot with the truth . . . I can't destroy him tonight. There's no harm in waiting until he comes home. Until I've confirmed what I already know. Until I can't shove the past into the closet any longer.

There's no harm in a secret.

Chapter 2

Izzy Cline

I didn't want to swim today. Why can't I, just for once, be a normal teenager? No pressure. No expectations. Why can't everyone just back off and give me a break for a change? I never wanted to be perfect, just normal. No one ever bothers to know who I am, except Travis, and even he's been pulling away, or maybe it's me.

I sit against my bedroom door. The image won't leave my mind. Mom standing at the sink, her broken cup in her hand, her shoulders slumped.

It's only a second until tears choke my own throat, bringing with them the burn that comes from fighting to keep them back. My chin quivers and my chest tightens. I don't want to care about what this will do to her. I've got my own problems. And they're huge.

I shake my head. What's *wrong* with me? I'm not one of those girls who bawls about her troubles. But then again, maybe the girl I am now *is* that kind of girl.

The few bites of Italian chicken with thick, spicy cream cheese gravy sit like rocks at the bottom of my stomach.

It's time.

I hold my cell in shaky hands and my vision is a total blur, but I manage to type out a text to Travis. *I need to talk to you.*

In a flash, his answer pops onto my screen. *What's up?*

I need to see you. Can you come over? I have to talk with him before Mom starts telling me what to do.

Now?

Yes. But not to the door.

Hmmm. What do you have in mind?

I just want to talk.

Iz, if you want to argue about that again, I'm not coming. I've already said I'm sorry. But it isn't just me.

We have a bigger problem.

This time his response isn't so quick. I've shocked him, and I don't even care.

The lump in the back of my throat grows, reminding me I am still alive. For now.

I'll be there in ten minutes. Keep the window open.

I tap my finger on the screen, but don't reply. What can I say?

Instead, I stand and pull my favorite teddy bear off the shelf, where he's collected dust, then click off the lamp. The glow from my computer monitor and the streetlight outside my window are enough to see by. I drop onto the mattress. If only I could disappear into the blankets and never return.

The window is still closed, but I listen for his tap with a mixture of dread and anticipation. How can I ruin his life like this? How can I ruin my own?

A knock at my door freaks me out, and I breathe deep through my nose to fight away the urge to puke. Thrusting my feet under the blankets, I pull the bedding up to my chin. "Come in."

In the light of the hallway, my dad looks older, tired. And he doesn't even know yet. "Isabella, are you okay? You didn't eat much dinner."

"Yes, I'm just exhausted. Good night, Dad." My chest squeezes. Now I'm a liar too. I cover my head in the blankets with only my eyes staring out. The voice in my mind screams for him to leave, to close the door and let me be.

"All right. I'm heading out. Let's spend some time together next week. I miss my girl."

"Sounds good." I bury my head in the pillow, unable to look for another second. My own pain is enough to drown me. How can I do this to my family?

The knob clicks into place, allowing me to open my eyes.

They'll never trust me again.

The tap on the window startles me, and I jump upright, dropping my feet onto the carpet. I squat to the floor, my bent knees smashed up against the baseboard, and I push the window open.

Travis's face glows in the dim streetlight that shines across our corner lot. "I thought you were going to open the window." The harsh whispered words push me back a few inches.

"My dad was here. Wait." Crawling to the door I press my ear to the cold wood.

Nothing.

I reach up and turn the lock, something I've rarely done before now.

Back at the window we stare at each other, but I don't know how to start the conversation.

"Can I come in?"

My gaze sweeps around the room I've called my own since before my second birthday. Dolls still hang over the edge of a wicker basket on the middle shelf of my bookcase. Behind the closet door, tucked into a corner, is the trunk that holds my long-outgrown dress-up clothes. A pile of stuffed animals, a zebra and giraffe among them, look down at me from the woven hammock in the corner. "I'll come out."

Pulling the fuzzy purple blanket from my desk chair, I swing one leg, then the other, out the window and slide the three feet to the ground.

As my feet sink into the soaked bark mulch that surrounds our house, cold seeps into my slippers. A gust of wind flaps the blanket like a cape.

But I'm no hero.

I pull it tighter, forming a barrier between us. A little too late.

"Come on, Izzy. Say what you need to say. I'm cold."

A striped cat runs across the street and leaps onto the neighbor's fence. Sweeping my gaze up to Travis's eyes, I stall there for a second or two, taking in the last moment before my words change our lives forever. "I'm sorry. I'm pregnant."

A shiver begins at my spine and shakes my body. My breath forms tiny puffs in the air.

Then he touches me. First hesitant, then with both strong hands. He pulls me into himself, surrounding me with his solid arms. "We'll be okay." His hand rubs over my hair, squeezing me tight against his chest. The beats of his heart crash in my ear.

He pulls away and brushes at my tears with the back of his rough thumb. "In a few months, I'll graduate."

Light floods the yard behind him as someone inside our house flips on the porch light. We jump back into the safe shadow of an overgrown bush.

I bite my lower lip then blow out a hard breath. "I'd better go." Holding his chilled face between my hands, I stand on my tiptoes and kiss his cold lips. How can I doubt he's the right guy? Didn't he just prove he is?

His gentle smile makes me want to fold back into his arms and pretend everything will be okay. That he's really the one for me, and we'll be happy forever.

I want to believe it.

Even if it's just for tonight.

◆ ◆ ◆

I wake up feeling just as tired as I was last night.

The full-length mirror hates me. I look like something between a rapper and a bum. From the pile of clean laundry in the corner, I grab Travis's sweatshirt. Three months until summer vacation. I'll never pull off this disguise that long.

Turning to the side, I suck in my breath. If only I wasn't so bony thin.

Water has seeped onto the windowsill where I didn't push it all the way shut last night. I sop up the mess with a dirty T-shirt then toss it back into the full basket. I don't even do my own laundry. How am I supposed to care for a baby?

The sky is gray outside my window. I'm lucky. It's been a long winter. But soon the sun will come out and everyone will strip off their layers. And my body is only going to get weirder. What will I do then?

Maybe I should just give in. I can strut around in a bright-pink tutu and crop top with the words "Another Teen Statistic" printed across the chest.

Heat burns my cheeks, and my skin in the reflection changes, growing pale with red splotches. How could I let this happen?

I press my palms tight into my sides, set my jaw, and look up at the textured ceiling. And God. How could He do this to me? Isn't He supposed to be the God of forgiveness? I screwed up. It was only a few times. I knew I shouldn't do it, and I was truly sorry, but God dropped this on me. So now, instead of another chance, I have a life sentence.

The guilt is immediate. It's not the baby's fault. It's not God's. It's mine. I'm the stupid loser.

I shake my head. This can't really be happening. I need to wake up. There's no way this is my life. Maybe the girls who slink out of school at lunchtime, spending time with their rotating boyfriends. Maybe even the girls who've never been to church, who make snide comments about my Christian values. But not me.

The walls around me shrink, squeezing me in. I have to go . . . somewhere. I grab for a swimsuit, another loss.

Yesterday's meet will be my last for a long time. Maybe forever. I can't continue straining my stomach muscles to sneak quickly into the pool so a crowd can watch the girl who's surely headed to the Olympics come in third.

I lift my shirt and place my hand on the lump that seems to have popped from below my hip bones overnight. Can there really be someone in there? The thought is creepy, like one of those movies Travis loves.

Three months ago, I thought I loved Travis Owens. I thought he was the only man I could spend my life with. The true love God had planned for me. And Travis said the same things to me. Well, not the part about God, but he said he loved me. I liked it. When we talked about the future—about me winning an Olympic medal, and Travis playing professional baseball, and us getting married—waiting didn't seem so important.

We'd never mentioned children, not then or in any other conversation. That was way too far in the future.

For that moment, nothing else mattered. We were only taking a step toward our forever.

Now it isn't a choice. We're tied together for the rest of our lives. And I'm not so sure he's the one. Somewhere along the way, my feelings for Travis started to fade.

Travis Owens is the father of my child. A baby who has no place here. A baby who should be the joy of my life somewhere far off in the future.

I pull my cell from my waistband. He still hasn't returned my text from last night.

The picture on the screen is us, arm in arm at homecoming, like two people who still have a future. All I wanted, my dreams, are slipping away. It's not fair.

Twisting my hair into a loose braid, I tie it at my shoulder, then yank at the neck of the sweatshirt. It's so hot. I can't stand it.

My friend Krista is always willing to shop. I'll pick her up and we'll go to the mall where everything is still normal.

The house is dead-silent. My brother must not be here. I step lightly through the hall and scoop up my mom's keys. Today it's better to ask forgiveness than to risk not getting permission.

"Going somewhere?"

My heart jumps into my throat as I spin around. Still dressed in her purple robe at ten in the morning, my mom grips her blue coffee mug with the snowflake prints. No steam rises from her drink. "I thought I'd go shopping with Krista." My stomach muscles shudder with the strain I automatically put them under.

"Izzy, I told you yesterday we need to talk. I meant it."

I search the room. "Where's Zachary?"

"I sent him to a friend's house for the day."

Tingles flash over my face.

"Sit down." Her tone is not compassionate or angry. It's dull. Almost empty.

"I don't really feel like sitting." My legs shake so hard I'm afraid I'll fall over. I lean on the counter, gripping the edge for support.

Mom stares into her coffee, as if she's waiting for the liquid to give her some sort of answer. Or she doesn't want to see me. "Is there something you should tell me?"

I can't keep looking at her. Turning away, I answer with another question. "What do you mean?" I've only bought myself a second or two, but I'll take it.

"Come on." A chair scratches along the wood floor. "This isn't the right time to play games."

Her hands fold over my shoulders and her cheek rests next to mine. The scent of lilacs always clings to her. When I was a child I'd wake in the middle of the night and call for her just so I could smell the flowery scent and drift back to sleep knowing she was there.

When did I stop wanting my mother's attention?

Hot and deep, the tears gush from my eyes. My shoulders shudder with the sobs until I can get a breath. "What am I going to do?"

"I don't have an answer for you. But we'll figure this out, somehow."

Turning, I stare into her eyes. Even through the blur I see the one thing I didn't expect.

Fear.

Chapter 3

Margaret Owens

The plastic bin pressed between my hip and hand bites into my flesh as I round the corner. At the table just left by three old farmers, I pocket my two-dollar tip, not even ten percent of their bill. Another reminder of my worth. Like the routine of breathing, I stack the sticky plates into a tower. My dark braid falls forward only an inch from a puddle of egg yolk from our famous and personally despised all-day breakfast. As I flip it back over my shoulder, my finger runs across some kind of cold goop. I swallow away disgust and wipe it off on my jeans. Ketchup.

Dishes crash into the tub. Returning to my home base, I heft the tub behind the counter and send it on a ride down the roller belt leading to the dish room. The coffee maker sputters with the final drop from the basket. Pulling the carafe of regular, I make my way down the line, hitting each customer's mug with a fresh shot of energy.

At the end of the row a hand slides over the cup a second before the first drop spills from my pot.

Officer Curtis Hobbs's deep-green eyes meet my gaze, and I shrink.

"How you doing, Margaret?" His round cheeks squeeze into a smile.

Without thought or sincerity, I nod. "I'm good. Is there something I can get you?" How can we possibly chitchat when it's only been two weeks since we met in front of a judge who held my oldest son's future in his hands?

He pulls his palm from the mug. "How about decaf? I've been wound kind of tight lately."

Tight? Not Hobbs. Life has a way of washing over him like rain on a

23

freshly waxed car. But that day in court? He'd been all business then. I can't really blame him. He was doing his job where I'd failed to do mine.

Exchanging the full-force coffee for unleaded, I fill his mug. Steam twirls up, but even the scent doesn't hold the charge of the real stuff.

"You hear much from that Marine son of yours?" He readjusts in his chair, correcting the balance of his belt hung with police equipment.

"Got an email last week. He'll know about his deployment soon."

His fingers wrap around his coffee cup. "How are you with that?"

I turn my back to him, putting a few steps between us, but the something about him I can't place does its work and melts a bit of my tension. He aggravates me that way. This same man dove onto my oldest, Kane, knocking him to the ground and breaking his nose in the process. But he is also the man who'd stopped Kane from making his next bad move.

My throat tightens like it always does when I let my guard down and think about what could have happened next. If the officer behind me hadn't done his duty, my son very well could be sitting in prison, a convicted murderer with no hope for parole. Instead he has five years for armed robbery. Maybe Kane can still get it together and have a life. I sacrificed any chance I had for one so he could live. Doesn't he owe me that?

"Margaret?"

I turn back to Curtis and balance myself with my palms on the counter. "Sorry. My mind tends to wander these days."

His hand covers one of mine for only a second, but the energy in his touch sends shock waves through my nerves. "I'm planning to make the baseball game tonight. Hope you'll be there." He slides a wad of money across the Formica. "That boy of yours is amazing. Heard he's been offered a scholarship. Is that right?"

My lips betray my mind and a grin takes over. I whip my long black braid behind my back, suddenly concerned about the few strands of white. "You heard right. Looks like Travis will be the first Owens man to graduate college."

"You should be very proud. You've done a good job." He pulls his hat from the counter and taps it onto his head. "Hey, we're having a lunch after church tomorrow to celebrate the first year since the big remodel. You should come."

Tired grabs me with powerful claws. "I wish. I'm working the Sunday lunch shift just like every other time you've asked me to church."

"I was hoping, I guess."

I pull a bar towel from the shelf below the counter and wipe at a sticky area where a child ate pancakes earlier. "Why are you always inviting me to your church?"

One half of his mouth tips up. "I like seeing you. You're fun and kind and, well"—his gaze drops to his coffee—"you're pretty."

My hand stops mid-swipe. Is he serious? I'm a mess. A waitress who works more than full-time only to leave this grease pit and clean other people's houses. I have four sons and no husband, and everyone in town knows the details of that derailment. My oldest son is locked up, and my second, Kyle, would be if he hadn't joined the Marines. The youngest hardly steps out of the cave he calls a room. If it weren't for Travis, I'd have given up and died a long time ago. One out of four. Not good numbers in the parenting game.

I try to look into his eyes, but I can't take the sincerity there. "Officer Hobbs, you don't know what you're talking about."

The door jingles. "Hobbs, you ready?" Officer Wade Denning swings a brown bag from his fingers, a bright grin on his face.

"On my way." Hobbs looks back at me. "Newlyweds. You see what I have to put up with." He winks. "See you tonight." He steps from the stool and ambles toward the door.

Before I can watch his tall figure walk past the outside of our picture window, Larry Bromell shoves the door open with his hip and struts to the counter, a large cardboard box in his hands. "Where's Carla? Shouldn't she be out here helping you?"

"She's in the back refilling the ketchups and mustards." And probably talking on the phone with her boyfriend.

"Well, go get her. I've got something for you both." His smile weighs heavy on me. The boss never drops good surprises in the middle of a workday. He doesn't even know what a good surprise looks like.

"I heard you." Carla tucks a loose strand of blond hair behind her ear and shoves her cell phone deeper into the pocket of her too-cute designer jeans. With long, carefree strides, she makes her way to the counter.

Turning my back to Larry, I flash her my best cut-the-attitude stare, but the girl tosses her hair and shrugs her thin shoulders.

Tape screeches from the top of the box, sending cardboard dust into the air and a shiver up my spine. Larry reaches in and pulls out a maroon dress with cream-colored buttons down the chest and an off-white apron.

Carla gasps.

"What do you think?" He doesn't wait for an answer. "These beauties are just what we need to give the joint an old-time diner feel."

An episode from the television show *Alice* flashes before me. Insult to my already injured life. Now I can not only be the source of the town's pity and gossip but I can look the part too.

"No way." Carla settles her fists on her hips. "I'm not wearing that."

"If you want to keep your job, you will." Larry's bushy eyebrows form one long woolly bear caterpillar.

Carla cocks her head, her eyes wide. "If that's what I have to do for this rotten job, I'd rather be unemployed."

Spoken like a girl with no responsibilities and two parents who still pay her real bills and protect her from the world. I keep my mouth in check by tugging my braid hard enough to cause a little pain. She has no idea how lucky she is. I've been taking care of myself since my mother was killed before my thirteenth birthday. As it turns out, men don't have the ability to take care of anyone.

"Your final check will be ready tomorrow."

"Fine." Reaching under the counter, Carla grabs her bag, flings it over her shoulder, and saunters out the door.

"Good riddance." Larry twists, popping his back. "Get the Help Wanted sign in the window."

The second hand ticks around the clock, my chest pounding with reality. "My shift ends in ten minutes."

"Not today, it doesn't."

"But my kid has a double-header. I'm already missing the first game."

He rakes his fingers through thinning hair. "My customers need service. And you, you need this job, so you'd better focus on prepping for the dinner crowd. Carol will be in at five. You can leave as soon as the rush ends."

Strutting out the door, he abandons the box of outdated uniforms.

What's the point of fighting?

◆ ◆ ◆

The door slams, rattling the thin walls of my rented double-wide and sending dust down from the ceiling. The clock says it's past ten, but it's really later. Every battery in this dump is drained, leaving the hands running slow.

Travis stomps into the kitchen and throws open the refrigerator. He grabs the milk and drops the jug onto the chipped counter. Mud covers one side of his blue and yellow varsity baseball jacket.

"Where've you been?" It's a question I'd learned to avoid with my older sons, but Travis is different.

"With Izzy. We got a milkshake after the game."

I slump onto our one stool. Another night with that snob of a girl. No. That's not fair. Izzy has never been downright mean. I'm sure she thinks Travis is too good for the likes of me, a miracle in the muck, and she's right. I can't argue. Travis can't stay blind forever to the horrid failure I am. Eventually, he'll wake up and see the mess he's come from, then walk away from it all. Walk away from me. Isn't that what I'd tried to do? "Take off your coat and let me run it through the wash. You can't go to school that way."

"It'll brush off when it's dry." He yanks a bowl from the cupboard and lets it clank onto the counter. He runs hot, a bit too much like his father.

"That's no way for a college baseball star to talk."

Travis turns, then leans back on the counter, his palms gripping the edge. "What makes you think I'm going to be a star?"

"They don't hand those scholarships out to just everyone, Travis."

Something in his features has changed. Maybe nerves. Maybe something deeper.

He shakes his head. "What if I want to do something else? Did you ever consider that?"

His words yank me upright, bringing me to my feet. I cock my hip and jam my fists into my sides. This will not happen. "I think about it every single day. Don't be a fool, son. We've worked too hard for way too long to walk away now. You have a chance here. Do you want to live like this forever?" I lift my hands and look around the shanty that I skimp and scrape to make rent for each month. Rolled up towels are taped to the base of the back door to keep water from coming in where the seal leaks. A blanket hangs over the front room window in place of curtains. If I only had the time or money, but I have neither.

Travis can have both.

"I know, Mom." His hand is heavy on my shoulder. "It's just, things aren't working out how I thought they would. And this isn't so bad." His mouth tips into a half smile. Travis pulls off his coat, and tosses it onto the counter. He gives my shoulder a squeeze then heads to his room with the cereal box, milk, and his bowl and spoon.

What has that girl done to make him doubt himself like this?

Holding the coat close to my chest, I breathe the earthy scent that always lingers on Travis. The smell means success.

The back door is swollen and I have to tug before it wrenches open. Outside the washer and dryer are protected from the rain, but cold weaves into the uninsulated shed. Once, when it belonged to someone else, this would have been a nice machine. The place where the knob used to be has settings for all kinds of laundry I'll never wash. I lift the white lid edged with rough rust and pull out wet clothes so cold they're nearly frozen. The dryer starts to hum along with an occasional squeak to remind me the bearings are about to give out.

Travis's jacket makes an odd clank when I drop it into the washer. I pull it back out and run my hands into the pockets. His cell phone buzzes against my palm. That was a close call.

The screen glows in the dim light.

Izzy.

My gaze glues on the door separating me from Travis. It's secure enough. I open the text, and as I read my heart pounds. *Thank you for being so wonderful about this.*

About what? I can't help myself. I need to know what's bothering my son. Crouching in the gravel in front of the washer, I scroll through his messages. The taste in my mouth grows sour and rage burns my skin.

No.

There's no way.

Izzy Cline is not going to take Travis's future away from him. He is going to be someone.

My jaw tightens.

This is my chance to make up for what I did to his father, a man who doesn't deserve my pity. But there was a day when even that drunk had a chance. Then he threw it all away to marry me. It didn't take long before he found the bottom of a bottle a more suitable home.

Not Travis.

Whatever it takes, I'll make sure he has a future.

Chapter 4

STACEY FREY

I should be excited. Today is the first day of our great new West Coast adventure. But it's also a Monday, and it feels like a Monday.

Keith turns the key in the lock of our new two-story Victorian. Before he can open the door, I rub my fingertips along the rough lap-board exterior, only a degree lighter than the dirt near the home we left in Tennessee. Up close, the color is darker than I first thought when we pulled up to the curb. The rich green of the yard has a way of muting the hue of the house.

For the last week, my nerves have swung from numb to tingling with pure excitement. Why does numb choose to visit me now?

The door swings open and Keith scoops me into his arms. Like the day we were married, he still steals my breath. "Whoa there." Lacing my fingers behind his neck, I offer him an approving grin, thankful I've resisted the urge to call my mama. This time is for Keith. He deserves my full attention. "We're hardly newlyweds."

"New house. New state. New job." He shrugs. "I'll call you my new wife." He steps into the living room, easing me back to my feet, his arms still circling my waist.

"Very funny." Shaking my head, I splay my fingers on the royal-blue T-shirt stretched across his chest. "You'll have to make do with your original wife."

I step back, leaving the warmth of his arms, and turn a slow circle in the stark-white room. My breath billows into the cold air.

The scent of freshly shampooed carpet and new paint punctuate the room with crisp, clean air unmarked by grief.

The house seems larger than it appeared in pictures from Keith's last of many visits to Oregon. Maybe too large. This is the home we dreamed of. But the life we're living isn't the one either of us imagined.

Stairs climb toward the vaulted ceiling, leading to a landing that looms above us like a judgment.

Three thousand square feet of empty.

Keith has done well for himself and this house is an extension of his success, while the sterility is a magnification of my failure to give him the one thing he asked of me.

I push haunting thoughts back down, refusing to ruin his moment with our reality.

We stop in the family room, Keith's hand weighing heavy on my shoulder.

Two people don't need a family room.

The cold glass chills my palms as I lean close to the French doors. Outside rain drizzles as if the sky is in mourning.

I straighten my pose, committing myself to Keith's happiness. Droplets roll down the climbing vines on a trellis. A garden would fill that space and bring a kind of life to our home. Bobbing my head, I start to envision the beds laid out in patterns, green sprouts bursting from the soil and producing an abundance of vegetables.

"The truck's here." Keith pulls away from me, breaking the spell of the painting in my mind. "Right on time," he calls over his shoulder.

So much for looking around. I haven't even been upstairs yet.

Keith slips out the front door, but I stay in the house, watching from the dry entryway.

Metal clanks and slams as the moving truck's back door rolls open, and three burly men begin to unload our belongings with the efficiency of ants.

Jumping back, I make room for our couch, a worn brown beast that should have been left to die in Tennessee.

"Where do you want this, ma'am?" A stocky blond man with a sticky Russian accent raises his chin to me.

I'm caught off guard with no plan for our home's layout. The rooms seemed different than in the pictures. Now that I'm standing here, I can see I need to rethink. "Y'all can put it over there." With my head, I gesture to the wall. The barren white begs to be covered by color and texture.

The scents of wet and earth and hardworking men quickly overpower the clean fragrance. Keith leads two box-toting movers up the stairs.

This house is truly beautiful. My mood takes another rapid shift, and I can't wait to see every square inch. I jog up the stairs and through the door to the master bedroom. There must be twice the space here as we had in Tennessee. The window looks down into our neighbors' yards. Evidences of children litter the grass. Trampolines and swing sets as well as a couple playhouses. This is a family neighborhood, children in every home.

Except ours.

From here I can see the bare dirt where play equipment was removed.

I shiver, trying to console myself with the extra garden space.

Keith's warm hands wrap around my shoulders. His silence speaks all the answers I need to hear.

A loud sniff breaks into our quiet moment. "Which room will be the nursery?"

I whip around, something in me ready to fight.

The oldest of the three movers stands in the doorway holding a cardboard box, the edges worn from being shifted from one cubby to another, the word "baby" scrawled across the side.

"The basement. Those go in the basement."

His forehead wrinkles. "You don't have a basement, ma'am."

Keith steps in front of me, ushering the man into the hall. "The room next to ours seems logical. Let's put that stuff in there."

Wrapping my arms around my middle, I can't stop the vivid images of the way the nursery used to be. The giraffe and monkey decals bringing the room to life. The crib pushed against the sky-blue wall. The mobile spinning with bright colored frogs over the bed that should have held our baby.

Like a flood, memories sweep over me, pressing me down with their power.

The call. The baby coming. Rushing to the hospital to see our son come into the world.

His cry.

His tiny hand gripping my finger.

The pride in Keith's eyes.

And the scream.

I wipe my hands over my face. Two years. Why does it still feel so fresh?

Keith steps back into the room. He stands toe-to-toe with me, my upper arms secure in his grip. "It's time we move on."

"I can't." My lungs squeeze tight as if pressed in a vise grip.

"Can't, or won't? Stacey, you know I love you with every bit of me. This is where we start over. We can't continue living like this."

"Losing a baby is not a little thing. How am I supposed to believe it will be different this time? I don't have the capacity for that much hurt." Anger and guilt collide in my chest. How can I deny him what he wants more than anything else? But how can I take the risk again? So many things can go wrong.

"You know I don't have the answer. Please, let's give this another try." Frustration wavers on the edge of his eyes.

"I can't forget him."

"No one's asking you to. I want you to make room for someone new." His mouth quirks into a sad smile. "What do you say? Will you think about it? Pray about it even?"

The tips of our shoes touch as I drop my head onto his chest. Drawing in the warmth of his scent, I allow my body to soften into his. "I'll think about it. And I will pray God makes it obvious if you're right about this." Grabbing handfuls of his cotton shirt, I pull in tight to him, tasting the familiar saltiness of my tears.

◆ ◆ ◆

Both my hands grip the shopping cart handle. I'm like Charlie Brown in the grocery store, always picking the one with the wobbly wheel. Other shoppers mill around, their carts easily maneuvering in the directions they're pointed. But me, no, I tough it out with this beast.

Pulling to a cockeyed stop along an aisle filled with shampoo and conditioner, I tug a list from my back pocket. We lack even basic staples in our new home, only a box of granola and last night's leftover pizza. Everything else we left with my sister in Tennessee. I'll start with flour and sugar, if I can find them.

The store spreads out in all directions, a maze without a map. This could take a while. Gearing myself up for another battle with the cart, I take the next turn. My arm burns with the effort to stay straight, then I lose my grip and the willful brute slams into a display of bottles, pacifiers, and sippy cups. This isn't just a buggy in need of repair. This thing is out to get me.

It's personal.

Dropping to one knee, I pick up the items and begin replacing them on their proper hangers. The candy bar I'd planned for a post-shopping treat is no longer tempting.

"Let me help you with that."

A shiver runs along my spine and down my arms. I look up at the first person who's spoken to me since Keith left for the office hours earlier. She reminds me of a woman I knew in our old church in Tennessee. Her curly salt-and-pepper hair is cut in a spicy style and her eyes sparkle as if they're reflecting her silver tresses. A long skirt flows down to her ankles in various colors with a modest smattering of sequins giving her the flare of a fairy godmother.

She picks up a pink bottle and threads it back onto the metal bar. "I've had that cart before. It's a doozy."

"Thank you." A week's gone by without a face-to-face conversation with another woman. Moving across the country seemed like a way to escape the sorrow, but I'm finding the loneliness to be a burden of its own. "I'm new here. Just moved in down the road." I turn to point in the direction of my house, but I have no idea which way that would be from inside the store.

"Welcome to town. Are you finding your way around okay?" The skin around her eyes crinkles with her warm smile.

"No. Honestly, I'm a small-town girl. I thought living outside Portland would be similar, but it's not. The city sprawls out everywhere. It's confusing. Do you live in this neighborhood?"

"Sure enough." She points to her cart, laden with baby clothes, all tagged with bright orange clearance tags.

"I don't understand."

She laughs. "I live at A Child's Home. It's right around the corner."

A headache brews behind my eyes. Something feels wrong. Feels dangerous.

"You should come by. Get to know the girls. We're always looking for volunteers and it's a great way to connect with people."

There it is. I finally meet someone and there are expectations attached. "What do you do there?"

"It's a home for girls who've found themselves with unplanned pregnancies. We provide a place to live, healthy food, education, and support while they make some very hard decisions."

Britney's tear-streaked face clouds my vision, her cries deafen me. Or are they mine? Our grief is so twisted together, untangling the threads of pain is impossible.

"Do you have children?"

No matter how I answer this question, I'm a liar. "No." You can't adopt a baby who isn't alive, even if his death took a slice of your heart and left you with arms that can never be filled.

The woman reaches out and touches me. Her hand is warm and soothing. "I'm sorry."

Can she see my thoughts? Are my memories so vivid a stranger can see the scene my mind plays out? "What?"

"You're grieving. Maybe it's because of my job, or maybe it's God jabbering in my ear. I see a lot of women who are hoping to adopt and a lot who are looking for answers."

"A Child's Home is an adoption agency?"

"No. We provide for the needs of the girls and we listen. Some choose to place, some to parent. We're right beside them, no matter which they choose. There's a caseworker from a local agency who comes in and helps to facilitate adoptions."

I rub the wrinkles out of my grocery list and prop it on the child seat.

"Let me give you my card." She fumbles around in her purse and produces a rectangle. Taking my hand, she places the paper on my palm and holds it there. "This is a big place, easy for someone to get lost, or feel alone. Call me if you need anything, even an ear to listen." She gives my hand a squeeze then lets go.

I nod, torn between flight and defeat. "Thank you." My eyes scan the writing. *Irene Smith.*

Before I can decide how to react, she's turned her cart and headed toward the checkout.

I look back at the card. Below the name and contact information is a Bible verse. *For you formed my inward parts; you knitted me together in my mother's womb. I praise you, for I am fearfully and wonderfully made. Psalm 139:13–14.*

For a moment, I can smell the newness of him. Feel the soft waves of his baby-fine hair. And hear the puffs of his breath. The tiny struggles for life. Then the stillness and the loud crack of my heart.

Chapter 5

JILLIAN

My finger runs below the line of Scripture printed on silky smooth paper, the focus for tomorrow's Sunday school class.

Again.

And again, I don't understand the meaning. Is there one?

Needles stab my right foot as I stretch from my cross-legged position at the side of our coffee table. The house is quiet, but my fears scream loud enough to deafen me to the work sprawled before me.

I bite down to stop the tears and pain sears through my lower lip. There isn't a chance I can teach a class about women of faith while my own faith stands, toes on the edge of a cliff, ready to plunge. Where was God when I was seventeen? Where was God when Izzy followed in my footsteps?

This was supposed to be a new life. I should have been able to start fresh. But here I am, sucked into the same problem with no good answer. Will this keep happening until I get it right?

I'm the last person who should be teaching.

It's not like I asked for this. Theresa Haskel skipped town for three weeks to spend time with her daughter and new grandbaby. As always, when no one else is willing to fill in, the job falls on the church secretary. Me.

My forehead thumps onto the open Bible, and I breathe in the woody smell of the tissue-thin pages.

How can a baby bring such joy to Theresa's family, yet devastation to ours? There must be another option for Izzy, another future. I will not lose my daughter, not even the tiniest part of her.

Stretching over my abdomen, my fingers remember the way my middle curved to make room for Izzy. And how it didn't for my first. A rumble sounds as if my body is still angry about the invasion.

There will always be an emptiness in me, a place nothing can fill because my mother pushed me toward the *easy* path. My mind skims over the old conversations with friends, with him. And I see the desperation in my mother's eyes. The fear someone would find out. From where I stand today, the look has a whole new meaning. Would I see her eyes if I looked at a mirror right now? Does the same terror play across my features?

I remember the days after, how minutes shifted from slow motion to fast-forward. Before I could make sense of who I'd become, I was hours away from my parents' home. I had a new man and a new life. And this man was different than anyone I'd ever met. He was a man of faith. The kind of man who grew up in church and didn't have anything to hide. The kind of man who would protect his family.

But I had a secret.

The front door swings open, smacking into the bumper on the wall. I jump to my feet and run my hands over my hair, swiping a finger under my burning eyes.

"Mom. You wouldn't believe what we did today." Zachary springs forward leaving the door open for Jasmine Monk to invade my sanctuary. A rush of cold air takes advantage and sweeps through the room. I snag the romance novel I'd set on the coffee table as incentive to finish the lesson and I slide it under the couch.

Zachary tugs at his T-shirt neckline. "We went to the place where they have the bumper cars, and we had pizza, and we ate cotton candy. It was the best time ever." He lunges for my middle and wraps his arms around my waist. "Thanks for letting me go."

"Sure, buddy." I plant a kiss on the top of his curly brown hair, so much like his sister's, yet permeated with the tangy scent of sweaty boy. "Go hang up your jacket."

Jasmine holds one hand on the doorframe and the other on her hip, tossing her blond hair over her shoulder. "You look run in. Have a rough day?"

My fingers press hard as I wipe them over my eyebrows. This woman is not going to get to me. It's like my personal mantra. I answer with a forced smile that tastes bitter.

"Maybe some sleep will help. Do you think you could be sick?" Her mouth transforms into a full-drama sneer, but her eyes smile at the prospect.

"Thanks, Jasmine. I owe you one." Stepping forward, I clench the knob in my fist and slowly push the door until Jasmine is forced to step back. Then, click, she's gone, leaving me with clarity. It's women like Jasmine I'd wanted to hide from all those years ago, and it's women like Jasmine who make me think maybe the choice I made really was the only choice that made sense. Because no matter what age, there will always be Jasmines to guarantee you never forget your mistakes.

"Can I play a video game?" Zachary shifts from one foot to the other, still reeling from a sugar-coated day. "Please."

"Sure."

His eyes grow big, and he leans closer as if he's heard me wrong.

"Hurry before I change my mind." I force my lips into a smile.

His arms wrap around me again, and I inhale the sweetness of his unknowing, unjudging hug. Then he's off to fight the bad guys. Precious boy. I can't imagine my life without him. Without Izzy either. Maybe that's why my heart won't let go of the one who isn't here.

My phone buzzes on the counter. Seven o'clock. Garrett calling from his office where he's catching up on work. Always on a schedule, always dependable. And always wanting to know everything. It's been a week, and I still haven't found the words to break his heart.

I can't do it. There's no way I can tell my husband how I've failed to protect his precious daughter. How can I explain Izzy faces the worst possible fate, and I missed the warning signs and neglected to put up the roadblock?

The buzzing stops. He'll try again in ten minutes. The man never gives up. His persistence convinced me to marry him and move here, but I'm strong too. I've never told him the real reason I don't speak to my mother, the reason our lives are completely separate. I've never given him cause to look at me and see the sum of my choices.

And I won't start now.

I can't.

Even if I have to live my entire life with this hollow void in my middle, I'll never invite disappointment into his eyes.

My choices were limited, but I can do so much better for Izzy. There's a way out there somewhere. An answer that will preserve her life. A hope that will spare her a broken future.

No matter how hard I concentrate, I can only come up with three choices. They're the standard three, the same ones I had. The same three every young woman in this position chooses from. And not one of them is really an answer. There isn't a miracle.

Tension pulses in my shoulders and my back aches as if I've aged twenty years in the week since that swim meet.

Placing a palm on the thin pages of my Bible, I stare as a tear splashes onto the words, wrinkling the surface. Izzy has a relationship with God and a daddy who loves her. I'd sacrifice my own life if it would save her. But it's not enough.

The phone buzzes again. My ten minutes are over.

Rising from the carpet, I take the five steps to where I can look down at the phone's screen. A goofy picture of my husband glows up at me. Another piece of my heart breaks as I pick up the phone and move it toward my ear. "Hello. We need to talk."

◆ ◆ ◆

Soothing music drifts over the waiting room, but my nerves continue to pop like fireworks. The worst two weeks of my life have ended here, in a doctor's office filled with cushioned chairs, warm-beige walls, and pregnant women. Definitely women. The other patients are, give or take ten years, about my age. My arms instinctively hug my own flat stomach. These are still *my* childbearing years, not grandma time.

A woman enters the room with a low moan, drawing all eyes to her and breaking the relative peace. Her husband, though visibly shaken, keeps a hand on her lower back as he guides her to a chair. Using his arm for support, she tips back into the seat like a board until she makes contact with the cushion.

"Will you be okay?" he asks.

She responds with a glare.

The man swallows and eases away toward the sliding glass window. He raps frantically on the divider.

Whisking it open, the receptionist greets him with what looks like a rehearsed smile. "Good morning, Mr. Stevens."

All eyes shoot back to his wife as she whines like a dying animal.

Izzy leans closer to my side.

"Oh." The receptionist pops from her seat. "You should have taken her to the hospital. I'll get the doctor."

"She wasn't like this when we left home." He holds up his hands imploring the audience of pregnant women to understand his plight.

The responses vary from shocked to terrified. The pressure of Izzy's grip on my arm tells me she's in the latter group.

Mrs. Stevens slides toward the carpet, her fingernails clawing at the armrests.

"Mom?" Izzy's palms wrap around my arm, tight.

"It's okay." What else can I say? Yes, this will be you in only a few months? No, it isn't the time to insert the sharp needle of truth. I pat Izzy's clenched hands, hoping the reassurance will lighten her grip and ease the pain she's inflicting.

Mr. Stevens kneels beside his wife. A drip of sweat snakes from his thinning hairline, past his temple, and along his jaw.

The door that leads to the examination rooms swings open and a nurse rushes in with a wheelchair. "Let's get you back so the doctor can take a quick look, then you'll be off to the hospital."

The woman looks up at the nurse. Her face is flushed and her eyes glazed as though she's left reality behind.

Together, husband and nurse lift her into the chair while her head whips back and forth between them.

Izzy buries her face in my side.

It's the first time I've felt her need me in months. I pat her back and kiss the top of her head, relishing the opportunity to have a purpose in her life.

Another scream, this one from somewhere in the woman's gut, and I have to hold Izzy back from climbing into my lap. The wailing of an ambulance grows louder, then stops.

They wheel the laboring mother through the door and the room falls silent. No one flips magazine pages. No one readjusts in their seats. No one swallows.

The clock ticks like a bomb, ready to explode.

"Isabella Cline." Another nurse, this one in pink scrubs, her red hair tied back in a ponytail, scans the room.

Izzy clings tighter and doesn't answer.

Peeling my daughter's fingers from my arm, I stand and pull her toward the door and the nurse.

Leaning in, Izzy whispers, "I don't want to go. Can we go home?"

"It's just a checkup. We came all the way to Corvallis for this appointment because you didn't want to do it at home. We're going to see the doctor." Of course, I would have suggested the drive myself if Izzy hadn't.

"I can't." Her face has lost all color, making her dark tresses and eyes stand out.

"Going home won't make you less pregnant. I'm sorry, but here we are. There's no reverse." I force my steps to follow the nurse, although I want to run as much as Izzy does.

The nurse's eyebrows scrunch. "I'll need your weight." She ushers us through a typical OB-GYN gauntlet including the cup to fill, then down the hall and left, into an examination room.

Another clock ticks. Another time bomb. Each click sits on my nerves, adding to the ones before it. Just when I think I can't take another second, a crash sounds in the hall, something hits the wall, and a woman screams. I'd forgotten about her. Voices are loud outside our door. I crack it open. Two paramedics wheel a gurney by me. Mrs. Stevens sits up, her face red as she strains.

"Try not to push. We'll be at the hospital in less than ten minutes."

The announcement doesn't register with the patient. Low grunts rumble from her chest. Ten minutes. I'm brought back to the night Izzy was born. Ten minutes might as well have been a year. There was nothing that could stop me from pushing my little girl into the world when the time came.

The doctor at the foot of the gurney holds up his hand. He lifts the sheet and his eyes widen. "We're not going to make it. Take her back to the exam room."

"Are you sure?" The younger paramedic looks to the older.

Mrs. Stevens takes in breath, pulls her knees to her chest, and proceeds to fully push.

At that answer, the gurney goes in reverse and disappears down the hall.

My hands are shaking. I remember it all. The fear. The pain. The regret. And the love so intense I thought I'd die under it.

When I turn back I see the object of that love slumped over, her legs dangling out from a paper gown as she sits on the edge of the exam table. Exposed.

She keeps her head down. "Is there something wrong with her?" The words are mumbled, but I can hear the waver of fear riding on them.

"No. She'll be fine once the baby is out. It's all part of the process." I'm only adding to her anxiety, but I can't lie. Childbirth is painful. In many ways.

"That is not at all what it looks like in the movies. I don't see how that woman could ever be fine again." She shakes her head. "I'm sorry, Mom. I can't do this."

Her meaning is a weight in my belly, but I won't acknowledge it. "Izzy." I place a hand on each of her bare knees. "You don't have a choice."

"Yes, I do." Her voice is just above a whisper and her shoulders begin to bob with soft sobs. "I'm sorry. I want to be strong like you, but I can't do this."

The room spins in a swirl of color. I scoot in next to my daughter. Paper crinkles under my desperate clutch. Strong. I've never been strong. Especially now. Especially then. Tears rush to my eyes and constrict my throat. "That's not the answer." But what is?

"How would you know?" Anger tints her words. She lifts her chin. "You don't understand what's happening to me. You don't know what it's like."

"Abortion isn't an easy answer." My heart thuds in my chest and my lungs grab for air. The past is upon me at this very moment. A lion, ready to kill. "Izzy, I—"

There's a tap at the door as it swishes open. "Good morning. I'm Dr. McConnel." His nose is bent toward the file he examines, his hair, too thick for his age, seems almost fake. "Your pregnancy test came out positive. I'll get right to the point." He looks up, taking us both in, then his gaze stops on me, judging my motherhood, my womanhood. "I assume this is not a planned pregnancy." He pulls a wheeled stool from under the desk and sits, squaring his shoulders over his knees. "We'll do everything we can to prepare you and to help you bring a healthy baby into the world. What you do from there, that's your call, but this is serious business. I want you to know what you're getting into. Have you thought about whether you'll parent or place this child?"

I can't breathe. The room is so small. And sauna-hot.

Izzy keeps her gaze from me. "What about the other choice?"

I want to scream, but my lungs are paralyzed.

Dr. McConnel scratches his head. "Abortion isn't something to be taken lightly."

If I could speak, I'd thank him.

He taps the chart. "We'll do a quick ultrasound to be sure, but by the dates you marked on the form, you're already past the first trimester. We don't do abortions here. You'd have to schedule that at another facility, and it would be a two-day surgical procedure."

Emotion sweeps from my toes through my middle and toward my fingertips and the top of my head. It's not joy. It's not happiness or elation. But some sort of relief that the decision to terminate couldn't be made today. It feels like the gift of a breath. A reprieve I can't quite capture to name. It's a kind of feeling I've never had the need to understand or identify.

I clasp my hands in my lap and whisper a prayer of thanksgiving in my heart.

Then I hear the sobs.

The sound is muffled by the sweatshirt Izzy clutches to her face.

I reach out my arm and let my fingers touch her leg, but I don't get up. How can I tell my daughter the only solution she sees for her pain is one that will haunt her? That I, the mother she thinks never made that kind of mistake, knows this too well. That though Izzy was the first of my babies to lie in my arms, the one who would call me Mom, she wasn't the first to live in my heart.

Chapter 6

STACEY

Hope Christian doesn't boast of superiority with a beautiful facade like the church we visited last week, but the other church, with its gorgeous architecture and towering copper cross, fell short with sanitized worship and wishy-washy teaching.

Keith grabs my hand in both of his, lifting my fingers to his warm lips. "I have a good feeling about this one." He winks.

At the boyish gesture my resolve breaks, and I smile back. "Didn't you say the same thing last Sunday?" I lean into his side as our feet crunch through the thick gravel parking area.

"Last week I said I had a feeling. That's very different than a good feeling."

"Nice save."

His hearty laugh eases my nerves. And the arm he uses to pull me even tighter to him soothes away any concerns about finding our place in this new town, thousands of miles from family and friends. As long as I have him, I'm home.

Making our way through rows of cars, we approach the modest brown building with the swooping roof that comes to a point in the middle. A rough cross is nailed near the front door with crude hardware. The hum grows louder as we climb the cement steps and walk inside.

The foyer, not much larger than our living room, buzzes with the ups and downs of conversation. A man with the build of a retired football player and a tie the color of pumpkin slaps the shoulder of another man. They exchange laughs, then he breaks away and aims for us like a programmed missile. "Hello, there." He extends his platter-sized hand to Keith. "I don't believe I've seen you here before."

Keith grips the man's hand in a masculine gesture that seems like an affirmation of his own size and strength. "First-timers. We just moved into town."

Tipping his head back the guy evaluates us at an angle, then wraps his arm over Keith's shoulder and tugs him toward a circle of people. My fingers are still intertwined in my husband's so I'm pulled along like a kite that can't make liftoff.

All conversation turns to us. Tiny prickles flutter over my skin. I attempt to step back, but Keith holds tight. The air in the crowd is muggy. I wipe my free hand over my forehead and try to pay attention to the string of questions.

A drum hits three solid beats and the worshipers pour into the sanctuary. *Sanctuary.* The perfect word, and exactly what I need.

Lined with actual pews, quilts in vivid colors hanging along the walls, there's a homey quality here, different from the packed foyer. A blue-haired old woman stops to tickle the toes of a drooling baby in his car seat. Mothers line their children onto maroon padded benches.

Keith starts for the front. He always does that, liking to be where he won't miss a thing. But I like to see the people. See how they interact with each other. How they worship. "Let's sit here." I cock my head toward a vacant pew three up from the back. "I can get a better feel from this row."

He kisses my head and sidesteps to our seats. "You mean you want an easy escape if this is another miss?"

Tightening my lips, I hold back another smile. "You know me well."

During the third song, as Keith closes his eyes and drifts into another world, noises distract me. I turn around and can't help staring. Four teenage girls, one with an infant and the other three clearly pregnant, shuffle into our row. And at the end of this unlikely church procession, the woman from the grocery store. Zipping through my memory for her name, all I can retrieve is the verse typed onto her card. The one I shoved into the kitchen drawer because for some reason I couldn't toss it in the trash.

The song finishes and the congregation sits, but my body stiffens. My knees don't bend. Keith tugs my arm, his touch restoring my mobility.

Next to me, a blond girl, a little too thin, lifts a baby from a teal sling. Even held out, the newborn's legs still curl into her belly. Placing the infant on her lap, head snuggled into the dip between her knees, the young mom adjusts her child's fuchsia headband.

Look away.

Long, butterfly eyelashes flutter over dark gray eyes. They gaze up at me. Look away.

The teen brushes her finger over the baby's puckered lips that turn looking for the promise of milk. So alive, she glows pink.

Keith's hand warms my leg with a gentle squeeze. Maybe he's right. Maybe the time has come. I tip my cheek onto his shoulder, and his breath, warm and moist, flows over the top of my head.

Excitement gurgles inside of me like tiny popping bubbles. I never thought I'd feel this again. The sensation rushes over me, making my skin dance with goose bumps.

A finger taps my arm, and I peer into the crystal blue of the mother's eyes. "Would you like to hold her?" Her voice is a delicate whisper, barely heard.

I touch my fingertips to my heart. This question is more than I can answer with whispered words. I nod.

She slips her hands under the infant's head and back then passes the bundle into my shaking arms.

Arms that haven't held a child since my son took his last breath.

But this is different. This little girl, with the tiny lips that seem to be nursing in her sleep, she radiates warmth. Her arms and legs twist, turn, and shift. She arches her back and a grunt pushes from her crinkled face followed by a rumble from below.

Keith's shoulders bounce next to me.

"Real mature," I say.

Ducking his head, he covers his face.

The girl reaches for the baby, her baby. "Sorry. I'll go change her."

I force my hands to give her back. The warmth of the baby somehow brought life into arms paused by death. "Thank you."

This pastor could be Billy Graham, and I wouldn't hear a word he says. Can we really do this? Will another birth mother choose us? Would the baby be healthy? What would we name him? Am I truly ready?

Images of a nursery, freshly painted mint green, a border of sky blue, soft yellow, or maybe pastel pink. I won't do the jungle theme again. That belongs to our first baby. But what design then?

Keith drops his chin to his chest. They're praying. Running my fingers between his clasped hands, I close my eyes and ask God if this is really the time to trust again.

When the prayer ends, people stand, shake hands, make plans. They greet newcomers and embrace old friends. A voice calls my name, and I startle. When I turn, the woman from the store is there, a smile lighting her face and sparkly lip gloss coating her lips.

"Stacey, right?"

I must look stunned enough for her to question the name. "Yes. I'm sorry I haven't called."

She waves her hand, thin circular bracelets clanking together like a wind chime. "You'll call when you're ready. Is this your husband?"

"Keith." He sticks out his hand.

"Nice to meet you. I'm Irene. Your wife and I met in the grocery store."

Keith glances at me, his lips pinched. I know him. He's trying to figure out if I mentioned this to him before.

I haven't.

A girl sidles up to Irene. Her explosion of a stomach rams the pew and she winces. Rubbing her hand in circles over the site of the collision, she cocks her head toward Irene. "Pastor Fields said he didn't know anyone with design skills."

"Well, we'll just have to run an ad. Sure would be great to find someone willing to donate the time though." She turns back to us. "I know you're new, but you haven't met anyone with graphic design skills looking to volunteer time to a good cause, have you? We need a new logo and flyer for the annual fund-raiser. The man who did the last ones passed on to glory." She raises a hand up flat toward the ceiling.

Keith pats me on the back, and I scream inside my head for him not to do it, but my thoughts aren't loud enough.

"Stacey did that kind of thing in her job back in Tennessee."

Light springs into Irene's eyes. "Well isn't that a special blessing. Do you think you could help us?"

I look toward the door, but there are too many people between me and freedom. "I guess I could take a look."

MARGARET

The familiar sound of Travis thunking dirt clods off his cleats on the cinderblock steps makes me straighten and try not to look as exhausted as I am.

I've waited for a couple weeks, wanting him to come to me with his problem or for it to just go away. He's tight-lipped, as usual, and the tension I see in his shoulders says we still have something to discuss.

He plows through the door, tossing his duffel bag on the floor. "Mom, shouldn't you be at work?"

Where else would I be? I'm always at the diner or cleaning someone's house. "I took the afternoon off."

His eyes open wider. I have his full attention now.

"Have a seat," I say.

Coming over to the stool, he grips the wide back but doesn't sit. "What?" No eye contact.

"You and I both know exactly what. Have you lost your mind?" I don't yell or even raise my voice. I just throw out the question. With my fingertips, I turn his face to meet my gaze four inches below his. "If word gets out about that girl's baby, do you know how it will look? What about baseball? What about your scholarship?"

"She's not *that* girl." His eyebrows lower, his father's fierceness reflects in his features.

"Well, she's certainly not *the* girl either. What were you thinking?" I'm getting hot now, the pressure to make him understand lighting a fire under my skin.

He shrugs. "I was thinking I love her. I don't know." With his full grip, he yanks his baseball cap farther over his face. "I don't know," he repeats.

I plop onto the stool, resting my elbows on the cracked counter and my face in my rough hands. "You've got to do something about this soon."

"There's nothing I can do except marry her."

My body tires under the weight of this problem. Somewhere deep in my gut, even my stomach tries to hide from his statement.

"Mom, please understand." His hand touches my back.

Spinning around, I face him. "*You* need to understand. Did you ever ask yourself why I married your father? Did you think this was the life I wanted?"

"You said Dad was different back then."

"He was. He was different until I got pregnant with Kane, and he married me and dropped out of college. Babies need diapers. They need food, and heat, and all sorts of other things kids like you and Izzy don't think about. Having a baby now will change you. And it will change Izzy. This isn't a game. You can't win at this."

He steps back.

Crumbs on the linoleum poke at my bare feet. I take a cautious step toward him. "You have a future. Don't flush it down the toilet like your father and I did. You'll end up living the same life you've been fighting to leave."

My words have hit a home run. The slump of his shoulders and the worry lines across his face tell me I've won. And it breaks my heart wide open. But Travis has to come first. He has to make it out of this dump. If he doesn't, my life will be a complete failure. My sacrifice, pointless. I'll die leaving only sorrow and brokenness as a sign I was here.

I clamp my fingers around the cotton of his shirt sleeve. "Let the hurt only be for now, not forever." Every muscle in my chest tightens at what I'm suggesting. There is nothing easy about this decision. I gave Kane life at the cost of my own, and he came into an angry world. Fighting good. Fighting love. Fighting the law. If Officer Hobbs hadn't stopped him, the life I protected could have taken another. Like claws that cut from the inside, the pain torments me every day.

Travis's head drops and the slightest shudder plays across his shoulders. Still my baby. He shouldn't be facing this.

"It's Izzy's choice. I'll do whatever she decides."

I bite back the urge to shake him. "Travis. She made the choice. She's trapping you here. This is how she's going to hold on to you. Don't be a fool."

Travis's chin drops down and his eyes meet mine. "Is that what you did to Dad?"

The verbal punch knocks my hands free, and I back away, tears pooling in my eyes and blurring the vision of his disapproval.

"I deserve this answer. Did you trap my dad into marrying you?"

My body shakes from my spine out to my toes and fingertips. I should have seen this coming. I should have expected the blow. I should have been aware of my guilt all along, but there'd always been someone else to blame.

"Did you get pregnant on purpose?" His voice booms through the house.

Turning my face away from his piercing stare, my gaze lands on Deven. When had he come out of his bedroom cocoon? How much has he heard? A Wii remote dangles from the strap on his wrist. He flings too-long hair from his eyes, his mouth half open as if his future depends on the answer to the question I've avoided for twenty-one years.

I search my boys for a way out, another chance. Travis looks like me, his hair and eyes dark, features so much like my own father's, but Deven is the spitting image of their dad. His copper hair lies in waves against his forehead.

A bar stool slams to the floor behind me. Wood cracks and the backrest skitters along the floor.

My heart crashes each beat.

There's fire in Travis's eyes. "The answer?"

Dropping to the floor, I hug my legs to my chest, surrounded by the wasteland I've created. "Yes. But you don't understand. You don't know what it was like at my house."

He slams the door on the way out, shaking our walls.

Chapter 7

STACEY

The address is marked clearly with white numbers, but I drive past the house and park half a block down the road anyway. Vehicles line the side of the street and fill driveways, families home from work and school for the night. I turn off the engine and step out of the car. This is my big accomplishment for today. Life is changing fast. Five days ago, we bumped into Irene and her "girls" at church, we decided to meet with an adoption worker, and I'd agreed to help Irene on a project.

Had I agreed?

One of my teal and chocolate-brown sandals touches the asphalt.

No, I don't think I did. I'm not even sure I spoke.

I replay the exchange between Irene and Keith, and my head begins to spin like during the original conversation.

My other foot hits the ground, this time into a puddle. Shaking my leg, I attempt to get some of the water off my shoe. Why did I get these silly things out today? It's rained almost daily since we've arrived in Oregon.

I head toward the stout brick house, larger than any other in the neighborhood, and obviously older. Cookie-cutter shapes line the edges of the roof and a boxy porch shelters the massive wooden front door.

My finger stalls over the doorbell, unwilling to push. I've made a mistake. And it's not even mine this time. Keith should never have said I'd do this job. No matter that I've been cooped up all week. No matter that I can't seem to find my footing here. Still. This should have been my call. I pull my hand back, ready to leave, but I've decided too late. The door opens.

And there she is again. The thin blond girl with eyes so light, the blue almost washes into the white. Her smile is instant, maybe already on her face before she saw me, I'm not sure.

She holds one hand splayed over the sling holding her baby, and with the other hand she waves. "Hello there. Irene said you'd be coming by. She's upstairs in her room. You can go on up." She steps away from the door and waits for me to enter. "See you later. We're off for our after-dinner walk." Bouncing down the steps, she jabbers to her baby as she floats along the sidewalk, her feet covered in pink rain boots with white dots.

Have I ever been so carefree?

The foyer is dark in a warm way, with deep burgundy paint you don't see in many homes anymore and plenty of rich wood. I push the door shut and it clicks into place. The floor is solid, but when I move there's a slight creak that makes me look all around to see if anyone has noticed me.

In the living room two couches face each other with an oversized fireplace at one end. There's some clanking behind the door that must lead to the kitchen and laughter floats out.

I take a step that way, but I'd rather find Irene and not have to explain to anyone else why I'm here or who I am, so I take light steps toward the grand staircase with the thick curling banister.

In a blur of purple and pink, Irene appears above me. "You're here. Great. Come on." She waves me up with her hand. "I'm still looking for my other shoe." As she turns, the back of her flouncy, ankle-length skirt flares up and exposes the sole of one bare foot.

I hurry to keep up with a woman who must be in her sixties but moves like a teenager. At the end of the hall she enters a bedroom and plops down on a quilt with a bright Amish star fanning out from the center.

"I've looked everywhere." She slides down to the floor and lifts the quilt, peering under the bed. "How could I have lost one shoe?" Standing, she fastens her hands on her sides and scans the room. "Maybe . . ." She yanks a box from the bottom of the closet. "I packed a few things last week." She rips the packing tape off the cardboard and rummages through the contents. "There it is." Holding the sparkly silver Toms shoe over her head, she looks like she's won a trophy.

"Are you going on a trip?" There's a suitcase in the corner of the room and more boxes flattened in the corner.

Her expression drops from elation to concern. "No. Moving out."

Chills crawl over my skin. "I thought you loved it here."

"I do. The board thinks I'm getting too old. Can't have an elderly old woman in charge, you know."

"You're hardly elderly."

"Tell that to those crotchety board members. All they do is sit around making decisions, never doing any of the hands-on stuff." She slaps her palm over her mouth. "I'm sorry. Shouldn't be talking that way. I'll have plenty to ask the Lord to forgive by the end of today." She slips the shoe on her bare foot, sits on the edge of the bed, and kicks up both feet, clicking her heels together.

"You said you have the flyers from last year?"

Irene grins. "You're all business." She pops up and pulls on a dresser drawer. Wood screams against wood. "Sorry about that. I need to rub more soap in there."

As she flips through papers, my gaze catches on a small picture frame. There's a man holding a little girl on his lap, a bunch of flowers in her grip. "Is this your daughter?"

Lines form along Irene's forehead. "Yes." The lightness vanishes from the room.

My mouth opens, but I catch myself before my next stupid question escapes.

Voices grow louder from the hall. A couple of girls peek around the corner. One knocks on the wall beside the door.

"What's up?" Irene grins, though it isn't as bright as before.

The girls exchange looks.

"Sierra, what is it?" Irene's voice is insistent now.

The girl shrinks at the mention of her name. "It's Nikki. She's angry again."

"More than usual," the other girl adds. "She said she was too sick to do her chore and tried to make Sierra do it. I called her out, and she threw up in the woodbox."

Irene cringes as my own stomach does an unpleasant flip. "Where is she now?"

"The big bathroom."

Nodding, Irene quickly steps around the girls, waving me to come along.

I start to remind her I'm only here to make a flyer, but she's down the hall where other girls huddle around a door.

"It's all my fault." Sierra hangs her head.

Irene places her palms on the girl's cocoa-brown cheeks. "No, it is not. Don't go blaming yourself for Nikki's temper." She waits until the girl makes eye contact, then smiles. "Girls, head downstairs. I'll take care of Nikki."

I start to follow the crowd when Irene's hand wraps around my arm. "Could you stay?" she whispers. "This is honestly the toughest girl I've worked with. She makes me wonder if the board may be right."

I nod, but my toes still point toward the stairs. I've never been a good one to have on hand in a crisis. I'm the little sister. The one everyone else takes care of. The one who can't quite make it on her own.

Irene raps on the door. "Nikki? Can I come in? I'm concerned about you, and so are the other girls."

"No."

"Let me see that you're okay, then you can have some time before we discuss this. Okay?"

"No."

Irene cocks her hip. "Nikki. Don't make me take this door down."

Irene isn't a huge woman, but I believe at this moment she can do about anything she sets her mind to.

"To live in this house, you are required to follow the rules. Am I clear?" Her voice is strong and unwavering, while my legs shake. She taps her foot in a steady rhythm.

The lock clicks but the door doesn't open.

"Thank you. We're coming in."

We're coming in? I squeeze my hands together. I'm only here to make a flyer. Doesn't anyone remember that?

The bathroom is enormous, like the size of a small bedroom. I step through the door but keep my back along the wall, my mouth silent. Nikki sits on the edge of an oversized tub, a giant mauve towel wrapped around her body and her clothes in a pile near the sink. She's filled the tub with water, the faucet still dripping.

I've never seen the girl, but I can see she isn't well. Her reddened face is damp, but I can't tell if it's from tears, sweat, or if she's splashed her face.

Irene kneels beside her. "I hear you're having a rough day."

Nikki lifts her feet one at a time and settles them in the steaming water. I cringe, but don't say anything.

"Let me run some cool water in there. It's not good for you or the baby to take a hot bath."

Nikki doesn't speak, but her jaw tightens, muscles twitching.

Turning the knob, Irene runs the water over her hand then swirls it through the bathwater like my mother used to do. "Are you feeling okay? Any contractions?"

"I'm not due yet, so back off and leave me alone. I just got a bug or something."

Irene eases herself onto the edge of the tub. She places her hand on Nikki's back and the girl jumps like she's been stung.

I should do something. At least make it known that I'm here. But I'm silent, watching them as if they're a program on television.

"It's okay. Stacey and I are here to help you."

The girl's gaze catches on me. She's like a wounded animal. Scared and dangerous at the same time. Stretching her back, Nikki starts to slip into the tub with the towel still tied around her. It floats up like a pond lily. She lays her head back on a plastic neck cushion, then her body squeezes forward. "I think I'm getting sick again."

Irene motions to the wastepaper basket.

For a moment I stall, then I step forward, bringing the can next to Nikki.

She spits, then moans deep.

Reaching her hand beneath the water's surface, Irene cups her palm over Nikki's belly. Her eyes go round, and I can hear the words she's speaking to me through her expression.

This girl is in labor.

Like a wave, I remember what it was like that day, and I'm pulled back, the memories taking away my air.

"How often are you feeling like this?" Irene asks.

Nikki grunts and shakes her head.

"Okay. Just breathe."

A moment later, her breath coming in pants, Nikki relaxes.

"Honey"—Irene pushes back hair from Nikki's face—"I think you're in labor."

Wild eyes shoot a glare. "No."

"You don't get a choice. That was a contraction you just felt. This is normal. You're going to be fine."

"What do you know? I don't even want to have this baby. I don't. I can't."

"Yes, you can. God is here with you. He'll help you through this, and I'll be with you too." She flips the drain and water starts to funnel out of the tub. "I'm sorry, but in case your water has broken, we need to get you out of the bath."

Eyes like saucers, Nikki looks toward her clothes. "I thought . . ."

As if accepting the fact she's in labor gives her body permission to have this baby, Nikki moans again, louder and longer, her face flaming with color. Her hand grabs my arm still holding the trashcan. Her fingers squeeze into my flesh, and I fight the desire to pull away.

Irene stands and pats my shoulder.

"Where are you going? Don't leave." Nikki echoes my thoughts.

"I need some help in here," Irene shouts.

Six faces appear from nowhere.

"Erin, get a robe for Nikki. Sierra, call the doctor and tell him we're on the way to the hospital."

Nikki shivers.

I wrap my arm around her shoulder, not sure what else to do.

"Help me," she whispers.

Irene pulls several towels from the cupboard and lays them at my feet, then she's out of the room and it's just me and this girl I haven't formally met.

I wrap a dry towel over her shoulders and rub my hands over her arms to warm her skin.

She grabs her belly with the next contraction and starts to sob. How long has it been since the last one? Maybe three or four minutes.

I help Nikki to the edge of the tub. Erin comes in with the robe and helps Nikki thread her arms into the holes.

Then another contraction. This time water gushes down the side of the tub.

"Three minutes and forty seconds," Irene announces. "We need to move. The car is out front."

I hadn't heard her come back into the room.

With Irene on one side and me on the other, we help Nikki up and into a pair of slippers. It seems like we'll never make it through the house. Twice we stop for contractions. When we get to the van, a towel is already on the seat. Nikki gets in and Irene reaches over her with the seat belt. She wails, but Irene doesn't stop this time. Before the contraction peaks, Irene is behind the wheel, her own buckle belted. "Stacey. I need you to stay with the girls. Insurance and board rules. My backup's daughter started chemo today. Can you do that?"

I nod, not really thinking about the question.

Nikki's head whips back and forth on the headrest. "No. No. I don't want to do this."

Without hesitation, Irene backs out and off they go, leaving me in charge.

But I'm only here to make a flyer.

Chapter 8

Izzy

Text me when you get here, but don't come in. I press send, then toss my phone onto my unmade bed. Dad and Travis fighting is more than I can take. Doesn't anyone care about what I'm going through? It's all about the baby, and it's not even here yet.

Rain drips down my dark bedroom window. I yank the blue poncho from its bag in the outer pocket of my backpack.

Cracking the window open, I suck in a full breath of cold, damp, outside air and try to remember the feeling of freedom. This room is like prison. I can't leave without seeing their sad and disappointed faces. My mom's eyes are always red, though I never see her crying, and the lines on her forehead have grown deep.

But my dad, that's tough. He hasn't looked me in the eye since before last week's appointment with the doctor. I don't even know when my mom told him, but it was obvious when he got home that she had. It's like he's preoccupied with his shoes and can't speak in sentences longer than four words.

Even Travis texts less often. He said he was in this with me, but every day he seems further away. Doesn't he even care how I feel?

His spark for me took a nosedive right after I told him about the baby. Or maybe it was before then. Maybe even the first night we'd gone too far. That night he'd gotten what he wanted, and I'd compromised. It was the beginning of our end.

At least Zach doesn't know.

I pick up the ultrasound picture with its already worn edges and the black and white image of my baby. Holding it to my lips, I try to believe this is real, but even though it moves around inside me, I can't imagine the kid in this world.

Lights shine outside through the sideways rain. His blue Mazda—a car that's older than we are—pulls up along the curb at the side of our yard.

Lifting my cell, I check for his text, but it hasn't come. I slip the picture into my pocket and rub my hands up and down my arms before threading the poncho over my head and climbing out the window.

Wet wind blows over me, ruffling the thin plastic.

My phone is quiet. Still.

The ground sinks under my feet. Wind whips my hair. Wet clumps of curls stick to my face. At least he won't be able to see the tears.

I yank on the passenger door. It doesn't budge. I tap a fingernail on the glass and he leans over and pulls up the lock.

A thin shiver runs across my skin.

I slide into the seat, wadding the poncho in my lap. Cold water drips from the plastic and soaks into my sweatpants. "Do you want to know how the doctor's appointment went?"

"I guess." His eyes stare straight ahead through the windshield even though it's covered with fog. "Do you want to tell me about it?"

I slap the wet hair off my face. "Not if it's too much trouble for you to listen."

"I didn't say that."

"You haven't *said* anything. That's the problem."

He turns toward me for the first time. His eyes are puffy and red and there's fear on his lips. "Izzy, you know I love you."

"What's that supposed to mean? Don't play games with me, Travis."

Looking away, he leans his head onto the window, drawing circles in the fog with his finger.

"Travis, I need to know what you're saying."

"There's something I need you to tell me."

I swallow hard, watching the numbers on the dashboard clock change.

"Was this the plan?" He rakes fingers through his hair.

My dinner hardens in my belly. "What?"

"The baby. Did you plan to get pregnant?"

I move so fast my knee slams into the glove box, sending needles of pain up my leg. "How could you ever ask that? I didn't even want to do it. And you think this is my big plan? Seriously? What do I have to gain here?"

He stares hard at me, his lips tight, his eyes narrow, an unfamiliar scent on his breath. "You didn't do this so I'd stay? You didn't want me to give up the scholarship and be here with you?"

"Of course I wanted you here with me, but not like this. I'd never ask you to give up your dreams. Can't you see what I could lose? My future is over. I can't just walk away. If you want out, fine, but don't dump it on me." My shoulders shake and the air in the car thins. "I can't believe you'd ask me that."

His hand reaches across the console and finds my leg, but his touch is cool.

I slap it away. "I need a break. I need time to decide what I'm going to do."

Shoving the door open, I lunge from the car and into the cool wind that at least holds some oxygen. Puddles splash my legs as I run through the yard. When I reach the house, I stop, leaning against the siding, and cry.

Behind me, his tires screech on the wet road.

Rain drips down my scalp and along my numb face. My fingernails bite into the paint on the side of the house, the only thing holding me up. In the wind, no one can hear me sob. No one, but maybe God, if He still cares.

A steady rhythm pounds behind my belly button. Does the baby feel my pain? Can this baby sense life falling apart before even taking the first breath?

I slip down into the muddy flower bed, wrapping myself like a shell around my baby. "Please forgive me. I'm so sorry." I rock back and forth, time washing away with the rain. "Lord, please don't leave me like this. Help me. Please."

A high pitch rings out over the howl of the wind. Coming closer, the flashes of lights and sirens scream down the road.

Jillian

Zachary puts the final piece in his Lego starship and holds it above his head like he's won the World Cup.

"Nice, buddy." Garrett ruffles his hair. "I'm amazed how fast you build those things. You'd make a great engineer."

Lowering the ship, Zachary turns toward his dad. "Like a train driver?"

Something bumps the wall between the dining room and Izzy's bedroom. I see her less each day. Only a few weeks ago, she'd be out here with the family. We'd play a game or watch a movie. Now she lives alone behind her door. And I can't reach her.

Garrett looks from the wall to Zachary, his mouth curved into a forced smile. "No. Like . . ."

The doorbell rings. I pull the last pot from the rinse water and drop it into the drying rack. Wiping my hands on a kitchen towel, I head for the door.

Garrett refolds his newspaper and beats me there. As he opens the door, cold wind rushes in and blows fear across my face.

"Wade?"

I hook my finger into Garrett's belt loop. Wade is a friend from church, but not so close I'd expect him to pop by on a Saturday afternoon. And definitely not in his police uniform. Behind him, rain sprays sideways, the setting lending a creepy factor to his drawn expression.

But my kids are all home, accounted for. Safe. Or as safe as we can keep them. And I have no other family. Garrett's parents live a plane flight away. Still, I'm scared.

"Come in." Garrett steps aside, but I release him and hold my ground until my husband pulls me back.

Wade walks into the house, closing the door behind him. He yanks the hat from his head and holds it in both hands, his gaze on his grip. "I really shouldn't be here, but . . ."

I shudder as Garrett's arm folds over my shoulder, pulling me to his side and surrounding my chill with his consuming warmth.

"I get the eerie feeling you're not here to chat about morning basketball."

As his hand brushes over his close-cut brown hair, Wade shakes his head. "I wish you were wrong. Is Izzy here?"

Cold runs through my arms, and I can hardly take a breath. What's happening? Teen pregnancy is bad, but not illegal.

No. Not one more thing. I don't think I can take it.

Garrett swallows. "Travis?" The beat of my husband's heart drums against my ear.

For a moment I can breathe again, then realization slaps me hard.

The silence speaks all the words I can't stand to hear. Wade's nod is like an executioner's ax.

"There was a wreck up the road. They life-flighted him to Portland." He shakes his head. "It doesn't look good. He was texting. We found the phone. *Iz, I l-o-v.* That's it. Don't know if it makes things worse or better."

I should thank him for bringing the news here, rather than waiting for it to find us through the town chatter, or across social media, but I can't speak.

Cold water washes over my body. Down the hall, Izzy's bedroom door is still. "Did they get his mother?"

"Curt is driving her to the hospital right now. She's a mess. Fell apart right there in the diner."

How could she not? A mother's worst nightmare. It puts Izzy's pregnancy in a whole new light. I wrap my arms around myself. At least I still have a child to hold. "I'll talk to Izzy."

Hands slide around my waist. Zachary's eyes brim with tears. I may not care much for Travis, but Zachary worships him. Dropping to my knees, I pull him tight to me. Life is so easily stripped away.

Garrett slaps a hand on Wade's back. "Thanks. We do appreciate your coming."

The door closes and the three of us are left in the heavy silence.

Slipping his hand into mine, Garrett pulls me up. "Let's do this together."

Zachary backs away to the couch and curls into the corner of the cushions, his bottom lip held tight between his teeth.

Each step toward Izzy's door seems to only move us inches. Yet, suddenly we're there too soon, like the end of a great book, but not. And I'm begging God for another minute before I tear what's left of my daughter's heart into ragged pieces.

Garrett drops a kiss on the top of my head. His touch is nothing like the shows of affection and caring I read about in my novels. His kiss is distant, distracted.

Instead of comfort, the pressure in my chest swells with the lies I hold between us. More than one lie, it's grown into a family of falsities to protect me from the person I was.

His hand grips the doorknob, and before I can stop him, he's in her room. The strength that left him when I told him about the baby is back in full force.

In the middle of her bedroom, Izzy stands cradling her cell phone, her hair dripping wet, the window open and a puddle running off the sill and onto the carpet. Wide eyes meet ours. "I keep calling. I send texts." Shivers shake her body. "The sirens?"

Garrett nods.

In an instant, the distance separating them dissolves and Izzy is a child in her father's arms. The sobbing racks her body and Garrett holds her up. No more words. Only the sound of her heart breaking.

I sink onto the edge of my daughter's bed, the pain of my teeth biting into my lower lip, the only thing keeping the nausea from taking over. My fingers dig into the mattress. Beneath one hand, something crinkles.

Picking up the paper I stare at the gray image that is my grandchild. Not even born, and he or she may have already lost their father. How will we ever be enough for this tiny baby? How can we possibly fill the gaps?

Izzy pulls back from Garrett. Her eyes are puffy and red, but her expression is determined. "You don't know what I did. I was so angry. I didn't talk it out. I let him speed off mad. Daddy . . . I don't think I wanted him to come back. I'm so sorry. I'm so selfish."

Holding her face between his strong hands, Garrett rubs his thumbs over her cheeks. "Baby, everyone fights. Everyone. And, usually, we have the chance to say we're sorry. Travis loves you, I know that for sure. This is not your fault. Don't ever let the devil get in your head that way."

"I love you so much, Daddy. I'm sorry I disappointed you." Her arms hang limp at her sides.

Garrett wraps her up in his embrace, one palm holding her head to his chest, gesturing with the other for me to join them.

But they're miles away from me. If they knew how Izzy is only repeating my mistakes. I thought having a father like Garrett would make all the difference. I thought Izzy would have the life I wish I'd had. But once again, I was wrong. I duck my head and step into my husband's side. His arm hangs around me like a heavy chain.

Chapter 9

MARGARET

"Margaret, wait." Officer Hobbs's voice chases me up the dim sidewalk. I don't turn.

Glass doors slide apart, and I run through the emergency entrance. Antiseptic, blood, cleaners . . . death, these smells attack me. Air catches in my chest, working my lungs to press past the constriction. "My son?" I pound on the clear panel separating me from a woman in scrubs.

A warm hand settles on my shoulder, sending a burst of shock through my shaking body. Turning, there's Hobbs. For the first time I see the smear of blood across his police badge. Travis's blood. I brush my fingers over the scarlet red.

Catching my arms, he stops me before my knees give way. "We're here for Travis Owens. He was life-flighted in."

"He's my son." My mind wills her to say he's fine, but her expression is unchanged.

"I'll page the attending doctor. He'll be right with you."

A sob jumps past my guard. Shouldn't the doctor be too busy with my Travis to come chat?

Hobbs's strong hands guide me away from the desk to a bank of chairs. He tries to ease me down, but I stiffen. I need to be ready. Need to see Travis.

The entrance doors open, and I turn toward the sound, somehow expecting to see my son. To have him say the whole thing was a terrible mistake. But instead there's only a dark-haired girl wearing a bathrobe shuffling in with an older woman guiding her. They make it to the magazine rack before the girl bends over with the deep grunts of a woman in labor.

"Can someone please help?" the older woman hollers to no one in particular. "Hang in there, Nikki. We're almost there."

The girl nods, but her eyes squeeze shut and her mouth forms a pinched circle. She drops her chin to her chest, gripping the arm of the chair she's bent over.

"Hold on, honey." The woman strokes Nikki's hair. "You can do this. I'm right here with you."

A nurse with a wheelchair speeds toward them. She takes hold of the girl's cheeks and forces eye contact. "Don't push. We need to get you upstairs."

The girl either doesn't hear or she doesn't care. She bears down even harder.

The nurse presses a button on her waistband and within seconds an announcement plays over the speakers and two men run into the room. They scoop the wailing girl into the wheelchair and rush her through the doors marked emergency.

For a second my eyes lock with the older woman's. I want to rush forward and let her hold me the way she held the girl, like a grandmother comforts a grandchild. Then the woman turns away, and she's gone through the same double doors, leaving me alone with the terror that rages through my veins.

"Mrs. Owens?"

Wearing scrubs and standing with his head and shoulders stooped, this must be the doctor who took care of Travis. And the news is written all over his quiet face.

Officer Hobbs pulls me to his chest.

"I'm sorry. We did everything we could."

The light above me swirls and tosses as the room shifts in the changing balance of my world. Then, from each side, darkness presses in.

STACEY

I flip the switch and watch as crisp orange and blue flames curve over an artificial log. The house already feels like a sauna, but I need the distraction of the fire. Something to stare at. Something that doesn't expose my complete incompetence. I killed as much time as I could calling Keith, but he's still tied up in some work issue and couldn't talk long. The fireplace screen screeches back into position, and I settle myself on the edge of the stone hearth.

Girls line the couches on either side of a deep red, Persian-style rug. I haven't been under such scrutiny since middle school.

"Do you remember me?" The blond smiles and clasps her hands in her lap. "I sat next to you at church last week. I'm Cate."

My head bobs to the rhythm of my heartbeat. "And you had the baby."

"We all have babies." A very pregnant teen points both hands to her beast of a belly stretching the fuchsia cotton of her maternity shirt.

My palm skims my permanently flat stomach.

A quick glance at my cell phone. Not even an hour has passed since Irene and Nikki drove away, leaving me in charge of a completely foreign world. I tap a fingernail against my front teeth, a nervous habit even I find annoying.

This entire day is a mistake. I should never have agreed to come. If only Keith were home and not on his first business trip with the new company. I could have him come over. He has the ability to be comfortable in any situation. But I'm a perpetual ocean of awkward. "I'm sure everything will be fine."

Cate snags a baby monitor from the table behind the couch and holds it to her ear. "Oh, yeah. They'll call us as soon as there's news. I'm so glad there'll be another baby in the house. Since Chloe and Seth left, I feel kind of weird. I'm the only one left who's had her baby."

"Is that unusual?"

Cate nods. "Back in January we had five babies and their moms, plus three more expecting."

It's like stepping into another world I didn't know existed. A time when unwed mothers were sent away. But these girls aren't being hidden.

They're loved by Irene, and there must be others.

I think back over last Sunday. The congregation welcomed the girls. They were a part of the family there. Maybe that's what I liked and hated at the same time. The church is as close as family.

The phone on the entryway table rings, startling me. When was the last time I even saw a landline?

Cate pops up with the others close behind. "Hello." Her face wrinkles. "No. It's not. Sorry." She ends the call and shakes her head. "Wrong number."

All eyes turn to me.

"Well, what do you usually do in the evening?"

"I know what we can do." A redhead who looks just barely pregnant tips her head toward the kitchen door.

"Excellent idea, Kaylee." Another girl winks and suddenly they're all disappearing through the door.

The girl with the wavy black braid settles back onto the couch.

"Aren't you going to join them?"

"No. I'm not really into the group thing." Her eyes cast down at the loose string she works with her fingers.

"I'm sorry. There are so many new faces. What's your name?" I can't help myself. I've come into this house with a commitment not to get involved, but there's something about her.

"Sierra."

"How long have you lived here?" I lean on the wide arm of the couch.

"A couple weeks. I don't know if I'm staying though."

"It seems nice."

"I don't think I want to raise my baby." Her gaze shoots up, and she holds it on me like an interrogation lamp.

Tingles run across my skin. I swallow at the hard lump in my throat. Is this the reason God sent me across the country? "That's cool." I search for words, scrutinizing every syllable.

There's no way to stop my mind from pulling at the memory of the girl who chose Keith and me to be the parents of her baby. She'll always be my hero. At only fifteen she knew she couldn't provide the family she wanted for her child, so she put him first.

"Are you shocked?"

"No. I was thinking about what a brave decision you're making."

"They won't think so." She looks toward the kitchen. Another howl of laughter echoes from inside.

Choices, no matter how well thought out, will always be questioned, especially by those who make a different choice. I think back to a near brawl my sister had with her next-door neighbor about the merits of being a stay-at-home mom versus a working mom. And there were battles over binkies, and education, and nutrition, and screen time. It's like women feel the right to rip each other apart as soon as a child enters the equation.

Isn't love supposed to triumph?

Izzy

I feel like a little girl again, curled up on the couch with my mother stroking the back of my hair. Almost safe. Like before my life fell apart.

But now there's a growing ball in my stomach. Not just the baby that flutters endlessly below my belly button, but fear. It's blowing up inside me. There's nothing my mom can do to make it better. No way I'll ever be okay again.

My dad's footsteps pace behind the couch as we wait for his cell phone to ring and bring news.

Not the ring I expect, but the buzz of vibration startles me.

I push myself up on one elbow, but he turns his back to me as he answers, the slow nod of his head cracking my heart in two. His hand comes away from his ear and his arms hang loose at his sides, the cell phone still dangling in his right hand.

He turns.

As if the punch isn't hard enough, a tear spills from my Dad's eye and brings with it new and deeper pain. I can see in him the horrible future I have in front of me.

He drops to his knees and pulls me close. "I'm sorry, Baby. Travis didn't make it. He was gone by the time they landed the helicopter."

Numb wraps around me and steals even the cut of the words I knew were coming. I'm in an empty place now, alone. Their voices echo from far away, but I can't reach them, can't see through the darkness. Like one of my racing nightmares when I'm straining to swim as fast as I can but I can't seem to find the wall, just keep pulling and pulling, the strokes going slower and slower, until my legs are too heavy to kick. Dead in the water. I'll stay here. Let my life slip away and be gone. Float through the nothingness until I find myself in whatever eternity God sees fit for someone like me. A girl who destroyed the lives of everyone who ever cared for her.

I drop further in.

Something nudges me. Pounds on me. I try to push it away. I want to go. To be away from all of this. I just want to be left alone.

Like a drummer's stick, the beat plays heavy and jars my whole body. And with this comes the pain, the weight of my new life.

I can feel the blanket lying over me, the harsh fibers claw at the skin on my arm. The couch cushion's hard edge presses into my hip. The smell of overcooked bacon from a long-ago eaten meal is thick in the air. The clasp of something over my ankle.

My breath grows jagged. The pounding won't stop.

I open my eyes. At the end of the sofa, my mother sits, her eyes closed and her hand resting on my ankle. The room is dim, but not dark. There's only the sound of the refrigerator humming.

And then it's back again.

I reach for my stomach. The hammering hits my palm.

I want to die. But Travis's baby wants to live.

Tears flood my eyes, squeeze my throat, and rack my chest.
Travis is gone.
The baby is real.
I am alone.

Chapter 10

JILLIAN

The once comforting scent of fresh-baked bread fills my car. Today it leaves a foul flavor in my mouth. Without turning off the engine, I step out, inventorying the food I've packed into an open cardboard box.

The trailer home is the picture of grief. Rain drips from rusted-through gutters. Moss greens the siding. The carport slumps in the middle. Under this semi-structure, worn boxes collapse into small hills of clutter. A porch light without a cover sheds a dim glow onto a twenty-year-old car that's been in more than one accident.

I stuff my purse under the front seat and reach across the console to lift my carefully packed box. A plastic container of steamed broccoli shifts to one side, tips, then settles again.

My first step toward the house lands me ankle-deep in a mud puddle. I gasp as cold stings my leg and pours over the top of my soft-leather loafers.

Why am I even here?

I've been a church member long enough to know the drill. Someone dies. Everyone brings food. The family barely eats.

The last thing Margaret Owens will need is broccoli, lasagna, and garlic bread. But this is all I can offer. Maybe her younger son will eat the brownies.

My gesture is futile at best. If I'd lost Izzy . . . I can't even finish the thought. It sours my stomach and stiffens my muscles. She could so easily have been in that car. She could be gone too.

Chilled wind brushes my cheeks, challenging the heat burning beneath my skin.

I walk past an open shed with a washer and dryer inside and up two cinderblock steps to stand by the door. Turning, I eye my three-year-old Camry with its seat warmers and dentless exterior. We don't have a lot, but we have more than enough. If I left my part-time job at the church, we'd have to cut back on extras, but we'd survive.

I've never given Margaret's situation a thought. I'm aware there's a story here, and I know it's bad. People talk. But I haven't even given her enough thought to listen to the gossip. I wonder if I've played this game so long that I really believe somewhere deep inside that I'm better than she is. How could I let my judgment be so harsh?

My mind takes the what-if path. What if I'd taken the time to know Travis's family? What if I'd been more involved? What if I'd been inviting, getting to know him, sharing our values and beliefs? Would Izzy still have gotten pregnant? Would Travis be dead? Would Margaret Owens be in the middle of the worst pain a mother can experience?

The door swings open, and my gaze meets hers. Dark eyes pierce me with what looks an awful lot like hatred. She's smaller than me, thin and an inch or two shorter, but the fire in her expression speaks of rage I don't have the power to hold off.

The length of time that passes, our eyes staring through each other, is undefinable. My muscles burn under the weight of the box. "I thought you could use a meal. Maybe. I'm sincerely sorry for your loss. We all are." Words fall useless to the cold cinderblock steps beneath my feet.

"If you're wanting money for the baby, you can forget it. I don't have any."

My neck stiffens, and I ease a step back. "What?"

"I know what your daughter did to my son. I know she wanted him to stay here. And I know that's the reason he's gone." Her dark eyes narrow.

I turn my head away, unable to muster sympathy while looking at her snarl. Concentrating on the tap, tap, tap of the rain dripping off the edge of the roof, I breathe in the damp freshness and talk myself into a semi-calm. At least enough not to snap her head off. "Mrs. Owens, I'm sorry you feel that way. You're wrong. I can't imagine losing a child. I'll pray for you."

But will I really?

"You'll never know what I'm feeling."

My throat narrows, nearly cutting off my breath. This woman doesn't know me. She doesn't know what I can empathize with and what I can't. And how dare she say that? I could have lost Izzy. But she's right. I'll never understand her grief.

"Travis was all I had."

For the first time, I notice the young boy behind her. His gaze drops to the floor and his shoulders slump. "That's not true. You have your other boys. And maybe more."

"I'm serious. I can't help you with the baby."

"May I come in?"

She cocks her hip, her swollen eyes exploring me for hidden motivations. "This box is really heavy."

Stepping to the side, Margaret Owens lets me past.

The house is cluttered but clean. Kitchen counters peel at the edges and the linoleum is pockmarked. Scanning the place for the overflow of food, I see none. The only sign of compassion is a vase of flowers by the sink. "Do you know when the service will be?"

"I don't . . ." Her cheeks flush.

I lay my fingertips on her upper arm. Muscles tighten under my touch. "I'm sorry. How can I help?" I'm not sure what's happened here, but I really do want to help her.

Her chin drops to her chest as she grabs tufts of her straight, nearly black hair in each hand. Sobs buck her shoulders.

I glance around. The boy is gone.

"You can help by just leaving me alone."

"If that's what you want, I'll go. But call the church in the morning. I'll be the one who answers. We can work out the arrangements together if you want."

Wild eyes turn on me, the lids raging red, but behind the anger there is desperation. How has this woman been so forgotten?

Margaret

Sun shines down on my back, burning through my T-shirt as I walk from the car toward the church. I hope God is getting a real thrill out of this twisted situation, the earth coming alive after a long winter, while my son lies stiff and cold in a mortuary.

I speed-walk through the near-empty parking lot and out of this poorly timed joke.

The church has changed in the over twenty years since I was a regular attender, but I can still see the past in the walls and doors leading to the sanctuary. The memories tear at my crushed heart. I was a little girl here. A little girl with a mom and dad and two brothers. But all that wonderful normal was wiped away in one selfish moment.

My body shakes, and I lean against the rough-textured wall. There's so much I wasn't able to give my sons. A mom and dad. A decent income. A place in the church. The respect of the community. A mother who was whole.

But Travis had overcome it all. He'd become a hero on the baseball field. He would have made it out of this town, if it weren't for the fact that I'm a screwup from a messed up family in a town that's all too willing to dole out punishment.

"Margaret?"

My gut squeezes tight with the urge to puke.

"I was hoping you'd come in."

I swallow the sickness back down. Seeing her does nothing to help me. "I think you mean well, caring for the *needy* and all, but I don't want your help." I set my gaze directly on Jillian Cline, showing my strength.

"Okay." She takes a half step back. "So, why are you here then?"

"I need to talk to the pastor about Travis's service. I can pay."

She looks away as if searching the hall for a hidden savior. "I'll take you to his office. When you settle on the time and date, I'll put together food and help for the reception."

"Just because your daughter is having my son's baby doesn't mean you have to be so involved."

Her eyes go wide, and she whips her gaze around the hall. "That's not it," she answers in a quieter voice. "It's my job. I do it for every service."

I've always known how my son was the smudge in Jillian Cline's perfect life. She has no idea what she missed out on. My son was the sweetest boy a mother could ask for.

Fire burns in my cheeks again. If only I could lie down on the dense carpet and die.

Jillian reaches her hand out like she's going to touch me again but pulls it back before she makes contact. "Follow me."

I have no choice, as usual. At the end of the hall a door is already open. She taps on the wood. "Pastor Gordon. Mrs. Owens is here. Can you see her now?"

"Send her in. Thanks."

Jillian sighs, clearly thrilled to be rid of me. Standing aside, she glides her open palm through the air toward the doorway.

The office smells of oiled wood and lemons. Books line one wall and bright sunlight reflects off a polished desk. This pastor isn't young or old. Probably about the same age I am. Or should be if I wasn't aged by my choices.

He pulls glasses from his nose and sets them near an empty mug. "I'm glad you came in, Mrs. Owens. Please, have a seat."

Gripping both armrests, I do as I'm told, keeping my fingers anchored into the smooth wood. "My son deserves a nice service. I don't have much money, but I can work off what I can't pay right now."

He raises a hand, his head shaking. "No need for that. You're a member of this community. Let us serve you."

"I don't need any handouts. I can make my own way."

"This isn't about charity, though I don't see any problem with one person helping another." He leans back. "Tell me about Travis, and I'll do whatever I can to make the service appropriate for who he was."

Was. The word bounces around in my head. I'll never be able to say Travis *was.*

My shoulders drop, and I cross my arms against my aching belly. "Travis cared. He cared about me when no one else did. He worked hard. He was going to college, you know. They'd offered him a scholarship." Lifting my chin, I look into his eyes. "Can you believe that? They were going to pay his tuition and everything. And he deserved it. And now . . ."

The pastor comes around the desk and kneels beside my chair. "I can't imagine the pain you're experiencing." His hand clasps my forearm. "Would you mind if I pray for you right now?"

I try to answer, but my mouth won't open or form words. Instead, I bow my head and wait for him to start.

"Father, God, our hearts are heavy with grief today, especially this woman who comes before you. Lord, we ask you to work in this situation, and bring blessings from Travis's life. And we ask you to hold his mother as she walks through the intense sorrow of losing a child. For the rest of the family, as they've lost a brother. We know this is a pain you understand. In Jesus's name, amen."

Tears drip from my nose and splash onto my hands. "I want to believe God cares, but life just keeps getting worse." My mouth can't contain all the words crowded inside of me. "I thought when I found out Izzy was pregnant and Travis was considering giving up his chance at college, I thought that was the worst thing that could happen to him. But then . . . then the police came, and they told me about the accident. I don't know what happened afterward, I just remember the doctor and the end."

"This isn't the end. God has good things for your future."

"How can I ever be okay when my son has no future at all?"

I keep staring at him, and he doesn't look away.

But he doesn't answer either.

JILLIAN

When I started my job as the church secretary, I felt useful, needed. After years of raising my sweet children, they had the nerve to grow to school-age, and I didn't know what to do with myself from eight until three aside from sinking into my books. It's not the kind of job that changes the world, but I put my all into each task.

And I loved it until my life was tossed into a giant blender. Who cares if the bulletin goes to the printer on time? I sure don't.

The clock ticks behind my desk in the front office. It's quiet here. No way to ignore my fears. I dial again. And again, no one answers.

Since we got the news, Izzy's spent her days in bed with the covers pulled high. It's all I can do to get her to eat enough to survive. Each day is worse than the one before.

I scan the room, glad no one is waiting. Each time I think of my daughter it's like the first day of kindergarten all over again. Moments after we arrived, Izzy wandered into the room, found a coloring book, and sat quietly at a table, alone. Her teacher gave me the everything-will-be-just-fine speech, but I cried all the way home, then off and on until I picked up my little girl at lunchtime. My heart was shattered without her. I thought that was a mother's pain. I had no idea.

I dial again.

From around the corner, Pastor Gordon sticks his head into the room. "Hey there, can we talk?"

I slam the phone down as if I've been caught in something devious. Had he been watching me wrestle with mommy guilt?

"How about in my office?"

My face flushes with heat. "Sure." I nod. "What do you need?" But he's already down the hall. The toast I had for breakfast turns to cement in my stomach. Pastor Gordon is not a formal man. He wears a collared shirt and jeans to work and prefers to do business anywhere but in his office.

Unless the situation is serious.

I pull a paper off the printer and set it on my desk before following him down the hall.

"Have a seat."

My heart rate increases with the lack of his usual smile.

He skirts around his desk, eases into his chair, and rests his elbows on the desk's shiny surface. "I'd rather have this talk with you and Garrett together, but I don't think this can wait. Margaret Owens told me Izzy is pregnant. Is this true?"

My body freezes, like some sort of paralysis is seeping through my veins and stiffening every muscle with its cold grip. This is the beginning. The news is out. No more hiding. No more peace. My full effort is needed to force my head to nod and with that slight movement the tears are released. I can't stop the flow. It's like the way I cried all those years ago, only deeper.

I can't see his face through the blur, but the tissue he offers tickles as it brushes my hand, and I take it.

"I was really hoping this was a mistake. How's Izzy doing?"

"Not well," I manage over shuddering breaths.

"Does she have a plan for the baby?"

I blink enough to make out his face. "What do you mean?"

"Is she planning to parent or place the baby?" He runs two fingers over an eyebrow.

"I don't know. It's so soon. There's no good answer."

He leans farther forward. "She's not considering abortion, is she?"

"It's too late even if she was."

"You'd be surprised. My wife has counseled women who terminated well into their pregnancies. I'm relieved Izzy won't be one of them. It breaks my heart to hear the grief these ladies are left with."

He has no idea how much I understand, but I'm not about to tell him my secret. It's more important to keep now than ever before. At a women's retreat a few years ago, I came so close to telling his wife, Lisa. What a mistake that would have been. Even if the conversation remained confidential, it would have started an avalanche. "Is that all? I have a lot of work on the bulletin."

"No. There's one more thing."

Lacing my fingers together, I dig my nails into my skin.

"I'm going to have to ask Izzy to step down from student leadership."

I gasp.

"It must feel like I'm being cruel, but I really need to think about the other kids too. We're teaching about purity, and Izzy is pregnant. How can we expect them to trust us?"

My hands form light fists. I want to fight this decision, keep even this small loss from touching my already wounded daughter. But I know, if we were talking about someone else, and if the conversation took place only a few weeks ago, I would stand beside Pastor Gordon, in full agreement.

My legs are as heavy as my heart. By the time I'm back behind my own desk in the office, the weight of our lives is like a mountain sitting on top of me.

"Jillian?"

My head pops up so quickly it tweaks a nerve that sends a jolt of pain down to my shoulder blades.

Claudette Hamond stands at the window to the office, her weight tilted toward the cane in her right hand.

"I'm sorry, Claudette. I didn't hear you come in. What can I do for you?" I hope my voice sounds steady, but all I can hear is the high-pitched squeak that comes out when I'm nervous.

"Just delivering a plate of cookies for Ethel. She's taking them over to the nursing home on Tuesday." She hefts a basket onto the counter between us then lifts out a plate stacked with oatmeal cookies, covered in plastic wrap. "Was that Margaret Owens I saw in the parking lot?"

I nod, not trusting my voice until I have another moment to gain my control back.

Claudette shakes her head. "That poor girl. It's been a rough life for that one. I went to school with her grandparents, you know."

"I didn't. Was that around here?" I push my chair away from the computer.

"Just down the road in Silbany. They lived right on the edge of the Indian land and were very involved with that community."

I nod, wanting her to continue, but afraid to look too eager.

"My late husband, Carl, was a mentor to Margaret's daddy. They all went to this very church, until Margaret's mama was killed in a hunting accident. Don't know what happened after that. The family just faded away." She shrugs. "It's a shame. And now that girl is going through another loss." She taps her finger on the plate of cookies. "Ethel will be by for these soon. Don't let the pastor at them." Her wrinkled face lights with a grin.

So many questions swirl in my mind. How old was Margaret when her mother died? Did her father remarry? Why did they leave the church? But Claudette has finished the part of the story she intended to share, leaving me somewhere between rage at the woman who poured out our secret and sorrow for the mom who'd lost the most precious thing in her world.

Izzy

I hold the sweater so tight my fingers ache. The loose knit hanging below my hips is the only thing keeping Travis's funeral from morphing into a public scandal.

There's a crowd already gathered in the sanctuary, mostly students and teachers. Is there anyone left at school? Is today even a school day? Every moment since I heard about the accident has been a blur. I'm not even sure where I got this sweater. I don't remember owning it or ever seeing it before.

My father takes my arm and leads me down the familiar aisle, but instead of our worship team on the stage, today there is a wooden box. And inside the box . . .

He was the boy I used to think I loved. The one I'd given my heart to, and the one I later regretted. That's the thing I can't quite swallow. I miss

Travis. He was my friend. We shared so much together, and now we share a child, but I don't feel like I've lost my one true love.

Shouldn't I?

Isn't that what all the staring people are thinking?

My dad guides me into a row after my mom and Zach. We're not in the front. Not even in the second row.

I blow out a breath. That would be too familiar. Too much like Travis and I were family. Too much like I'm the mother of his child and the girl who ruined the last weeks of his life. Maybe even the girl, yes definitely the girl, who caused his life to end.

Tears run hot down my cheeks again. How can I possibly have more? But these are tears of self-pity, and I hate myself for each drip as they roll off my chin.

Mrs. Owens and her youngest son, Deven, sit alone. I'd expected to see at least one of the older brothers. Don't they let you out of jail for a day when your brother dies? Is his dad here? I don't even know what the man looks like.

Behind his mom sits Officer Hobbs, bent forward next to Officer Denning. His chin is tipped to his chest, his hand wipes over his head. He reaches for Mrs. Owens's shoulder. Even from here, I can see her flinch.

My body begins to shake like it does when I step out of the pool after a hard race and my skin collides with cold air.

They're looking at me. All around the room, people are looking at me.

"I can't do this." I start to rise, but my dad's firm hand holds me in my seat.

"If you leave now, you'll regret it."

What's one more regret? But I stay.

From my mother's bottomless purse she pulls six tissues—two for me, two for Zachary, and two for herself.

The room falls silent. I hadn't noticed the piano music until it quit.

Pastor Gordon starts talking, but I don't want to hear anything he has to say. I lean into my dad's side. He's warm. I'm icy cold.

The baby kicks.

Tears flow.

Reaching my hand into the sweater pocket, I finger the edge of the ultrasound picture. I'm crying for my baby. This child will never know what it's like to have a daddy. Never have his warm side and strong arm for comfort.

My child will never know what it's like to be part of a complete family, all because I compromised.

Chapter 11

STACEY

The violet folder holding my designs for the logo and flyers is tucked under my arm, and for the first time since I've arrived in Oregon, the sidewalks are completely dry. If it weren't for Irene's refusal to communicate via email, I wouldn't be here on such a beautiful afternoon. I'd be off exploring the city. Or not.

At least I wouldn't have stepped foot in this house again.

And I really want to want that. I mean, my first experience was like cliff-diving, but the girls, especially Sierra, touched my heart. I catch myself. This isn't a baby store. I'm not here to find my child. I'm here to do a job. Once that job is done, I'll be on to something else. Whatever that is.

I tap on the door.

After a couple minutes, I tap again.

The hiccupy wails of a newborn funnel down from a second story window. I look up, but the sun is fading, and I can't tell if the glass is open. Finally, I turn the knob and push it open.

Girls are piled on the two couches. Another plows through the swinging kitchen door, a huge stainless steel bowl of popcorn held at her hip.

Behind one of the couches, Irene leans forward in an armchair, lamplight illuminating the baby hat she knits.

"There's a baby crying."

All eyes turn to me.

"Stacey, I'm so glad you came. We have some making up to do with you." Irene gives Nikki a nod toward the stairs, but the girl looks away as if she doesn't get the reference.

Irene sets the knitting in a basket on the floor, stands up, and positions herself behind Nikki. Placing her hands on the girl's shoulders she waits without a word, more patient than I've ever been. But I can see Irene is wearing thin too when she tips her head up like she's pleading with God for a break.

With one finger, she taps Nikki's shoulder.

"What?" She twists to look at Irene, her expression less than respectful.

Irene waits a beat before answering. "You need to keep the monitor on. The baby needs you."

"He's fine. Children need to learn their mothers aren't going to come running every time they cry. And, anyway, I'm tired. I just had a baby." She turns her head away.

The folder slips from my grip and skitters along the floor.

Irene walks around the couch and stands in front of Nikki, her arms crossed, her body bent slightly forward with a large pendant swinging like she's about to perform a hypnotism.

My attention is drawn to Sierra who shrinks into the corner of the couch as the conflict rises.

Collecting the folder, I stay on my knees near Sierra. Maybe the presence of someone else will soothe her in some way. Or am I only making it worse?

Irene clasps her hands together. "Your son is a newborn baby. All you teach him by not caring for him is that his needs will not get met by his mother."

My jaw drops open. The words are clear, brutal, and . . . true.

"I take care of him fine." She stands, broader and taller than Irene, then takes a step too close for comfort.

With her thumb, Irene slides the dial on the baby monitor to maximum volume.

Tiny frantic wails shake my heart and make me want to scale the stairs at superhuman speed. I would never let him cry that way, but I don't have a son to soothe. The unfairness of it has a bitter taste.

"Go get him right now." Irene takes her own step forward. She's not a big woman, not tall or thick, but I get the feeling she isn't someone to mess with.

How would I handle a situation like this? Could I be so brave?

Everyone is watching now. I skim the audience. It's like a death scene. Cate holds little Marianna close to her chest. The young mother's eyes are brimming with tears.

"I'll do it." Sierra climbs from her corner, tossing the maroon blanket on the couch behind her. She's up the stairs before anyone can respond.

"See." Nikki's eyes narrow into a glare. "Sierra is willing to help. At least someone has compassion around here."

I bite my lower lip. It's the pain that stops me from unleashing a wave of condemnation all over the girl.

"Nikki." Irene stops. Breathes in and out. "Nikki, you and I have a mandatory meeting coming up. I'm pulling in a board member. You will not miss it. Am I clear?"

The soft lilt of Sierra's voice drifts through the baby monitor. I imagine her rocking the baby back and forth as her voice rises and falls, rises and falls. His screams quiet into tiny gasps then slurping as Sierra must be feeding him a bottle.

Nikki snatches the baby monitor from the end table and lumbers toward the stairs.

A shiver runs across my skin. "Is she safe?"

Irene gives a little nod then guides me toward the hall that leads to her office. "Nikki is angry. Her parents are meth addicts. She's practically raised herself and her little brother. But even he's on the street now. I had to fight hard with the board to get her into the house. A friend took a special interest in her and thought we might be able to give her a chance. But, I don't know. Maybe I was wrong."

"What would have happened if you'd said no?"

"Hard to say. She'd probably have had the baby with no home to come back to. The father's been out of the picture since before she even knew she was pregnant. I was praying she'd take this chance." Irene brushed a hand over her cheek. "It's so hard to watch someone throw away their future. And even harder to watch her do the same to her son. Maybe tomorrow will be different."

"Maybe."

The red tinge in Irene's cheeks tells me she isn't counting on this miracle. And why would she?

"Well, that's more drama than we usually get, even here."

I hand her the file.

Gray curls bob as she nods at each image. "These are great. Carrie will be in tomorrow morning. Can you bring these and meet her here?"

"Carrie?"

"She's a board member. We need approval from one of them before we move forward. Oh, and I have something for you." She steps into her office and pulls a stapled packet of papers from her desk. "Here. You should give these to Carrie tomorrow too."

Application for volunteers. My jaw opens, but when I start to protest, she's already gone.

◆ ◆ ◆

The only thing breaking up the days of unpacking are these trips to A Child's Home. I can't believe I'm back again this morning. There's something about this house. It heals and hurts at the same time. It's like a weird addiction. Like the people who cut themselves to release . . . something. I don't know. Even my thoughts have become a swirl of confusion.

The twelve-passenger van pulls out of the driveway as I lock my car parked along the road. I planned to be a few minutes late and miss seeing the girls altogether, but punctuality is like a curse sometimes. I can't help being on time.

The sun shines down on me. Maybe the golden rays are a sign things are changing. I sure hope so. Keith and I have an appointment at an adoption agency later. I can't even think about it now. I shake my head and step up onto the porch.

Inside, the house is oddly quiet, almost eerie.

A door closes and the wood floors creak as someone comes my way. As she draws closer, a hollow rhythm and soothing voice join in.

Irene startles when she sees me in the entryway. "Hush now." She pats the baby in a faster rhythm.

Beneath the baby-blue knitted blanket, his body squirms.

I actually itch to hold him, but my brain is screaming not to get too close. He's not mine, will never be mine.

Tipping him away from her chest, Irene stares into his gray eyes. "Time to eat, isn't it?"

"Shouldn't Nikki be doing that?" There goes my tongue again. It's really none of my business. I'm suddenly aware that I'm still carrying the volunteer application in my folder. Why haven't I tossed it into the recycling bin?

The look on Irene's face is enough to answer the question. Before I can decipher her movement, the baby is in my arms.

"I'll get the bottle. You keep this little guy happy." She rubs her finger across his lips. "It shouldn't be too hard. He's a sweetie."

I settle on the couch and really look at him. He's nothing like my baby boy, but he's still precious. He's a perfect miracle. Why can't Nikki see how lucky she is to have a healthy, thriving son?

He squirms and his chin quivers. Slipping my pinky into his mouth, he latches on and sucks with passion.

Nikki makes her way down the stairs, her hair wrapped in a green towel and the robe she borrowed the night she went into labor tied tight around her waist. She walks right past me and toward the kitchen. Just as she reaches the door, it swings open and Irene emerges, a five-ounce bottle in one hand and a towel in the other.

In a flash Irene's smile drops into a frown. "There you are."

"I was in the shower."

"Nikki, you can't leave a baby alone on the couch. Any number of things could happen."

The girl looks back and seems to notice me for the first time. "Looks like he's fine to me."

"That's not the point. I was here. But what if he slipped into the cushions? He can't help himself if he gets trapped."

She shrugs. "I guess I just forgot. I wanted to shower, and I forgot to put him in the cradle thing. It won't happen again."

Irene hands me the bottle. Should I give the baby over to his mother now? But Nikki fiddles with the towel, not seeming to care who shares this moment with her son.

The front door opens and a woman with dark hair highlighted by flyaway grays and topped with a pink and purple knit hat steps into the room. Her eyes blink hard behind round glasses. On the dining room table, she drops a thick stack of files. "Good morning. I'm early. Hope that's okay." Her voice is like the ups and downs of a bird's song.

"Come on over." Irene waves her closer. "I have two new people for you to meet."

She tugs off thin gloves and stuffs them in her pocket, then leans over my shoulder.

"This is Stacey, she's the one who's doing the artwork for us, and this"— she runs her hand over the baby's head—"this is our newest arrival."

I reach a hand out from under the baby to formalize the introduction.

"This is Carrie Wattly, one of our faithful board members."

"Wow. He's gorgeous. What's his name?"

Irene looks to Nikki.

"I haven't decided yet."

I gasp a little too loud, but Carrie doesn't flinch.

"Do you want to hold him?" I ask.

She looks to Nikki. Why didn't I think to do that?

As if she couldn't care one bit less, Nikki shrugs and drops into an armchair.

Carrie takes the little bundle and speaks hushed words into his ear, like a prayer or a blessing. "This is what makes the effort worth every moment."

Nikki steps forward. "I'll take him now and go upstairs."

My heartbeat skips. I'm not sure why, but I can't stand the idea of her taking him away. Will she look after him? Will he get the rest of his bottle? It's silly. She's his mother, but anger is so close to the surface with Nikki. It's like it fills her and she doesn't have room for him.

Irene raises her hand. "Wait, please. This is the perfect time to have our mandatory meeting."

Nikki's face goes pale, but she sits, the baby lying across her lap.

I pick up my file and search the room. Where can I go?

As if she can hear my thoughts, Irene touches my arm, which only makes me want out more. "Have a seat, Stacey. You're one of us now. No secrets in this house."

One of them? My life is moving forward without my consent. But I do as I'm told. Obedient to a fault. I believe my mother would actually be proud.

Irene sits on the edge of the couch, hands folded, and bows her head. "Nikki, you know the rules of the house, correct?"

"Yes." She doesn't make eye contact with any of us, not even her son.

"One of those rules requires you to take good care of your baby."

Her chin shoots up. "Cate asks for help. Why is it okay for her?"

"You've stumbled onto the answer yourself," Irene says. "Cate *asks* for help. We can't have you leaving him around and letting him cry when he needs something. One of the top goals here is to help you bond with your child. Nikki, do you feel like you've formed an attachment with him?"

Dark eyebrows squeeze together. "I'm not a bad mother."

Carrie shakes her head. "That's not what we're saying. Irene and I have discussed the situation, and we believe some extra time with Nurse Tower and Virginia may be helpful. They volunteer time to you girls because they really want to help."

"You think I'm crazy?"

I reach my hand out to rebalance the baby on her lap. The girls talked about Virginia the night I'd been on duty. Only Cate had anything positive to say about the therapist, but sessions are part of the house requirements.

"No," said Irene. "No one thinks you're crazy. Virginia's job is to help you deal with your hurts and give you a plan for your future. It's amazing how our relationships with our own moms and dads affect the way we raise our kids." Something changes in Irene's expression. She clinches her hands tighter and looks away.

"I just don't think I need that," Nikki says.

Carrie kneels down next to Nikki. "I'm afraid it's not that simple. We're going to require you to do these things, or we'll have to ask you to move out. Do you understand?"

Goose bumps pop up along my arms. Where would she go? Who would care for the baby?

"I understand I have to do whatever you say." Sarcasm oozes from the words, but at least she seems to get the serious nature of the situation.

Carrie leans closer. "We're not trying to trap you. You have the freedom to leave here any time you like. I hope you'll choose to stay. But while you're here, there are certain rules you must follow. If you don't follow the rules, you give us no other choice." Carrie runs a hand over her long hair. "Nikki, I know you came in late in your pregnancy. Did anyone talk to you about adoption?"

Her lip slides up in a snarl. "Yeah. But I said no."

"You can still choose to place your baby. It's not too late. I want you to know that."

My heart beats faster and my face turns hot. I hold myself firm on the couch, but I want to jump up and tell her how much I want a baby. How I could love him as if I'd given birth to him, but I promised myself I wouldn't go there. Not here. Maybe not anywhere.

Baby Boy fusses.

"I've got to change him." Nikki scoops him into her arms and climbs the stairs.

Carrie plops onto the couch. "She's a tough one. Any idea if she'll come around?"

"Tough? You wouldn't believe. I just need to get through to her heart," Irene says.

My mouth opens and, of course, my resolve to stay silent is once again broken. "Do you really think there's a chance? I mean, she doesn't seem to care most of the time. She's angry. I don't think I've ever known anyone so mad at the world."

Irene nods. "The thing is, the anger is there to hide what's really going on. It's a secondary emotion. There's always something else behind its mask. I think she's scared." She looks at Carrie. "So, what do you have for me?"

"You're not going to like it. These are the only four applications we didn't have to reject on the spot."

"Applications for what?" I ask.

Irene rubs her fingers into her forehead. "To replace me."

The room turns cool.

My mind swirls with so many more questions, but I hold them back for another time.

Irene flips through the papers Carrie handed her.

"You wouldn't believe the responses we got. Like no one even read the ad. Seven were from men. Seriously."

"What about this one?" She taps a paper then holds it up for us to see.

"I knew you'd like her. She was my pick too, but I took a call on the way here. She's withdrawn her application. It seems, you'll love this, she just found out she's pregnant. Unplanned."

Irene tosses the papers on the floor. "I guess I'll be here for a while." The whisper of a smile dances on her lips.

◆　◆　◆

My thoughts are still on Nikki when Keith and I arrive for our afternoon appointment. I follow him up the steps to a home renovated into a business. There's something about this kind of place I like. I imagine how the house looked before, who lived here, what happens in the rooms I can't see.

The chimes on the door jingle and Keith pushes it open. Inside, soft music is pumped into what must have been the living room. No one sits behind the desk stationed at one end of the gray-blue room with bright white accents.

I tug at a loose string hanging from the sleeve of my yellow sweater. It helps control the shaking of my hands.

"Settle down." Keith kisses my forehead. "We've done this before."

"Is that supposed to help me? What if this turns out like last time? Or worse?" But I have no idea what I mean by that. There is no *worse*.

"That's very unlikely. We can't stay in a holding pattern because of what happened." He starts to say something else, but a woman walks in, breaking me free from the moment.

"Are you Mr. and Mrs. Frey?"

There's no one else here. "Yes."

"Please come with me." She leads us down a narrow hallway and into a bedroom converted to an office. Two wooden armchairs with deep blue cushions are arranged in front of a modest desk. On the wall hang a hodgepodge of pictures, all of babies and children. "I'm Gina Bane, one of the caseworkers." She watches us for a moment.

Swallowing hard, I shake off the desire to run.

"So, you're interested in adoption. What brought you to your decision?"

No beating around the bush here. It's a flashback to our original home study. Every detail of our lives from birth forward laid out for all to see.

Keith drops into a chair. "Actually, we chose to adopt three years ago."

And here comes the sick ache in my chest.

"So, you already have a child?"

"No. We were matched with a young lady, but when our son"—Keith hesitates for the slightest moment—"when he was born, there was a problem. He died later that day."

I look away. Keith hides his pain well for strangers, but I can see it flaming just below the surface. Breathing deep, I examine the shag carpet, the stacks of books beside the desk, the half-wilted plant that's set near the trash can, and the paper circles from a hole-punch that litter the floor like snow.

"How long ago did this happen?" Gina asks.

I want to scream that my son wasn't a *this*, but looking crazy here isn't a smart move.

"Two years. We lived in Tennessee then."

"So, you haven't been through the process here in Oregon. Mrs. Frey? Can I call you Stacey?"

"Yes." I force my gaze back to her face and push a smile into place.

"Do you feel you've had enough time to grieve your loss?" She tips her head and straight brown hair cascades over her shoulder.

My heart beats hard. If I mess this up, I can't imagine how much it would hurt my husband. "No." If only I could suck that one word back into my mouth, but it's too late. "I don't think there will ever be enough time in one life to move past the love you have for a child. When they put him in my arms, he became a part of me. And then he was gone. I'm sorry." I peer into Keith's worried eyes. "I don't think I'll ever get over losing him, but I do think there's room in my heart for another baby."

"That's exactly what I was hoping to hear."

Keith's eyes widen.

"If you're ready, we can get started on the mountain of paperwork. We'll need you to come to a one-day training, but depending on my conversation with your caseworker in Tennessee, we may be able to forgo that piece. I'll need a copy of your home study, and we'll see about getting it updated and approved in Oregon."

Pulling me into him, chair and all, Keith wraps his arms around me and plants a kiss on my cheek.

Chapter 12

JILLIAN

Walla Walla onions and green peppers fill the kitchen with spicy sweetness as they sizzle in my pan.

It's a game.

Pretend we're all okay, while the world crashes down, destroying everything we've worked for.

It's a game I'm not winning no matter how hard I plan every move.

I feel him before I hear him, another side effect of a home ready to implode under the pressure. Zachary snuggles into my side and watches me move veggies around the skillet as if dinner will magically solve our problems.

"Looks good, Mom." His soft blue eyes are so very much like mine, but with the beauty of innocence. How can I keep him stainless?

I smile down at him. "What are you talking about? You can't stand green peppers and onions." With my pinky, I pull back a strand of his hair.

Shrugging his shoulders, he squeezes closer. "It looks good in a purely artistic way."

"Nice save, kiddo. Why don't you set the table?"

Without argument, he takes to the task. What I wouldn't give for a normal complaint about now.

The growl of Garrett's engine climbs toward our house. It sputters to a stop. A moment later he's inside shedding his shoes and coat, then he's beside me, breathing in deep over the pan.

"You'd think I hadn't fed you guys in a month."

His eyebrows rise. "We're hungry after a long day of work. Isn't that right, Zach?"

Zachary's head bobs. "School is a crazy business, Dad."

Garrett plants a kiss on his son's head. He's a good dad. Devoted. Nothing like the man who was my father in name only.

He's dead now. At least that's what I heard a few years ago. The news didn't affect me. Does that mean I'm cold, heartless?

My son plays dramatic with mock disgust then goes back to his chore.

"How's Izzy doing? You think she'll come out for dinner?" Garrett empties his pockets of change then deposits the money in the coin bank.

I press my fingertips to the bridge of my nose. "She's only been out of her room to use the bathroom. It's all I can do to get any food in her at all. I've made another appointment with the doctor. Maybe he can get through."

"This has got to stop." His jaw sets and his military facade steps forward.

My own posture straightens. "There's not much we can do." I drop my volume. "I'm worried about what she's doing to the baby. She's lost a lot of weight."

"Hey, Zach. I almost forgot. I have a candy bar in my truck for you. Run on out there and get it."

Zachary looks from his dad to me, unfooled, but unwilling to give up chocolate for information.

The door snaps shut and Garrett turns to look at me. "I spoke with a buddy from the guard today. He told me about a place in Portland where girls who have unsupported pregnancies live."

My joints stiffen. "Izzy is not unsupported."

"Yes, but my friend thought they might make an exception under the circumstances."

"No. She needs to be here where we can watch over her. Not in some turn of the century hideaway for unwed mothers. She needs us."

"Jillian, this isn't a judgment on you. I'm trying to find a way to solve a very difficult problem. And the house is supposed to be very nice. There are a few pictures on the website."

"That's the thing. We can't solve this. There's nothing we can do to make this go away. It's not like we can turn back time."

"I get that. But she's slipping further and further from us. She may need to get away for a while. At least there she could get the training and education she needs and not have to face Travis's death at every turn."

The sweet smell turns acrid. Flipping off the burner, I pull the smoking vegetables from the heat. "So much for fajitas."

"Jillian, I don't want her to go either, but we need to consider all the options." A curl forms a perfect scoop on his forehead. He'll need a haircut soon. Sometimes he looks so much like Izzy it grabs my heart.

The beginnings of an idea form in my mind. "We can tell people she's visiting family or something."

"And what happens when she comes back with a baby?" he asks.

"Maybe she doesn't." I drop my gaze to the floor.

"What?"

Cold pours through my body. I can't have my daughter living every moment of her life wondering about where her baby is and if it's okay. But I also can't bear to have her hurt day after day by people's judgments. "Maybe she chooses to place the baby for adoption. I don't know."

"No. She's our daughter and we'll see her through this." Garrett's jaw muscles jerk.

"Don't I have a tiny say in my own future?"

I spin around.

Izzy is dwarfed by the comforter wrapped around her shoulders. Her eyes are red like they are most of the time now, with dark circles underneath.

"Of course you have a say." Garrett tucks matted curls behind her ear.

"Then I want to go. I can't be here any longer." Tears rush forward, spilling down her cheeks. "I need to get away."

Garrett pulls her into his arms, leaving me out in the cold.

I try to force my feet to go to them, to show Izzy I'm here to support her, but all I can see is my daughter being erased. Will I ever get my baby back?

IZZY

The house for pregnant girls is huge. I've never been in one so big, but it's also ordinary. Green lawn, white porch, pretty much like the others on the street except for the small sign along the walkway. Honestly, if it weren't for the mess I'm in, this is the kind of house I'd print and paste into my notebook. Character without being snobby.

When I move in, I won't bring my notebook of dreams. It's still tucked into the drawer of my nightstand where it's been since the day I found out I was pregnant.

I look from our empty van to my dad, already at the door. Mom didn't come. She made up an excuse about Zach's class, but I've seen the panic in her eyes. She feels like my coming here means she's failed. And she sure hates to fail.

"Come on, Princess." He rubs his hands up and down his arms. His gaze slips past me and down the street.

I haven't bothered to hide the bulge today. Now I regret the decision.

My belly curves out over my sweatpants and my purple swim team T-shirt stretches over my middle. Will it ever go back to its original shape?

Will I?

Dad knocks on the door. His shoulders sag like he's had a hard day at work followed by one of his Guard weekends.

But he hasn't.

It's just me. And all the problems I've brought to our family. They'll be better off with me out of the house. Today is supposed to be a visit to help us decide, but I already have. I'm leaving home.

The thick door creaks open, the sound giving me shivers. The woman on the other side is older, probably about the age of my own grandmother.

I swallow a wave of sickness. How will I ever face Grandma and Grandpa Cline? Do they already know? Are they still coming to visit this summer?

"Good afternoon. You must be Isabella and Garrett." She pulls glasses from her nose and lets them fall to her chest on a gold chain. "Please, come in."

The entryway widens into a living room with a fire crackling in the fireplace.

"This is our main living area. Usually there are girls hanging around in here, but they're not home from school yet." She holds her glasses up and checks her watch. "Follow me and I'll show you the kitchen."

I yawn. This is more action than I've had in weeks. What day is today? I follow but let my dad ask the questions. None of it really matters anyway. They talk for the longest time about the meals. Can't they see I have much bigger problems than what's for dinner?

Hello, I'm pregnant. My baby's father is dead.

Dead is permanent.

So are babies.

Noises buzz in from the swinging door.

"That will be the girls. Isabella, let me introduce you."

"Izzy," I say. Isabella makes me feel like a child.

She cocks her head. "What's that?"

"My name is Izzy."

She smiles then leads us into the living area.

A blond girl sets a car seat with a baby in it on the couch, then flops herself down. "Ah. Home."

"I don't want to hear it," says another girl. "At least you can put your baby down." She rubs her palms over a huge belly. Gigantic.

My own bump is expanding wildly each day. If I grow that big, I'll burst.

The blond opens her eyes. "Oh, sorry." Popping up, she steps toward us. "I didn't know we had company. I'm Cate." She turns the car seat around. "This is my daughter, Marianna."

"Nice to meet you." I stare at the baby, so calm, and the girl seems relaxed and unworried. I'll never be like that. Never again.

Cate looks to Irene. "Have you shown her upstairs yet?"

"Go ahead. That will give me some time to chat with her dad."

Cate lifts Marianna from the carrier.

The baby yawns and pulls her legs toward her tummy.

"Anyone else?" Cate scans the others.

"I'll go." The girl must be about as far along as I am, but short and stocky, like a gymnast.

Cate waves them on. "This is Sierra. She hasn't been here long either, but she's already part of the family."

Sierra looks away. She doesn't respond.

"So, here we are. The upstairs is mainly bedrooms. With five of us, you'll have to share a room."

I nod, but I've never shared a bedroom in my life. The thought sticks in my mouth like a bad taste. I peek into a room with two twin beds. The walls are a cool blue with bright white trim around the window. Two desks, one large dresser, and a closet. That's it. "Where do you keep all your stuff?"

The girls exchange a look that confirms I'm a total outsider.

"Come into my room," Cate says. She opens the door and lets me and Sierra in first. "Go ahead, have a seat." She points to a double bed against the far wall.

The room is pretty much the same as the other except the bed is bigger and there's a crib at one end. On the white dresser sits two framed photos. One of Cate and Marianna in the hospital and the other of an ultrasound. It doesn't look any different from the one they gave me. Maybe it's an elaborate joke. The ultrasound machine plays a prerecorded video. Travis never died. I'm not pregnant. I tap my fingers on my stomach. It taps back. So much for the fantasy.

"Would you like to hold her?" Cate offers the baby to me, assuming my answer.

My mouth goes dry. How can I tell her that babies are about the scariest things in the world to me right now? I'm not one of those babysitter types. I swim.

Before I can coax my mouth to answer, the baby is in my arms. She stretches a tiny fist out like she's looking for a fight, then dark eyelashes flutter, and she stares up at me.

My breath catches. In a few months, it will be my son or daughter lying in my arms. That's how things can get worse. What am I supposed to do with the baby when it's out? What if the kid cries?

My right side warms as Cate settles alongside me. "It's going to be okay. I was scared when I got here too."

Sierra still stands in the middle of the room looking like she doesn't know what to do with her hands. "She's right," she says in the faintest voice. "It's the best place in a rough situation."

"Do your families visit much?" I ask.

Sierra ducks her head.

"Most of us don't have much family." Cate wraps Marianna's tiny fingers around her own pinky. "You're so lucky to have a dad who cares enough to come here."

I nod, shame washing over me. I really am very fortunate. The trouble I'm in is my fault and my fault alone.

Cate leans back on the bed. "When I first came here, I didn't know anyone, and I was scared to death. My boyfriend broke up with me the moment he found out about the baby, and my aunt told me I'd have to find somewhere else to live. She said I was a bad influence on her kids." She pats my leg. "But the people here, especially Irene, they see me as a daughter of the King. Do you know Jesus?"

The thud and crash of my heart must be loud enough to hear in the hallway. "Yes." But I wonder, do I really? And, seriously, who talks like that?

"Then you know He loves you even though you're in a mess."

Sierra blinks away tears. She catches me watching her and turns toward the pictures, pretending to be interested.

Cate walks over to her and pulls her into a side hug. "It's going to be okay."

I doubt she's right, but the baby is starting to warm my arms, and with her coos comes a sliver of hope.

Chapter 13

Margaret

I weave my car around potholes and toward my house. There's someone already there. Headlights shine shadows around the double-wide. But it's the lights on the roof of the car, even though they're off, that stop my breath. It's a patrol car. Waiting for me. What now?

I cut the engine and demand my shaking legs to step from the car. Sick rolls over in my stomach and up my throat. Slamming the door shut, I wipe my hands on the apron of my uniform.

From the dark, a familiar figure steps forward.

My knees buckle, and I grab the side mirror for support.

In an instant he's there beside me, just like that awful night. His hand reaches around my upper arm and holds me steady. "I'm sorry. It's okay. I didn't mean to scare you. I'm such a clod." He shakes his head. "I thought it best if we dealt with the situation here. Can we go inside?"

"It's okay?" I'm staring straight into his eyes. I'll know if he's hiding something horrible.

He nods.

I force a deep breath. "Deven?"

"He's with me. He's safe."

I turn my face away and tug my arm free, wiping away the tear that made it past my guard. "I'm fine."

His boots crunch in the gravel. "Come on out." This time his voice is full of strength and authority. Much like the voice he used with Kane. He opens the back door.

My youngest steps from the squad car.

I can't look at him. At the door, I open the house and find the air inside as cold, if not colder, than outdoors. Sliding the thermostat up, I flip on some lights. Not the kind of place you'd invite company, but it's what I have. Plopping my purse onto the counter, I turn toward the fridge. "Can I get you anything to drink?" I scan the shelves. I don't even have milk.

"No thanks. Deven and I had a run-in tonight."

We're going to get right to it, I see. I close the fridge, keeping my palm flat on the cold surface. "What did he do?"

"It's more what he was about to do. I caught him with a rock in his hand, and an eye on a window downtown."

"I wasn't going to do anything." Deven's voice cracks on the last word. The next sound is his door slamming.

I turn to the counter, my work shoes sticking to the linoleum either from something I've stepped in at the diner or a mess I haven't cleaned well here. It doesn't really matter. What's the point? "What are you going to do?" My voice sounds flat even to me.

He scoots out a stool and sits. "Nothing. Nothing as far as legal consequences anyway."

"What do you mean?"

"I mean I'm not writing him up."

"Thank you." It's all I can do right now to take in enough oxygen to survive. Dealing with court again? I can't.

"He could use a man's influence."

Heat flushes my face. "Couldn't we all. But guess what." I flip my palms up. "There isn't one, and the chances of me bringing home anyone worth being around are pretty slim."

His eyes dart around the room. "I'm not suggesting anything like that. I meant, if it's okay with you, I could check in on him."

I stand straighter, crossing my arms at my chest, and look him up and down. "Why would you do that?"

"Because I care about you. And Deven."

"What do you have in mind?"

"I work with the middle schoolers at church. I could take him with me to youth group. Maybe we could catch a burger every now and then."

I loved church when I was Deven's age. Youth group was the best part of the week. But I failed to give my boys what I'd had. Flashes of their father go off like firecrackers in my mind. The violent mood swings, the alcohol, the day he walked out and never looked back. The church won't want me soiling the sanctuary, but maybe Deven would be okay.

"What do you think?"

"Will the church mind?"

"Because you're not a member?"

"Sure." I pick up a pile of mail, flipping through the envelopes.

His hands warm my arm. "Trust me. They'll love him. I wouldn't let anything happen to him."

He's too close. Too warm. But my legs won't obey me and step back.

Officer Hobbs moves away.

Swallowing, I touch the place his hands just left. A lifetime has passed since a man has been so gentle. Travis's lifetime. Guilt hammers my bones. How could I allow his touch to bring me comfort, to make me feel the slightest fraction of life, when Travis, my very own son, will never be here again? "I think you should go now."

"Did I do something wrong?"

"No. I need to put some food on the table and get ready for tomorrow." What a joke. There's barely a cracker in the house. I made it to work today because my job was on the line. The grocery store will wait. For what, I have no idea.

"I could help." His words sound almost desperate, pleading.

I shake my head. Throbbing bobs behind my eyes. With one hand, I press hard into my forehead. "I'm too tired for help. Thank you."

"Do you mind if I say goodbye to Deven?"

"Be my guest, but when he's mad, he doesn't care for company."

Hobbs knocks on Deven's door. "Let me in, please." No request, just polite clarity.

The door opens an inch and Hobbs pushes it the rest of the way, walking in, but not closing it behind him.

One child at home, and I can't even handle him.

* * *

I drop two full grocery bags on the counter in my empty kitchen. Keys slip from my fingers and clank to the linoleum. "Deven. Officer Hobbs will be here any minute. Come eat."

Light shines under his bedroom door.

"Deven, come on." I pull a new jar of store-brand crunchy peanut butter and a loaf of bread from the bag, and grape jelly from the refrigerator. I open the jelly lid and huff; tracks of peanut butter are swirled into the translucent purple. "I'm making you a sandwich."

With a butter knife, I spread peanut butter across the slice, the scent rich and sweet. My stomach growls. I sweep my finger along the top of the jar and pop it into my mouth. For a moment the sensation is wonderful, and then I see Travis doing the same thing when he was in middle school. It grows heavy in my mouth. I spit the glob into the sink and rinse it away.

"Deven. I've had enough. Get out here . . . Please." I wipe my hands on my uniform apron and walk the short distance to his room. He doesn't answer my knock. Blowing out a heavy breath, I turn the knob and open the hollow door.

Sunk into an orange beanbag, Deven stares at a television set. His reflection looks back from the dark screen. The mattress on his bed is bare, with sheets and blankets bundled in a pile at the end. Laundry litters the floor along with wrappers, shoes, and unfinished homework.

"Did you hear me?"

He doesn't budge, doesn't even seem to notice me.

"Deven. Don't ignore me."

Eyes flash my way. "Doesn't feel very good, does it?"

"What?"

"Being invisible."

I shake my head. "I don't know what you mean." I never do.

"Travis could see me. He knew I was here, and he cared. But not you." He jumps up and storms out toward the kitchen.

"That's not true. You don't understand what I'm going through." I dig my fingernails into my palms. "You can't understand what it's like to lose a child."

"You mean I can't understand what it's like to lose your one good son. And you, you don't understand what it's like to lose all three of your brothers, your father, and your mother. Try that one on." He flings the refrigerator door open against the counter, clinking bottles stored in the door. From the bottom shelf, he pulls a slice of pizza wrapped in plastic wrap. Where did that come from?

There's a knock at the door.

"That will be Officer Hobbs. Behave yourself tonight." I try to pull off a stern warning look, but the jab to the gut I've just taken still stings too much.

"Fine. I'll do anything to get out of here." Opening the door, he pushes past Hobbs, stomps through the carport, and jumps into the pickup's cab.

Hobbs stands on my top step, his usually expressionless face flashing shock.

I cock my hip, pressing one hand into my side. Who does he think he is, judging me?

As fast as Hobbs lost control of his features, he straightens again. "I'll have him back by ten. Is that okay?"

"Sure."

"You all right?" His arm extends like he's thinking of reaching for me, but then he shoves both hands deep into his pockets.

I shrug my shoulders. "Just the normal preteen drama." The lie stings my throat. For a second too long our eyes lock, and I know he knows. Maybe it's his police training. I'm stripped of the protection of my lie when he's here. Uncovered. Vulnerable. And a tiny bit safer.

"A night out may do him good. You want me to talk to him?"

"I wouldn't even know what to suggest you talk about." I step back. "I've got groceries to unpack. Thanks again."

He takes my not-so-subtle hint and heads for the truck.

From the kitchen window, I watch as Hobbs swerves to miss potholes. Why does this man care what happens to us? Why does it matter? Deven's been without a father since before his first birthday. At least Bill came in and out when the other boys were young. Deven was the last straw. When he was born, Bill decided he'd had enough of fatherhood. His ideal family meant a home, a wife, a meal, and a six-pack. Not bills needing to be paid, plumbing that leaked, and tiny miracles that always needed food.

I shrink. No. It can't be possible. What if I actually blame Deven, on some level, for Bill leaving? What if, somehow, he's right, and he's spent his life being ignored by the person who should see him more clearly than anyone else in the world?

I pick up the jar of grape jelly and hurl it at the floor. Glass explodes purple lines along the cupboards and across the refrigerator door. Bill broke the first two boys, Izzy took the third, and Deven, I was the one who destroyed him.

◆ ◆ ◆

I didn't talk with Deven when he came home last night. I guess I needed more time to sit with the truth. Lying awake until sunrise gave me the time. And waiting all morning for him to wake up has given me even more.

Steam rises from the pot. I lean over, letting the moist heat blanket my skin. When I step back, the air feels cooler, almost chilled, like at a baseball game. Tears pop to my eyes. Again. Turning on the faucet, I run water into my cupped palms and splash it over my face. How long will it take before I can manage a day, even half a day, without tears? When will I be able to move without my feet feeling like they're dipped in cement? And, if that day comes, will I be able to stand myself for letting him go?

Stripping the top from the cardboard box, I dump macaroni through the steam, and then slice hotdogs into coin sized bites, dropping them into the jumping noodles. I stir the pot, watching the ingredients expand in the raging heat. Change by circumstances. Altered by scorching temperatures.

My mind slips away into deep thoughts, memories, and regrets. They take control, grip my heart and my soul.

Every parent is supposed to do better than the one before them. From what I can remember, I had a good mom. And my dad was decent until my mom was killed and he gave up faith and family for scotch and women he picked up at the bar but grew bored of within the week.

He became a beast, yelling at anyone who had the nerve to be noticed. I couldn't stand him, and I hated who he'd become.

That's when I came up with the idea. It took years before I knew how intentional the pregnancy had been. It was my escape, my chance to be rid of the pain of punishment he doled out just because I was there. And I stepped right into the same mud with Bill. Made the same rotten choices in a husband and father for my children. I took my own sorry circumstances and dished them out to my kids.

Twenty years have sped by, and I hear from my dad rarely, almost never. He has another child, a daughter, but I don't even know her name and I'm not sure I care.

And now I rarely hear from my oldest boys. Prison, marines, there's little difference. They might call if I had money to send them. But since they know I don't, why bother? What's there to talk about anyway? Kyle called from Bridgeport, California, when he heard about Travis. Yes, he was fine. No, he wasn't coming to the funeral.

The timer rings, and I jump, startled out of the mire in my mind. Straining the macaroni and hot dogs over the sink, I let the steam burn my skin, the pain keeping me present for the moment. We're out of milk, so margarine is all I have to mix with the orange powder from the packet. The mixture slaps around the pan as I mix full circles with a chewed up spatula. It looks gross, but it's Deven's favorite.

Sitting the pot on a wooden trivet, I gather a couple bowls and forks. "Deven. Lunch is ready."

He's behind the closed door again. Hidden from me and isolated from life. I've done that. I made him who he is.

I knock first, then push the door open. This stops here. No more lost children. Not in this family.

Shoots of red-brown hair peek out from the cocoon of an almond-colored comforter. The radio plays in the background, a rough song with even harsher lyrics. I press the power button and quiet the room.

He rolls over, his sleepy eyes narrowed into a glare. "What did you do that for?"

"I don't like you listening to that junk. Lunch is ready. Come on out. I think we should talk." Before he can fire off an answer to my demands, I turn and leave.

The clock ticks. No Deven. I dish up the bowls and plop the forks into the sticky mess then carry them on one arm like I do at the restaurant. I open his door, then turn the radio off again. Without asking permission, I sit on the edge of his mattress. "Here you go." I set one of the steaming bowls near his nose.

"What's this?" His voice is deep and groggy.

"Lunch. Your favorite."

"Breakfast is my favorite."

"I mean your favorite lunch dish."

He sits up, his chest bare. He's still scrawny and lean, a child with the anger of a full-grown adult. He stabs the fork into the bowl over and over until the tines are stuffed and then shoves the bite into his mouth.

"I think we should talk about the things you said last night."

"Why?"

"Because I care about you. I've done a lousy job showing it. I'm sorry."

He leans back against the wall. "I shouldn't have said those things, and I don't want you paying attention to me now just because I'm the only one left."

I nod. "Okay. That's fair."

"And I want you to stop messing with my radio."

I wrinkle my mouth. "I can't commit to that one, but I'll try to respect your likes and dislikes."

He pushes the bowl across the bed. "Then you should know I don't like macaroni and cheese."

My shoulders slump with the punch. I've given him Kane's favorite. This is not a good way to start over. And no way for me to show him I love him for who he is.

Chapter 14

JILLIAN

Garrett grabs my hand and guides me toward the church. "I know you don't want to be here. Honestly, I'm not feeling it either. But sometimes, especially in the tough times, we have to come to God even if it's only in obedience."

"We should be with Izzy."

"Izzy should be with us." His grip tightens and his steps quicken. Zachary has already rushed through the front doors.

The list of "shoulds" keeps getting longer. If I could only wake up and realize the last few months never actually happened. Then I'd have the chance to do things differently. I'd warn Izzy. I'd be clear and strong, not wavering in my stance. I'd be honest, because before this, honesty may have made a difference. Even if my honesty started a crack that would turn into a canyon and devour my marriage, it would be worth the pain to save my daughter. To keep her from falling off the same cliff.

Garrett shakes hands with a man from his Bible study. My husband's face, to anyone else, appears calm and secure. But I can see the tension in his jaw, the slight drop of his shoulders, the almost imperceptible slowing. Eighteen years of marriage. All that time I've held tight to my secret. Now is not the moment to break.

Jasmine saunters up, and cocks her hip. "Where's Izzy?"

Her makeup is so thick I could scrape my fingernail along her cheek and leave a ditch behind. Instead, I paste a smile on my face while containing my screams inside my head. "She's resting at home."

"Resting?"

"Yes." Why do I have to elaborate for someone who only cares to get a savory taste of gossip?

"Well, it's no good to lie around wallowing. She needs to move on. Pull herself up. When my father died, I wanted to drop out of all my volunteer duties, but then I thought of all the poor people who would be in such a sorry place without me." She shrugs. "What could I do? I'm needed. Maybe Izzy needs to volunteer somewhere."

I bite down on the tip of my tongue, blood flavoring my mouth with a coppery tang. What right does this pompous woman have to tell me what my Izzy needs? "I'll take care of my daughter, thank you very much." I yank my hand free of Garrett's and make my way to our regular row in the sanctuary.

In here the buzz of conversation softens to a hum. I drop into the seat and duck my head, feigning interest in the bulletin, but the words are a blur on the page.

By the time Garrett settles in beside me, the angry tears are pushed back. My cold hands still shake with the rest of my body.

His open palm presses into the middle of my upper back more like pressure than support. "What's going on with you?" he says beside my ear.

I turn to him, darting my gaze around to make sure no one is listening. "Are you serious? Our lives are falling apart. And you're actually asking me what's going on with me? Didn't you hear that woman?" Fire blazes across the back of my neck. His hand burns my skin. I shift free of his touch.

Pressing his palms together, he looks down on me, his eyebrows knit together, his jaw set. "Can't you let stuff like that go? Why do you always take it so personally?"

My mouth opens, but the fury raging in my bones takes all my energy and drains my mind of the ability to respond.

The drum beats and the music begins. It pierces my eardrums and rattles my core. The room grows tight as people filter in, pressing into rows. I gasp for breath, my rib cage narrowing, aching. The woman behind me belts out the words off-key. I pull at my collar. The heat. Someone has bumped up the thermostat.

Garrett lays his hand on my leg, but I slap it away. "I have to go."

"Where?"

"I have to get out of here." I grab my purse and head down past singing people with perfect lives. At the foyer I keep going, bursting out the doors and into the cool, moist air, my breath coming in desperate heaves. Cold fills my lungs. What happened in there? I glance back at the doors, but I can't return.

STACEY

I set the tray of sandwiches in the middle of the long table then stand back to evaluate the lunch spectacular that Irene and I have created. My shoulders relax, and I smile. Today I actually feel useful.

I haven't found a job yet. I haven't even looked.

Keith keeps encouraging me to explore my dreams. I love to paint. I spent a year in art school before I had the realization that bills aren't paid by passion. That took me to graphic design. It's nothing like holding a paintbrush to canvas, but at least there's a creative element.

Irene floats in the front door. "And they're off." She scoops her hand through the air.

There is a transforming peace with Nikki heading off to a doctor's appointment with Nurse Tower.

"Oh, Stacey, the table looks beautiful. Maybe this is enough to distract the board members. I need them in a good mood today."

I'm about to ask why when the door opens and the house is filled with the unusual boom of men's deep voices.

I recognize Pastor Lawrence from church, but dressed in a blue button-up, jeans, and no tie, he looks even younger than I remember. The other man is the one who first approached us in the entry.

"I'm telling you, Robert, the Beavers have a solid team come next fall.

You'll be eating your words for Thanksgiving, along with a side of roast duck."

"You're overconfident, man. Not a chance." Robert twirls a University of Oregon key chain around his pointer finger.

They stop when they see me, offering greetings and small talk.

Another group filters through the door.

Irene sidles up. "You know Carrie. That's Lyra and Brenda with her."

I nod, suddenly not so excited about the flower arrangement and colorful fruit salad.

Lyra pushes an umbrella stroller with a sleeping toddler bundled into the seat. "Sorry. The babysitter canceled at the last minute. Now she has the flu." Her chin wrinkles. "I think that's my fault. Sorry I couldn't help out last week, Irene."

"No problem. Stacey keeps coming to my rescue."

Robert stands behind one of the chairs. "We're all here, so let's get to business."

I shrug. He's clearly not a man with an eye for pretty things. The thought makes me smile.

Pastor Lawrence leads us in prayer then the food is passed around.

Robert opens a file beside his plate. "Looks like the first order of business is a potential new resident," he says around a large bite of cream cheese and cucumber sandwich. "Did everyone get a copy of her application?"

Around the table there are murmurs of agreement and shuffling of papers. Except for me. The only paper in my folder is a copy of some potential logos. I don't even know why I'm here. Irene could easily show my designs.

Lyra wipes a crumb from her chin with a lavender paper napkin. "I'm confused about this girl. She lives with both parents who seem very supportive. She's involved in her church, a good student, and an excellent athlete. Any chance the family is trying to hide the pregnancy from their community?"

"I was wondering the same thing," Brenda said.

"This house is designed to help young women learn skills to be great mothers," said Carrie.

"And to be a ministry." Pastor Lawrence pulls at the hair above his ear. "Irene. What do you think? You met the girl. Frankly, I'm surprised you sent the application on to us, but I trust you have a good reason."

"I do." She leans her elbows on the table.

Irene and I have spent the morning talking about Izzy. At this moment, I realize I'm attached to her. I bite my bottom lip and whisper a prayer in my heart that these people will understand Irene's conviction. There's something important happening here. Something I don't understand but feel passionate about anyway.

Irene rubs her fingers over a dangly earring, a habit I've noticed she has when she's about to get serious. "Izzy Cline looks like she has it all. She even worked in leadership in her church, but she made some bad choices, and now she's pregnant. I wouldn't bring this to you if that was the whole story. Izzy's boyfriend, the father of the baby, went to her house one night. He and Izzy argued. The boy sped off. He made another bad choice. He didn't pull over. Instead, he typed a text to Izzy, lost control of the car, and died."

Even knowing this already, my heart sinks further. I actually ache for this girl I've never met. Ten years ago, I was the picture-perfect Christian girl. The cheerleader and youth group leader. My boyfriend was the hunky guy on the basketball team. We didn't sleep together, but we could have. It would have been easy. Of course, it appears I wouldn't have gotten pregnant, but that's no consolation.

Irene laces her fingers together and brings both hands toward her face. "My answer still would have been no, but then I had the opportunity to meet her and to speak with her father alone. It's all her parents can do to keep her eating enough to stay alive. When Izzy heard about our house, she asked to come here. I don't know if we're the answer, but I feel God wants us to try."

Lyra's eyelids flutter. "What about the boyfriend's family? Are they involved?"

"There's only the mom, and she's had a tough time of it. Mr. Cline has reason to believe the boy's mom thinks Izzy got pregnant on purpose to keep her son from going to college on a baseball scholarship. She won't be a support. In fact, she may be one of the main reasons for getting this girl out of town."

"What about other family she could go to?" asks Carrie.

"Mrs. Cline is estranged from her family and Mr. Cline's relatives live in Minnesota. They don't want Izzy to be so far from home."

Carrie tucks a strand of hair behind her ear. "I'm not sure I can vote on this one yet. I need some time to pray. Would it be all right if we emailed our votes in to Robert?"

All around the table, they're nodding. I want to stand up and demand they approve her right now. Walking away will put distance between them and Izzy's story. What if this is a way to cushion the blow, and they're all just fixin' to say no.

"So, Stacey, you have some images for us?" Robert moves on like Izzy is only a name typed on a form.

I stare back at Pastor Lawrence. Who cares about logos? This girl will forever be changed by their decision. My spine goes straight, and I clench my fists. I need to be here. I pull the volunteer application from my bag and slide it across the table.

◆　◆　◆

I slap a photo down on my kitchen counter littered with a dozen others. "These are so empty."

"Empty? What do you mean?" Keith leans over my shoulder, his breath brushing my neck.

"They make our lives look void."

"Because there's no baby? I think any birth mother who looks at our book will understand the fact that we have no children. That's kind of the point."

I sigh, deflated. "Our last book was filled with pictures of nieces and nephews. We had family gatherings. We had something to offer."

"I see what you're saying. But I don't see why we can't use some of those pictures again. It's not like we're never going to visit. And our families will come out here too. Your mother is coming next fall, right?"

The frustration doesn't leave, but the effort he's making to sound excited about my mom's visit warms my heart. "You're a real trooper."

"What?" He leans back, his hands spread open and amusement sparkling in his eyes.

My mother's a dear woman. Too dear. She comes in and does her best to fix every hurt, mend every wound, and she does it with food. So much food that by the time we flop into bed each night, we'll be bloated and ill. I can't help but be drawn back to the days after we lost the baby. Most of the meals my mom cajoled me into eating didn't stay down. Some hurts can't be healed no matter how much our mothers want them to be.

I squeeze his cheeks between my thumb and first finger then plant a kiss on his puckered lips. "I love you."

"Yeah, I'm a pretty good guy." He grins and pulls me into his arms. "I love you too, even if you think a life with just me is *empty*."

"That's not what I meant." I lightly slap his back. "All right, now let me go. We need to finish this so I can drop it off tomorrow."

He kisses my forehead and releases me, his smile sweet and serious.

"Now what?" I ask.

"I'm glad we're doing this. I feel like we're back from some sad journey. Like we're us again."

Tears tickle my nose, but I'm quick to bring them under control. "I still think about him, but you're right. And you were right, it's time to move forward. Thank you."

"Anytime, babe. How about I make pancakes and you keep working?"

I nod. The kitchen hasn't been used to its full capacity since we moved in. When we were first married, I loved creating amazing meals for my husband. But somewhere along the way I shifted to pasta, breakfast foods, and takeout, only making a true meal once in a blue moon.

And he never complains.

I set aside a photo of the new house, one of the two of us with the Columbia River in the background, and another of Keith hugging a painted cow statue. The last one really shows who he is, and why I love him enough to travel across the country with him.

A thought flashes through my mind. This is what I want my letter to convey to potential birth mothers. We may not have current pictures of children surrounding us, but we have each other. And Keith Frey will make the best daddy ever.

I slide my laptop into place. Opening a new document, I begin my letter again. This time I write about the first time we met, the moment I knew I loved him, and how we long to share our love with a child. Words flow, telling the story of our dreams for the future, for coaching soccer teams, bandaging little scrapes, watching first band concerts, snapping pictures on prom night. My heart is on the page, raw and vulnerable, but honest.

We may not have the most attractive book, but I'll feel good knowing that what I've shared is completely true. The decision to place a child with us shouldn't come from manipulation. I want any birth mother to know I love her for her choice and we're not perfect, but we'll do our best.

And it's all in God's hands.

A shiver runs across my skin. Equal parts elation and nerves, but mainly satisfaction.

Chapter 15

Izzy

Rolling over again, I can't force myself back to the safety of sleep. My room is bright with sunlight. Why do I keep leaving the curtain open? Travis isn't coming. He never will again.

I prop myself up in the corner, one shoulder against the wall, the other on my headboard. The skin on my stomach itches. My room is now my safe place and my prison. Heaven and hell. Good and evil. Grief is so heavy, but sometimes when the sun is out, like today, I wonder if fresh air would lighten the load. But then I try to get dressed and my pants won't zip or my jacket won't close, and it reminds me my room is the only place I'm free from judgment.

Last week I had another ultrasound. I'm having a girl. A daughter. I thought knowing this would help. It doesn't.

There's a light knock on my door, probably my mom trying to make me eat. I know I should. I'm losing weight in every place but my stomach.

"Come in."

Leslie Stanton's head peers around the corner of the door.

I grab for blankets, yanking them up to my chin then pull a pillow over my middle, hugging it like a teddy bear. "Leslie? I thought you were my mom."

"Zach let me in. He said you were still in bed, but you wouldn't mind if I came back."

My brother's life still revolves around Legos and action figures. He's oblivious to how bad things really are. "Sure. It's okay." But I wish she'd leave.

124

Leslie closes the door behind her. She pulls the desk chair out and turns it toward the bed. "How are you doing? You haven't been to school in weeks. I hear your mom is homeschooling you for a while."

"Yeah. I'm fine." I have to hand it to her, she's brave. She's the first friend to visit since the funeral. The one I worked with in youth group leadership, and the one I should be honest with, but also the one I can't stand to disappoint.

Lines crease her forehead. "I hope you'll be back at church soon."

I'm torn between shock that it's been so long and surprise that it hasn't been much longer. Time doesn't work the same way anymore. It's as much out of my control as everything else. "I haven't been feeling well."

"It must be tough, but you know we all miss you, and we want to help."

I run my tongue between my teeth and lips. Sure they do. They want to support me because of Travis's death. What about when the whole truth is out there? It's funny how you don't think much about the rumors of teens sleeping together, but on the occasion when a girl becomes pregnant, everything changes. No one wants to be around her. It's like she's carrying the plague. Get too close, and it could happen to you. I was one of the girls to turn up my nose. If only I could take it back. If only I could take so many things back.

"I'm sure that's what everyone says, but I mean it. Anything I can help you with, I will. I miss you, Iz." The edges of her eyes turn down like a sad dog's.

"Thanks. I know you care. It means a lot, but really, I'm doing much better. Just waking up is all."

A smile bursts across her face. "Great. I have my dad's car. Come with me to get a new pair of shoes." She hops up.

"Now?" I pull the blankets tighter.

"Of course. Throw on some clothes, and let's go. It's warm today. You could probably get away with shorts and a T-shirt." She sits down hard on my bed. "Come on."

"I don't think so." My heart is racing and my cheeks warm.

"Why?" Her voice shifts into a higher pitch.

"I'm not ready. It's too soon."

Leslie grabs the blankets and yanks. "It'll be fun, I promise. I'll even buy you an ice cream."

My fingers ache with the death grip I have on the fabric. "No." My voice is snappy and it frightens me even more.

Dropping her hold, Leslie leans back. "All right. I'll go then." Her mouth droops at the corners. "How about you call me when you're ready?" She leaves my room without looking back.

The front door slams, and I free my fingers from the comforter. What have I done now? Why am I holding so tight to a secret that will eventually go public?

The phone rings in the kitchen. I pull on my robe and shuffle out of my cave. Rounding the corner, I catch my mother's panicked expression.

"Yes. That's good news. We'll let you know what we decide." She drops the phone onto the leather couch and stares at me. "That was the house your dad took you to visit. They approved your application."

I nod. Fresh air.

"I think we should give this some more thought. What are you going to do up there where you don't know anyone? What if you need us?"

I step forward, opening my arms and hugging my mother. At this moment she needs me more than I need her. "If I need you, I know you'll be there."

Soft sobs echo in my ear. "Any time, baby."

JILLIAN

I pull another T-shirt from Izzy's dresser, snap it open and hold it up. Too few of these clothes fit her even now. Tossing the soft fabric back into the drawer, I nestle onto the mattress next to my daughter and her suitcase. "How about a few of my things until we can buy you some maternity clothes?"

Izzy buries her head in her knees, closing herself off again.

"Honey, this is hard, but I've been thinking, maybe this is for the best. You can come home after the baby is born and have a fresh start."

Her pale face turns to me. "You really don't get it, do you? I have to keep this baby."

Pain grips my heart, stealing the oxygen from my blood, and leaves me weak and unable to fight. Not even in one of my sappy novels would everything turn out rosy for a character in Izzy's position. She'll die here from the regret, the stares, and the guilt. "I'll be back in a minute." My legs shake as I stand, but I make my way to the door. Shutting it behind me, I sink into the carpet. Where is the answer? What is the plan? I have to do something to fix this for Izzy. There must be a way to make it all okay again.

"I'm going to take a shower," I holler through the door.

It takes the walk through my own room, into the master bathroom in the back with both doors closed behind me, forming a false barrier between myself and the world, but I finally feel alone, and safe. I turn on the fan, the heater, and the shower. Stripping off my clothes, I stand in front of the mirror. The nausea has left my body as deflated as my heart. My hip bones point through the skin with its unhealthy pallor. No wonder Garrett is growing more distant. The woman in the reflection is sick. Broken. Izzy looks healthier.

Turning from my reflection, I step into the hot water. At first I recoil, then allow my body the chance to adjust to the burn, and I'm in. Steam fills the air. Another door between me and my reality, and that's the one that allows the dam to burst. Sobs wrack my shoulders, my back. I suck in air, but my lungs scream for more. Pressure pounds in my temples. My nose swells shut and salty tears run down my cheeks and in through the corners of my mouth.

My knees buckle, and I drop into a mass on the tiled shower floor. I can't do this. Can't feel this. I can't handle the pain.

High moans weave from my lips, echoing through the confined space.

A situation with no good answer. No answer at all. How can I watch my child suffer? Where is the hope I can pass on? Where's the God I raised my daughter to believe in?

When I met Garrett, I was broken, searching for answers to questions I still refuse to ask myself. I followed him to church, said the right things, and believed God was there. We had a Christian wedding and raised our children in a Christian home. Is this some kind of joke a mean-hearted monster created thousands of years ago?

What have I given my life over to? A faith as make-believe as Cinderella?

I've thought these questions before, but they were soft, a whisper. Now, with my daughter's future on the line, they scream in the front of my mind. What if everything I ever taught her is a lie?

Pounding cracks through my cave. "Jillian? Are you okay?"

Garrett shouldn't be home from Zachary's Cub Scout paper drive for another hour. I shake in the warm water, kneeling under the spray. "I'll be out in a minute. I'm fine." Another lie to add to the mountain of dishonesty.

Chapter 16

STACEY

"Here you go, ma'am." The kid behind the printer's counter slides an eight-and-a-half-by-eleven-inch box across the counter toward me.

Ouch. When did I grow into a ma'am? "Thanks." I turn my back on him and walk to the closest table. Pulling the lid off, I examine the flyers. Maybe it's because I believe in this work, or maybe I've taken extra time on this project because I'm painfully bored eighty percent of the time. Whichever it is, they turned out fabulous. Along one side of the paper, pictures document some of the success stories from A Child's Home. A girl's graduation. A mother and child outside playing together in lush spring grass. A young woman grasping a diploma with a smile glowing on her face. How could anyone not encourage this program?

The buzz in my pocket startles me. I pull out my cell phone. The caseworker from the adoption agency. I cringe. No more paperwork, please. "Hello."

"Hi, Stacey. This is Gina Bane. Is this a good time?"

People all around me punch codes into copy machines. I might as well be alone on an island for as much attention as they give me. "Sure. Did I forget something?"

"No. You've already been approved. It's funny how long it takes people to accept the fact that the paperwork is truly over, for the time being."

"That's good news." I tap my toe, holding the phone with my shoulder as I start to fit the lid back on the box.

"I'm actually calling because I met with a birth mother this morning.

She's a very sweet girl. Just turned eighteen. And she's due the end of the summer. Anyway, I gave her a few books to look through."

The queasy waiting and wanting feeling rushes over me. Knowing it's out there is the worst part. "That's great news, but is it possible to not tell us when you share our book? It makes me crazy, and I can't sleep. It's the wondering."

"I understand. That's my policy unless I'm told otherwise."

"Did Keith ask you to call?"

"No. So this girl . . ."

I wince. Doesn't Gina get it? Bless her heart, I don't think she's listening. Every drop of information makes the rejection that much harder.

"This girl, she's very decisive. She chose you and Keith right away. She said it was . . ."

The phone slips from my shoulder, hits the floor, and bounces under the paper cupboard. Dropping to my knees I sweep my arm under the space until my fingers touch on the cold metal. I slap it onto my cheek, startling myself with the thunk against my jaw.

"Stacey, are you there?"

"I'm here. Sorry. I dropped the phone. What does she like?"

Gina laughs. "Your letter. She said you're the only couple who sounded genuine, not like a diaper commercial."

My heart beats hard against my rib cage. "I'm so glad." The words are so little, so meaningless against the appreciation swelling in my chest.

"She'd like to meet the two of you as soon as possible. What do you think?"

"Yes. I think, yes."

"Great. How about tomorrow morning at ten, my office?"

"We'll be there."

Shoving the cell phone into my pocket, I turn circles looking for someone to tell, someone who'd care that I'm about to be a mama. I grab the box and my purse, fly through the door, then run for my car. This isn't the kind of news I want to tell Keith over the phone.

Traffic crawls as I make my way down the four-lane street, my fingers clamped on the steering wheel, my chin not far behind. The office complex is only two blocks away now. The tallest building visible, but the light is red.

I swing the Bluetooth device over my ear and speed-dial Keith's number.

"Hey." His voice is cheery, but there are other voices in the background. "Can I call you back in a few minutes?"

"No. I mean, I'm pulling into the parking lot. I need you to come down for a minute." I keep my voice level, but my heart pumps wildly.

"Are you okay? What's going on?"

"I've got to go so I can park. Bye." I press the off button. Another ten seconds on the phone, and I'd give up the surprise.

The rain this morning was heavy, but now the sun shines and reflects brightly on the wet asphalt, making the ground look golden. In the rear-view mirror, I see him throw open the door and dart my way. I step out of the car, squinting into the sun, the warmth of its light seeping through my sweater and heating my back.

He reaches me before he speaks. "What's going on?" Worry wrinkles his brow and darkens his eyes.

A smile takes over my face before I can control my dancing emotions. "She called."

"Who?"

"Gina. The agency. She called."

"And?" His eyes widen and his mouth falls open, his hands tight on my upper arms as he searches me for the answer.

"We've been chosen." Saying the words out loud brings happy tears to my eyes. "A birth mother looked at our book and chose us."

"Already?"

I nod.

"Walk with me." He cups my elbow in his hand and leads me to a fountain. Water spouts from high in the center, filling a giant bowl where it cascades over the edges. Fully peaceful. "I didn't even know our book had gone out."

"Neither did I." I could jump up and down like a pogo stick if I weren't so afraid I'd never stop. "She's due in August, and she wants to meet us tomorrow morning."

His features grow thoughtful. Keith looks up into the sky, blinking. Without looking back down he pulls me into his arms and holds me tight.

I wish we could stay here for hours talking about what will happen next, redrawing our dreams, but life goes on and Keith bounds back upstairs to a meeting.

And I have someone else to tell.

It doesn't take me long to drive to A Child's Home, but finding Irene is a harder task. When I reach the top of the stairs, I'm struck by the melodic jingle of laughter coming from Sierra's room. The door is open so I tap it with my knuckle as I walk in.

"Hey there." Irene drops down onto Sierra's bed. "I was just telling our girl here that she's about to have a roommate."

"Izzy?" I'm almost afraid to ask.

Irene nods. "The board gave approval for Izzy and for you. Looks like our little family is growing."

My chest swells with my own news, but I don't want to tell Irene here, with Sierra in the room.

Sierra bites her bottom lip.

"Aren't you excited?" I ask. "I loved sharing a room with my sisters. Of course I was the youngest, so they may have had a different take than I did."

"What if she doesn't like me?"

"What's not to like? She'll love you. Why would you wonder that?" I ask.

Her gaze goes from me to Irene. "It's just . . . Nikki said you only took me because you had to."

Fire replaces my other emotions.

Irene stands and paces a few steps before responding. "Nikki doesn't know what she's talking about. We'll be getting to the bottom of this right now. Sierra, no one has the right to talk to you that way. You come to me if she says anything else."

Sierra's eyes go wide. "Please don't tell her I said anything."

"Why on earth not?"

"She'll think I'm a tattletale."

There's something else. I haven't been here long, but even I can feel the unsaid words hanging in the room.

Irene steps in front of her. "Do I need to remind you of house rule number four?" She taps her foot. "There are to be no secrets. Do you understand why we have that rule?"

Sierra shakes her head.

"It's for your safety. You deserve to feel safe. Is Nikki asking you to keep a secret for her?"

Silence speaks volumes.

"Sierra, do you trust I want what's best for you, for Nikki, and for Baby Boy?"

She nods.

"I need you to tell me what's going on. Please don't force me to go to the board," Irene says.

She wouldn't do that, would she?

The words hit hard, and Sierra's chin snaps up. "Please don't."

"You have to make a good choice here." Irene stays strong where I'd crumble.

"Nikki goes somewhere. She leaves the house in the middle of the night."

"The baby?" asks Irene.

"No."

The facts start to slide into place, and I understand. "You're taking care of the baby for her, aren't you?"

Her head bobs.

◆ ◆ ◆

I tuck a loose strand of hair behind my ear. Why did I let that woman cut it so short? I'm a ponytail kind of girl. No equipment, no products, no stress. I check my phone, still ten minutes before Irene and I are scheduled for our coffee and chat time. Finally, I can tell someone else about the baby.

The shrill beep of Irene's horn startles me. She's not the kind of woman to be impatient, a trait that makes her well-suited for her job. But something's different today. The horn screams again, then her door creaks open. Grabbing my soft, yellow sweater from the last cushion of the couch, I toss it over my arm and dash out the door before she can make it to my porch.

I open the passenger door then slide into the seat. Boxes fill the back, but she's made room for me here.

"Sorry. Change of plans. We have to act quickly if Nikki has any chance." She thrusts the stick shift into reverse, grinds the gears, then shoots out onto our quiet cul-de-sac.

My hand grips the armrest on the door. With my other hand I check the security of my seat belt. "I take it we're not going to coffee."

"Nope. We're on a bigger mission."

"Do you really think this is a good idea?" I ask.

"No. It absolutely isn't. But this is the only one I have right now and taking a witness seems prudent."

She merges her tin can of a car onto the freeway.

My fingernails dig into the soft vinyl.

"Nikki's been disappearing, a lot. She left the baby with Sierra last night and didn't return this morning." Both of her hands clench around the steering wheel, one at ten and the other at two. Her elbows are locked, her shoulders pressed tight against her seat as if she's bracing for an accident.

"Do you think she'll change her mind?"

"No. But I'll be hog-tied if this girl is going to make me stop believing in miracles."

Businesses flash by outside my window. Why is her faith so strong? I've known Irene long enough to know she's alone in the world. She has no family, no friends her own age, and no husband.

My elbow slams into the console as we veer off the freeway and into a neighborhood I've never visited. Within blocks, the scenery morphs into the setting for a dark movie, apartment building after apartment building with broken-down cars and trash decorating the thin strips of grass. A child runs into the street, chasing after a ball. Irene hits the brakes hard, jarring us forward. When the boy looks our way, instead of signaling his thanks, he glares straight at Irene.

"There it is." She points at a building that looks like the last three we've passed, and then parks the car. After one deep breath, she tosses her keys into her bright, floral-patterned purse. "You don't have to do this with me. I understand if you'd rather stay here."

A car pulls up, stalling beside us. A man, his shaved head a billboard of tattoos, bends toward his steering wheel and looks us over through his passenger window.

My heart races. All I can do is stare back, unable to force my features into a less obvious response.

He revs his engine and squeals forward and around the next corner, leaving a trail of exhaust behind.

"I'll go with you." I press the button and my seat belt pops free.

Irene would step in front of a wrecking ball to protect any of her girls. I have no chance of talking her out of this.

As we walk up the sidewalk, I regret my choice to follow. I can feel eyes staring at me through blinds and from across the street.

Irene hands me a scrap of paper. "Will you check the address? I didn't bring my reading glasses."

Unfortunately, the numbers match. I give her a nod but don't speak. My voice would surely shake the same way my stomach is trembling right now.

She taps the apartment door. Muffled sounds come from inside, but no one answers. With a squeezed fist she pounds again then rubs her forearm. "Nikki?"

The door opens and with it comes a puff of skunky-sweet marijuana smoke. I step back, but Irene holds her place.

A man, tall and slender, leans against the doorframe. "What do you want?" Behind him a baby howls. "You one of those social workers? Tara, I think this one's for you."

"I'm not a social worker. I'm looking for Nikki Conway. Her mother gave me this address."

"Does she want to see you?" He sneers down at Irene as if the request came from a dog.

My feet want to run. But I force myself to stay.

Irene crosses her arms in front of her chest.

I cross my own arms and try to look as convincing. The worst thing he can do is murder us, and well, Irene's clearly sure where she's headed. "Is she in here?" My voice cracks.

Nikki comes up behind the man's bare arm. "Hey, I'm doing what I was told, finding a new place to live." She doesn't even acknowledge me.

Irene positions a wave of hair behind her ear. "This isn't at all what we discussed. I told you we'd help you find a safe place."

The man steps forward. "What are you thinking, coming to my house and making your sassy statements? What makes you think you're better than me?" His giant palms form fists, punctuating his questions and making a threat at the same time.

Irene stretches to her full height, which isn't much to speak of. She's easily a foot below him. "Not better, but absolutely safer." She peers around his torso. Somewhere deeper in the apartment the baby still cries.

I force my feet forward, until I'm standing directly beside Irene. Drugs are strewn across a coffee table, ashes spilling from a plate.

"Where do you think you're going?" He moves so close he's now staring down at the top of our heads, the stench of his body doing as much to block the door as his stance.

Irene stretches her hand out toward Nikki. "I think you should come with us."

His palm sinks into Nikki's shoulder, his eyes shooting arrows at us. "I think you better be going on . . . Alone." Stepping back into the apartment, he shuts the door. A series of acidic shouts follow.

My strength evaporates in the warm air, leaving my legs shaking and my mouth dry. How can Nikki choose to live like this over the future she's been offered?

Irene starts for the sidewalk.

"We can't just leave." I didn't want to be here in the first place, but now the last thing I want to do is leave. Driving away means giving up. I may not be too fond of Nikki, but I'd never wish this life on anyone.

"There comes a time for each of these girls when they have to make a decision. I may not agree with what they choose, but it's not my job to force them to think like me. It's only my job to point to God. He's the one who can truly change lives."

I stare at the sky. Soft white clouds drift overhead, but toward the west, darkness creeps over the mountains.

Once we're back in the car, Irene's shoulders slump forward. She keeps her gaze out the window, but I can tell it's a tear she's brushing away with the back of her hand. "They've left us no choice. There's a baby in that apartment. And drugs. I have to make a report." She pulls into the street and off we go, leaving Nikki behind.

Irene hands me her phone. "Look through my contacts and find Child Protective Services."

I find it right away. "Now what?"

She raises one eyebrow. "Make the call."

A tremor runs across my skin. "Me?"

"I'm driving. And this is important."

I press the button and listen to the phone ring. Finally, someone answers. A someone with a very unenthusiastic, uncaring voice.

"My name is Stacey Frey. I'm calling with Irene Smith from A Child's

Home. We've been to an apartment with a child inside and obvious drug use."

"Whose apartment was this?"

"I'm not sure."

"Okay, what is the name of the child involved?"

"I don't have that either."

"Ma'am, you're giving me little to work with. What are you reporting?"

"I'm reporting a child in danger." My face starts to burn hot. I rattle off the address.

"All right. There's no need to get upset. I'll file a report and have someone check into it."

"When?"

"When, what?"

"When will someone check?"

"I can't discuss that with you. Did you have anything else?"

I slam the phone shut then look to Irene. Her mouth is turned up in a half smile.

"What?"

"It's nice to see someone else have to make the call." Irene taps my knee. "It's frustrating. We have another avenue we can take, but it's always good to start with the people who are supposed to do the job."

"Will they take that baby?"

"Probably. Maybe that'll be enough to scare Nikki into coming back."

I can't believe what I'm hearing. Even after what we've witnessed, Irene is still working to let the girl back into the house.

Chapter 17

JILLIAN

After two hours on the freeway, the last thirty minutes in heavy traffic, we turn into what Garrett describes as a neighborhood. Windows are decorated with iron bars. Cars are parked in garages. There are no children playing in front yards or dogs chasing balls. The houses, while beautiful in their craftsman style, stand menacing as if each person who enters is suspect.

I work the button in and out of the hole on my taupe dress coat. "A person could get lost here." I turn back toward Izzy. She's leaning against the window behind Garrett's seat.

"There's nothing wrong with blending in." Her hand presses into her abdomen.

Izzy and I, we've never been like the mothers and daughters on television or in the movies. We have a connection that surpasses rising hormones and growing independence. Until the pregnancy, we saw things the same way, understood each other. But now everything I say seems to have a different and offensive meaning to her. What should have taken years, the separation of our relationship into two separate people, has happened over the course of a few short weeks. And the ripping apart has left raw wounds.

Garrett pulls the car over to the curb. A deep porch centers on a wooden door with an old-fashioned knocker. The paint along the steps is worn through where feet scuff.

We sit, all staring at the house that will steal my daughter at least for the summer. This place has the power to do what I can't for my child.

Izzy can live here, place her baby, and return to her old life as if nothing happened. Isn't that what I tried to do? Maybe this is the only way to get back what a foolish mistake has taken from her. I reach my hand between the seats and touch Izzy on the knee.

"You can't make this go away." Her mouth is a straight line, and her gaze doesn't connect with mine.

"What are you talking about?" But I understand every word she throws at me.

"You think you can hide this. Maybe no one will ever know. But even if I did place her, I'd know."

I nod. "I want you to think about your future. You don't have to give it up."

"No kidding, Mom. Can't you just accept that I'm doing the best I can?"

"I want you to think ahead. In twenty years, will you regret your decision?"

Her chin juts forward and her head tips to the side. "How am I supposed to know what I'll regret when I'm old? That's more than double my current age. Have you never trusted me, or is this new since you discovered the horrid creature I really am?"

I suck in a breath and look to Garrett, but he turns his face from me, something he does a lot these days. "You don't understand what I'm saying."

"No, Mom. You don't understand what I'm saying." She flings the door open, yanking her sports bag with her, and stomps toward the house.

"What am I doing so wrong?"

Garrett looks down at me, his face red with restrained rage. "How would I know, Jillian? You've never trusted me enough to let me in." He pops his door open and follows his daughter, leaving me alone in the car.

I've never trusted him? The rebuke clings to my lips, ready to leap out at him, but the truth of his words refuses to allow their release. I turn my gaze away from my daughter and husband standing at the door. He can't understand. The secrets I hold, they're because I love him. It's my way of protecting him from the pain of my past. It's never been about trust.

Opening the car door, I drop one foot to the curb. Garrett holds his daughter in his arms, his way of protecting her. Because my way hasn't worked. Another reality that hits hard, knocking the wind out of my lungs, beating my sore muscles. This is all my fault. The sins of the mother. They've come back from the place I hid them, attacking full force. How can I ever make it up to Garrett and Izzy?

Sniffing back tears, I straighten my shoulders. The cycle has to end here, somehow. And I have to find the strength to make it happen. I owe it to all of them to fix this. Izzy can come back from this. I will not allow it to define her life. And she'll have her mother's support the entire way.

As I take the first step to catch up with them, Izzy opens the door and enters another world. My heels click along the sidewalk as I speed to catch up. The door clicks shut behind me. A large window stretches across one wall of the living area. Light shines in through gauzy curtains, but the dark wood and maroon paint give the room a sinister appearance. Somehow, I pictured something more like the church nursery. Bright walls and oversized animal decals, boxes of toys along the wall.

A woman steps in through a swinging door. "Hello. You must be Izzy." She dries her hands on the kitchen towel she carries.

Izzy looks around. "Irene said she'd be here to show me what to do."

The woman nods. "Something came up. Irene had to go, but she'll be back later. I'm Carrie, a board member."

If this Irene woman is so responsible, why did she run out when she knew Izzy was arriving today?

The door swings open again and three girls walk into the room, their chatter stopping at the sight of the newcomer.

A pregnant girl holding a tiny baby wrapped in a blue knit blanket comes closest.

"Izzy, did you meet Sierra when you visited?" Carrie asks.

Izzy's eyes turn as round as saucers and her mouth hangs open. "Is that your baby?"

A sad smile lightens Sierra's face. "No. I . . . He's . . . I'm watching him."

My gaze sweeps the room. Pregnant. Pregnant. Carrying a baby . . . and pregnant. Where is the mother of this little one? Are they running some kind of childcare here? Are they expecting to make a profit off my daughter? My jaw clinches. No. This isn't right. My daughter should be with me. I glance back at the door. Thoughts flood my mind. I can picture myself taking Izzy away from here. Then I see the looks. I see Jasmine's sneer, and the other kids laughing and cheering at the fall of someone who seemed to have it all. I feel my daughter break.

And I see what Izzy's been telling me. Home isn't an option. It twists my heart until I think it will rupture inside my chest.

My phone rings in my purse. I pull it out, planning to silence the device, but the number on the display is the friend who has Zachary for the day. "Excuse me for a moment. I need to get this." I step closer to the door and answer. "Hello."

"Jillian, I'm sorry. I know you're taking Izzy to her aunt's, but Zachary had an accident."

My heart stops for a moment, a chill running across my skin. "What happened?"

"He fell out of a tree. We're at Immediate Care right now. Looks like his arm is broken and he may have a concussion. He keeps asking for you."

"I'll be there as soon as I can." I hang up, my heart torn into two ragged-edged pieces. How do I choose between my children?

IZZY

Sitting on the edge of my assigned bed, I struggle for anything to say to my roommate. The weeks of silence that followed admitting I'm pregnant and Travis dying have left me unable to make conversation. "So, when are you due?"

Sierra tucks her hands between her knees. "September. But . . . Never mind."

"What?"

Her head drops, and she picks at one of her fingernails. "I'm not keeping the baby. I've decided."

"Wow. I think that's great you know what you want to do. I wish I did."

Her gaze works its way up from the floor to me. "You don't think I'm being irresponsible?"

"Seriously?" I stand and walk over to Sierra's bed. Easing onto the mattress, I put a hand on her shoulder, then pull it back. What am I supposed to do with all of this? "I think you're very brave. It takes a lot of courage to put your baby first like that."

"Thank you. Are you thinking about placing your baby?"

I clasp my hands together and stare at my fingers. It wasn't long ago that it was Travis's hand linked with mine. "I thought I would when I first found out. Actually, I thought about getting an abortion. But it was too late. I'm really glad now." Tears swell in my throat, making it hard to talk past the lump. "My boyfriend died. I think I need to keep her for the sake of Travis's memory." Tears rush me every time I say his name. Travis. He'll never hold his daughter or any other child. And it's all because of me.

"That's awful." Sierra leans closer. "About your baby daddy, I mean."

I nod, but it's so much worse than awful. I'm not sure a word has been developed to describe the ache I have inside of me. The intense guilt.

"What's your family say?"

"Mom wants me to place the baby. She thinks I can start all over like nothing happened." I rub my hand over my round stomach. "I don't think I'll ever be the same. How could I act like nothing happened? And I can't walk away now anyway."

Sierra stiffens. "I'm not walking away."

"That's not what I meant." Shifting, I turn toward her. "I owe it to him, that's all."

"I guess, but he'll never know."

My mouth goes dry. "What about your baby's dad? Does he have an opinion?"

She stands. "We better get downstairs. It's almost time for dinner." Without waiting for me, she walks out the door.

I really stepped into a mess with that last question. If I could, I'd take it back.

The memory of my last moments with Travis hits me again. If only I could make those words fade. Travis would have been back. He would have taken care of us. I know him. *I knew him.*

Before I head down to dinner and have to face the whole group, I run a brush over my hair. The next months will be easier if I can make at least one friend. I'm tempted to text Leslie, but I haven't told her where I really am, and I'm not ready to hear the shock in her voice. It's too much to bear the feelings of others on top of my own.

The brush clatters back onto the dresser, and I walk out the door, nearly colliding with the perky girl, Cate, as she comes out of her room across the hall.

"Hi, Izzy. It's taco night." Her eyebrows rise like this is the highlight of the week. From what I've seen, Cate reacts like this a lot. She's barely older than I am, she has a baby, and she's thrilled about everything. What's the deal with that? "Oh, the nurse is coming in tonight. She's great about answering questions. You'll love her. She'll tell you all about how big your baby is and what he or she is doing and what comes next."

"She," I say.

"What?"

"My baby is a girl."

"Nice. Do you have a name for her?"

My mind spins. Does Cate's brain work as fast as her mouth? "No. I don't know." Truth is, I have nothing.

Cate stops at the top stair. "You don't know what?"

For the first time in weeks a smile cracks my face. "Anything. I don't know anything."

Cate laughs and pats her baby's back. "I talk too much. Sorry."

"No. I like it. I think I may have been missing people. I've been cooped up."

"Well, you've got us now, and we're family. Come on." She jogs down the stairs with the baby held tight to her chest.

Something about Cate gives me a tiny ray of hope. Maybe there's good still ahead.

Chapter 18

STACEY

If I had to pick a word to describe Oregon, it would be *coffee*. The people here in the Pacific Northwest love their mountains, their coast, and their trees, but above all, they adore their coffee.

Back in Tennessee we had an occasional cup in the morning, but it never extended to an event in itself. In the weeks since the move, I've had to give up my RC Cola, a daily habit I've had since high school. The people of the Pacific Northwest don't know what they're missing. It's a rare commodity here, so I've had to take up coffee, the West Coast drink of choice. There's a coffee shop on every block, all boasting a better brew, and I've visited every one of them within a ten-mile radius of my house.

It's become a hobby for me, a challenge to find the best, or at least what my inexperienced java buds love the most. And I believe I've come to the place that has it all. A few miles from our home I discovered an independently owned shop with a flair for the arts. The first time I visited, Inspire Coffee dug its claws into me. It's not only because the baristas mix up toasty drinks with flavors made to savor, but because it does just as promised. It inspires.

I cut the engine in my car, pull my laptop from the seat behind me, and head inside. My foot catches the entrance door before it slams shut, the spring being broken. Music floats down from a loft above the open seating area. At one end, a stage stands ready with equipment for tonight's performance. Along the walls paintings hang in neat rows. This week's display revolves around the ocean, from whales to lighthouses. I pull out my phone to snap a picture, sending it on to Keith with a quick message about visiting the ocean before the baby is born.

Our baby.

The thought warms me and grabs me into a great big hug each time.

I meet the gaze of the barista, a dark-haired girl with a blunt cut and black-framed glasses. "I'm thinking white mocha today."

"Great choice." The girl grins and writes my order on a yellow sticky pad then takes my money. "I'll bring that out to you."

The door opens again and Irene enters. She weaves around tables toward me. Her usual easygoing nature hasn't come with her. I can't help but see the tension drawn across her forehead in tight worry lines.

She hugs me then places her own order.

We sit at a table near the corner, alongside a shelf where people can leave and borrow books. Paper covers the tabletop and a cup of colored pencils sits in the center. I select a grape color and begin to sketch a child digging in the sand.

"You're very talented." Irene's head is cocked and her attention stays on my hand. "I want to apologize."

My hand stills. "For what?"

"The other day we were supposed to do this. You had something big to say, and I dragged you off on a pointless mission instead. I do that. I get so wrapped up in the house I do a lousy job of showing the people I care about that they're important."

I drop the pencil into the cup and rest my hand on her forearm. "No hard feelings. In fact, it gave me a couple days to enjoy the anticipation. Besides Keith, you're the first person I've told." The reality fades my smile. Why haven't we told our own parents about the baby?

The dark-haired girl sets a foamy drink in front of me and a cup of tea by Irene.

"Thank you," I say.

She nods and walks away.

I curve my hands around the hot stoneware and bring the drink to my nose, inhaling the mixture of spicy and sweet blended with the earthy texture of coffee. Sipping, I let the richness lie on my tongue for a moment before I swallow. Anticipation. The ingredient that enhances every flavor.

Irene hasn't touched her cup. Her face is lit with a full smile like a mother enjoying her child. "How much longer will I have to wait? Waiting isn't a delight for some of us."

I cough on the coffee that shot down the wrong tube when a laugh got in the way. Swiping the foam off my lips with a paper napkin, I regain myself. "You're sure you wouldn't rather wait until next week's coffee date?"

The lightness has returned to Irene's eyes, and I'm amazed at how it comforts me. "Now would be good."

"Okay." I lean forward. "You know Keith and I decided to restart the adoption process. Thank you for the recommendation, by the way."

Irene nods and waves me on.

"Well . . ." I can hardly talk through the smile. "We met with a birth mother who wants to place her baby with us."

"Praise the Lord." Irene presses her palms together. "This is wonderful news."

I pinch my lower lip between my thumb and finger. This is why I haven't told anyone else. At this moment sadness seeps into the story, and I don't want to face what I've lost.

Irene's eyes narrow. "What is it?"

"Guilt, I guess. It's about the baby we lost in Tennessee. I can't help but feel we're leaving him behind again. And it's not the same with this birth mother either."

"In what way?"

"Well, when we were matched with Britney, there was an instant bond. I took her to every doctor's appointment, attended her high school graduation, shared so much of the experience. It was early in the pregnancy when we were matched. I really wanted to know who she was. In some ways, we walked through it together. I miss her so much."

"Did she change her mind?"

"No. Britney was solid about her decision. She wanted her baby to have a mother and a father. It's not that she didn't love him. He had her whole heart. So much so that she was willing to let hers be broken."

"She sounds like a mature young woman." Irene cocks her head to the side.

"She is. We still exchange emails every so often." A woman walks in with a toddler in a stroller. He slurps from a sippy cup. "When Britney went into labor, she called us. Keith and I rushed to the hospital. It took hours and everything progressed just as expected. Then Braydon was born. He cried. Then he stopped."

Irene's eyes shine with tears. She holds a hand over her mouth.

"The doctor called a code blue. Everything went crazy. Even though everyone was rushing around, time slowed."

"I'm so sorry."

I nod. I've heard those words so many times, but the honest compassion in Irene's voice spurs me on. "They brought him back. I thought they'd saved him, but then the doctor gave us the bad news. Braydon wouldn't live to leave the hospital. I thought Britney would ask us to go, but she wanted us there too. We took turns holding him . . ." I brush away another tear. "Three hours later, he stopped breathing. Britney and I were each holding one of his tiny hands, and he just slipped away."

Irene's chin quivers. "What a blessing his short life was."

"You're right, but most of the time I forget to be grateful for his short moments with us."

"There's a purpose in every life. Even a life ended quickly."

A smile breaks through my sad memories. "I'm so proud of Britney. She's a college student now. She accepted Jesus two months after Braydon died, and now she's seeing a very kind, Christ-loving man. She told me in her last email, she thinks he's the one."

"And it all worked together for good. I'm sorry about your loss, but I'm also encouraged by your story. Thank you. I really needed that today."

"Is everything okay?"

Deep worry lines divide her features. "They arrested Nikki for drug possession."

"What about Baby Boy?"

"Children's Services is picking him up this afternoon. I don't know what I'm going to say to Sierra. She's gotten very attached to him."

JILLIAN

The yeasty scent of fresh-baked bread saturates the air. I've always found comfort in the kitchen, mixing yeast, flour, and sugar with whatever ingredients the recipe calls for and turning the solitary items into something more than the sum of each one. It feels hopeful.

Bread. That's the solution I pull out when life is feeling hopeless and out of control. I've made a lot of bread over the last couple months.

I tap Zachary's door, then push it open. His head is curled to the side of his Transformers pillow, his arm in a cast rests on top of his stomach. Garrett brought the little television into his room and the old version of Superman plays on the screen while he sleeps.

Leaning over him, I take in the sweetness of this child. His dark hair clings to the moisture on his sweaty head. I brush my thumb over his cheek then pull a fleece blanket up to his chest. Broken bones and scrapes heal, but what about broken hearts? They seem to ache forever.

Shutting the door, I leave him to sleep with the sounds of a superhero saving the world, as if it's that easy.

In the kitchen I beat my fist into another bowl of dough. The doorbell rings. "Just a minute." I rub my hands clean on a kitchen towel then, without considering who could be on the other side, I open the door.

Three of Izzy's closest friends stand on the step. "Hey, Mrs. Cline. Is Izzy home?"

I'm slammed like the dough I've been taking my pain out on. "She didn't tell you?"

Leslie strokes her long braid. "I send her texts and snaps every day, but she never responds. We were hoping we could convince her to go to a movie with us."

"I'm sorry. Izzy's out of town." Did my voice just shake? Can they see my struggle and fight for the right words? "She's visiting my Aunt Frieda. She lives up north. She needs help. Not in good health."

With a flood of questions only teenage girls can produce, they swamp me. "When will she be back?" Leslie asks.

"Not . . . well, she's got the summer swimming thing. She'll be gone until next fall. I'm sure she'll write, or text, or email, or something. You know. She needs some time to get back on her feet. Helping my aunt will be good for her. I'll let her know you came by, okay?"

Before I can dig myself further into this endless pit, I close the door and press my back against its smooth surface.

"What are you doing?"

I whip around.

Garrett's jaw is a strong line, his arms are crossed and his biceps bulge. "Some girls came by for Izzy."

"Jillian. I heard it all. What do you think you're doing with that ridiculous story?"

I cross my own arms and set my own jaw. "I'm doing what I have to do. Do you think it's better for Izzy to come home to a town full of gossip?"

"They may just notice the baby in her arms. Our granddaughter."

The image flashes through my mind and cracks off another piece of my heart. There are some things I can't consider, can't even let myself see. "There may not be one there. She has options. She can place the child in a home where it can be cared for by people ready to be parents, and Izzy can come home and be just like she was before."

"You can't control this."

I stomp toward the kitchen, flipping a snarl his way. "At least I'm trying."

"There's one big difference between trying to control our lives and living them. One has God in it and the other has you playing God."

The front door slams. From the kitchen window I watch him jump into his truck and screech off down the road. That must have been what Izzy saw when Travis took off. The day he died.

I hug my arms around my chest, willing the shivers to stop. My world is cracking beneath my feet like thin ice. Any moment I'll plunge down into the frigid water. The first moments will burn with bitter cold, then I'll slip away, my heartbeat slowing with my respirations until finally all life fades away, and my body rises to the surface, an empty shell.

My hands drop to my sides and I melt onto the kitchen floor, my back against the hot oven door.

The timer rings.

More bread, done.

Chapter 19

Izzy

Sierra paces across our room, patting Baby Boy on the back and talking softly.

The air in here is stale and hot. I want to rip the hair right out of my head to distract myself from the kid's cries.

I'm not really a baby kind of person, but that never mattered before. I figured when I had my own, I'd feel differently. But it hasn't happened yet. What's wrong with me?

Finally, he burps, and that must be what he needed, because he settles down. After a few more passes by my bed, Sierra sits down next to me, her eyes glued to the baby, her finger absently stroking the birthmark on his ear.

And she's the one who's placing her kid? It doesn't make sense. Sierra would be a great mom.

The room cools when I look up and see Irene and Stacey standing in the hall. Those expressions say everything. They're the same looks I saw on the faces at Travis's funeral. It's grief and pity and helplessness.

Irene enters first. She kneels next to Sierra, but my roommate doesn't acknowledge her. "We have to let him go."

Sierra shakes her head. "I can't do it. I was supposed to take care of him. I promised."

I rest my hand on her shoulder. It's all I can do.

"It was never your responsibility." Irene holds Sierra's cheeks in her hand and lifts her chin so they make eye contact. "I'm so proud of you for caring for him. He knows he's loved because of you. But he needs the chance to have a family, not live in a house where people come and go. Either way, we don't have a choice. The board would like to skin me for keeping him this long. There's a caseworker downstairs. She'll take him to a temporary foster home until they can find a family member or a more permanent foster home."

"Why didn't Nikki place him when he was born?" Sierra's sad eyes fill with fresh tears. "He'd have a family now. She doesn't even care about him."

"I think she cares about him as much as she's able to care about anyone," Irene says.

"I wouldn't do this to my baby. I'd never make him move around like that. And I'd have given him a name."

I'm struck by how much he doesn't even have an identity.

"What would you call Baby Boy if you could name him?" asks Irene.

Sierra runs a fingertip along his chubby cheek. "I'd call him Caleb. It means wholehearted."

"You've given this some thought," Irene says.

Her shoulders shrug. "I call him that. He needed a name."

"You're right. You are a precious gift, little Caleb." Irene rubs his fuzzy head. "And so are you, Sierra."

Wiping away a tear, Sierra sniffs. "We should take him downstairs now."

Stacey, Irene, and I follow Sierra. She carries the baby close, his head nestled in the crook of her neck.

At the bottom of the stairs the caseworker taps her foot on the hardwood floor. Her lips are pinched and her eyebrows raised.

She's not removing this child from a meth-house or a filthy shack.

Irene touches my elbow. "I'll go get his formula."

"We've already packed it." Cate holds out a diaper bag so full the top won't zip. "His binky and blanket are in there too."

"I'm under the impression this boy doesn't have a name." The caseworker flings the bag over her shoulder.

Settling her hands on her hips, Irene cocks her head. "You are under the wrong impression. His name is Caleb." She looks to us and we nod as if we've known this all along.

"I see. Well, Caleb, we should be off." She reaches around Caleb's body, but Sierra holds firm.

Easing him from her shoulder, she plants a kiss on his forehead and then whispers words I can't make out before placing him in the car seat.

The caseworker looks across the silent group. "He's going to a very nice home, and we'll be sure he's taken care of. Honest. I'm not the bad guy here." She threads her arm through the handle and lifts the baby to hip height. "I can't give details, but I'll let you know when he's settled in a more permanent home."

The door shuts behind her, leaving us all staring at the last place we saw baby Caleb.

Sierra's chin quivers. She bends forward, keeping her eyes away from the group. "I'm going to my room for a while." And she's gone before anyone can respond.

I've only been in the house for a few days, but already I'm overwhelmed with the pain of my roommate.

◆　◆　◆

"Mom, I hear what you're saying, but this has to be my decision. Even the counselor said so." I lean back onto my bed, careful not to drop the phone. "No matter what I choose, I can't make this go away. People are going to know. I'm going to know."

Sierra steps into our room, her arms piled with thin books.

"I've got to go now." I hang up before my mom can make her next well-planned argument.

Sierra takes a step backward. "I'm sorry. I'll come back later."

"No." I scoot off the edge of the bed. "Don't go. It's your room."

"And yours. It seems like you could use some time."

"My mother thinks she knows exactly what I should do. Travis was right. He always said she was ruling my life. But this is my choice, right?"

Like I've stunned her, Sierra's eyes go wide. "I guess."

"This is my baby, and now with Travis gone, this is my decision alone. Right?"

She sets the stack on the desk and sits in the matching chair.

"How can she just expect me to give my baby away?"

Sierra's chin dips.

I press my fingertips into my forehead. I'm such a jerk. "That's not what I mean. Really, Sierra. I don't think you're doing a bad thing, I just don't think it's the right thing for me."

She nods, but her gaze stays down.

"Are you studying? Can I help you?" It's a very small gesture after trampling on the only friend I have in this world.

"They're adoption books."

"What's that?" I pick up the top booklet.

"Pictures and letters and stuff put together by people who want to adopt a baby. These are the people who met the criteria I chose. Now I'm supposed to look through them and decide who's best to be my baby's mom and dad."

Why do those words sting me like a shot? Maybe it's because Sierra feels she can't do this on her own. Maybe it's because my daughter won't have a dad. I try to push away the thoughts, but the future only makes the now worse. Will anyone ever be able to love me again? How will I make a living? Will my entire future be focused on putting food on the table and never having my own life again? Will I turn bitter like Mrs. Owens?

"Would you look at them with me?"

The offer is so personal, so intimate. I squeeze her hand. "Thank you. I'd love to." I settle myself on the carpet, the bed at my back.

She divides the stack in half and hands me the top section.

The first book has a deep blue cover surrounding one picture of a couple with mountains behind them. He's tall, with dark hair and round

156

glasses. Her skirt brushes the ground, her long hair is in a braid draped over her shoulder. Their letter is distant, like a textbook. I toss it to the side and pick up the next one.

A couple vowing to raise a child to be free-spirited. No violence. No boundaries. And no way, if you ask me. I imagine my brother growing up like this. He's wild enough with steady rules.

I toss it on top of the first one. "Are you finding any you like?"

"A couple are okay."

"What are you looking for?" I fan the three I haven't opened yet. "I'm overwhelmed already."

"The counselor helped me to figure out what was most important to me. I want a family who wants lots of kids. I want marriage to be important to them. They need to love this baby no matter how he or she got here. And they need to be forgiving."

"I like that one."

"And I want them to be Christians. Not the kind of Christians I used to know, not the ones who just say they are. I want someone like Irene and Cate. I'm so jealous of them."

I run my fingers along the pointed corner of one book. "You're jealous because they're Christians?"

"Yeah. I would love to be like them." Her shoulders curl forward.

"What's stopping you?"

"You wouldn't understand. You grew up going to church. You know all the stuff, the things to say, how to do it. I'm not like you. I'm a mess."

I roll onto my knees, placing my hands on Sierra's feet. "I'm right here in the same house as you. So is Cate. And from what I hear, she came from a horrible background."

"You just got turned around." Sierra edges away.

"Believe me, it was more than one little wrong turn."

"What happened to you?" Her eyes go wide. "I'm sorry. It's none of my business."

I shake my head. "No worries. It wasn't some big tragedy. I got all caught up in myself. I don't know. The reality is, this could happen to anyone. It doesn't matter how much your parents are worth or which neighborhood you live in. We all make choices." Suddenly I'm overwhelmed by all I have to be grateful for and, at the same time, all I've lost. Silly things like shopping with friends, my flat stomach, my place in the world. They're the things I miss most. I still wanted others to see me as someone who had it all figured out. I wanted their jealousy. Then Sierra knocked those thoughts out of the park. Her words make a home run. "It's not about where you come from or where you've been. We're equal."

"How can you be so sure? You barely even know me." She works a clump of hair with her fingers. "I've done some horrible things. You wouldn't understand."

"You aren't your mistakes." I use the chair to help me stand, then I run my fingers through Sierra's hair the way my mother used to do with mine.

Chapter 20

MARGARET

I set the only board games we own on the counter, then put the popcorn in the hand-painted bowl that used to belong to my grandmother. It's the first time in years that I've taken this piece of family history out of its box. And it's about time.

"I've got the pop." Deven hands me a can and cracks the top on his. "Now what?"

"Now we play." I'm starting our first family game night at the suggestion of Hobbs. Tuesdays, every week, until further notice. "What's your choice?"

He picks up each of the four boxes, one at a time. Monopoly, checkers, Twister, and Life. "Do you know how to play any of these?"

"All of them."

He questions me with his eyes. "All right then, checkers."

I pull the top from the box and unfold the board. "Red or black?"

He chooses black.

"Is this the kind of thing you've been doing with the youth group?" I take my turn.

Deven moves his checker. His lips part with a grin. One tooth on the top has grown in twisted to the side, giving him a mischievous look. "No, Mom. Last week we played Xbox. And the week before, we did something called Fugitive. We took turns trying to get from the start to the finish without being caught by the police."

My mouth falls open and the pounding of my heart echoes in my ears.

"Don't worry. They're pretend police. It's just a game." His eyes sparkle as he slides a checker closer to my side.

"Officer Hobbs knows you're doing this?"

"It was his idea."

I've got to talk to that man as soon as possible. This sounds nothing like the youth group I went to when I was a kid. But then again, look how I turned out. I jump my checker over two of his.

"Ouch."

"I told you, I know how to play."

The phone rings, an uncommon interruption.

"Hello?"

"Mrs. Owens?" The voice is unfamiliar.

"Yes," I say.

"I'm calling from Child Protective Services."

My hand goes numb, and I fumble with the phone, nearly dropping it. What now?

"Is your maiden name Conway?"

"Yes." My neck warms and I start to sweat.

Deven sets his checker down, his eyebrows pinch.

"And your father is Howard?"

"Yes." I keep answering questions, but we're not getting anywhere. "What's this about?"

"Your sister has been arrested on drug charges. She may make bail, but we have custody of her son for the time being. He's currently in a temporary foster home, but we'd like to place him with a family member, if possible. You're the only person who met the criteria. Would you consider taking him in?"

This must be a joke. I've never even met my sister. In fact, until this moment, I wasn't completely sure she existed. No. This isn't my problem. I look over at *my* son. We're finally making a little progress. He's still eyeing me with questions I have no idea how to answer. "Doesn't he have a friend he could stay with?"

The line is silent.

"Maybe a neighbor?"

"Mrs. Owens, I understand your family isn't close. The child in question is only two months old."

I swallow hard, my gaze locking on Deven's. "What about work? I can't take him with me."

"We'll help with expenses and childcare costs. Please, Mrs. Owens, think about this tonight and get back to me tomorrow. We can do an emergency certification. You'll then have two years in which to complete the Foundations classes."

Two years? That's a long time. "Okay, I'll think about it."

I scribble down the number and hang up.

"What?" Deven leans forward, his palms pressed into the counter. "What happened? Is it Officer Hobbs? Is he hurt?"

I put a hand on his shoulder. "No. Nothing like that. Children's Services wants us to take in a baby. Your cousin to be exact."

"I have a baby cousin?"

I shrug. My family is far from close. Finding a cousin must sound as normal as running across a space ranger on the way home from school. "It's news to me too. The baby is in foster care right now. I don't know what to do."

"He can sleep in my room." Deven leans back into his seat.

My cheeks burn with the hot tears that sting my eyes, and I pull him around the counter and into my arms. "When did you become such a caring boy?"

He wriggles away. "I'm not. Yuck, Mom."

"So, you think we should say yes. That's crazy, you know."

"Officer Hobbs talked to our youth group about how sometimes we feel better when we help out other people. Like when we do a job for somebody, we get even more than we give. Maybe this kid will help us get better too. Like about Travis and everything."

"I don't know about that, but I'm not sure I can live with the guilt of not taking him either. Let's think about it tonight. Maybe we can have him for a trial visit."

"Or we can keep him forever." He grins. "I'm kind of tired of being the youngest anyway."

The youngest. In most ways Deven is now my only. Kane won't be out for years, and Kyle has sent exactly one letter home since joining the Marines last year. Okay, he did call when he got word about Travis. Even Kane called home then. But it wasn't like they'll be sitting at the table for Thanksgiving or hanging a stocking above the woodstove. To them family means a drunk father and a frazzled mother. It means screaming, crying, and poverty. It means promises that can't be kept and people who don't come home.

Is that the life this baby is doomed to lead?

We don't have much. Not much money. Not much room. But the one thing I've learned from losing my husband and three of my children is that stuff doesn't matter. People do. Why couldn't I have learned that lesson before they were all gone?

STACEY

My feet are planted on the asphalt in front of Willamette OB-GYN. Another look at my fingernails. The mauve polish I painted on this morning is begging to be picked off. I check my cell phone again. Maybe a quick call to Keith. He'd know what to do. He always knows what to do in crazy, socially awkward situations. He'd make a silly joke, and I'd fall into the temptation of his distraction.

But Candice is uncomfortable with Keith joining us at her doctor's appointment.

I cross my arms and scan the parking lot. What if she changed her mind? What if she's been in an accident? What if something truly awful has happened? The adoption process has turned me into a maniac, and they say pregnancy is rough.

The uneven rattle of a car badly in need of a tune-up hits my ears before I spy Candice behind the wheel. She parks nearby and shimmies herself to the edge of her seat then uses the door handle to hoist herself up. "Wow. That gets harder every time. Sorry I'm late."

My teeth clamp down on the inside of my cheek. "No. You're right on time." I hold the office door open for Candice and follow her into the waiting room. Approaching the desk, I pretend I don't notice the scowl on the receptionist's face, bless her heart. "Candice is here now." I paste an extra sweet smile on my lips.

"Have a seat." She doesn't return my gesture.

Running my tongue along the bottom of my teeth, I search for something to say. Anything to start a conversation and break this uncomfortable silence. The more I scan my brain, the less I find to draw from. What did I expect, that all birth mothers would be exactly like Britney? That we would have an immediate bond? That we would hit it off with an instant connection because we share love for the same unborn child? "So, did you have a good lunch?"

Candice cocks her head.

"I mean after our meeting on Saturday. You said you were having lunch with a friend."

"Yeah. It was good."

"What'd you have?"

"A burger."

"Great." Well, that took me a long ways.

The nurse walks in and brings the sweet relief of interruption. "Candice, we're ready for you."

Like a spring, I jump to my feet, too eager, but too late. With my eyes, I try to convey to the nurse how important it is she not leave me alone in a room with Candice. My message must not translate well because she narrows her eyes and returns my pleading with a weak, somewhat suspicious smile.

"We'll be doing an ultrasound today. Did you want to know the gender of the baby?"

Candice shrugs. "Whatever Stacey wants is fine with me."

My jaw falls open until I slap it shut with my right hand. "I think that would be fun." Eyeing Candice, I'm hoping for a glimmer, just a flash of emotion to say I've done something right. That she and I are on the same team. But she's already consumed by her smartphone, and I'm all alone.

The nurse rolls her eyes, not even bothering to turn away from us first. "Take this." She shoves a lidded plastic cup into Candice's hand. "Head into the bathroom and give us a sample."

Without a word, Candice leaves.

The nurse opens a door and ushers me into an exam room. "We have a consent form from Candice so we can speak with you. Is there anything you wanted to know?"

My heart thumps harder. "Is the baby healthy?"

"So far everything looks great. Candice doesn't come off as very interested but she assures me she's been taking her prenatal vitamins and she's never missed an appointment. Late, always, but missed, never." She turns her stool toward me and scoots closer. "I'll let you in on a secret. We actually schedule her thirty minutes later than the time we give her." She pulls a tray on wheels over to the ultrasound machine. "I'm glad she found you. Candice has been anxious to move forward on an adoption plan."

A plan. That's exactly what this feels like. Keith and I are part of Candice's plan. Nothing more. With Britney we'd been her cheerleaders, her support. We'd formed a connection from sharing one of the most precious of all feelings, love for a child.

I keep my eyes trained on a poster about the benefits of breastfeeding. How am I going to break this nasty habit of comparing? This time will be different in many ways. Some I'll struggle with, but others will be miraculous, like the birth of a healthy baby.

Candice walks back in. She's changed into a gown she holds together in the front with one hand while tugging at the hem with the other. She scoots onto the table, and the nurse covers her legs with a white cotton blanket.

"Go ahead and lie back. I'm almost ready." She snaps off the lights. The room glows from the computer screen. "This is my favorite part of the job." Opening Candice's gown, she squirts a squiggly line of gel around her bulging belly button.

Candice grips each side of the table, her eyes closed.

I step closer. "Are you all right? Does something hurt?"

She opens one eye. "I'm fine. Just bored is all. How long do you think this will take?" Opening the other eye, she studies the nurse.

"Not long, but I think you'll find this interesting."

"I saw my mom's ultrasound when she was pregnant with my little sister. It was just a bunch of static on the screen."

"You may feel differently this time," the nurse says. "It's completely different when it's your baby."

Candice turns her head to the opposite side, apparently fascinated by a pole holding a blood pressure cuff.

With the ultrasound wand, the nurse pushes the gel around. Something moves. Like a wave on her skin, it happens again.

"Baby isn't so sure about this." The nurse types something on the keyboard.

Candice doesn't respond.

A moment later the image sharpens, and I see the baby. Near the mouth, a tiny hand is balled into a fist. So small. So perfectly formed.

I touch Candice's shoulder, completely overwhelmed by the miracle. "Look."

She doesn't move.

After taking what feels like a hundred measurements, the nurse stills the picture. "There you have it. This little one is definitely a boy."

My gaze jumps from the screen to Candice. She's holding her bottom lip between her teeth, her head still to the side. If she heard, there's no indication.

The nurse looks closer at the screen. She moves the wand again and takes new images of the chest.

"Is everything okay?" I swallow the walnut-sized lump suddenly lodged in my throat. "Is he okay?"

There's no answer.

The room starts to spin, and I grasp the counter for support.

She presses the wand harder, forming a hollow in Candice's abdomen. "I think everything is fine. Just a weird angle. Dr. Hudson will check over my images, but I don't see anything to worry about."

Combing my fingers through my hair, I peer down at the table. Candice is staring at the screen, her mouth open and a tear trailing down her temple.

Chapter 21

JILLIAN

"Good morning, Curt—or should I say Officer Hobbs? What brings you to church on a Friday morning?" He's intimidating in his police uniform even after the years I've known his gentle spirit. The gun on his belt and the badge shining from his chest set him into a different class than the goofy man I see working with middle schoolers. "Not that I mind. It's pretty lonely here on the pastor's day off."

His face lights with a childlike smirk. "Then I suppose it's a good thing it's you I'm looking for."

For a moment the skin on my face tingles, and I'm swallowed by dread.

Then he crosses his arm and becomes a boy in a policeman's costume. A friend.

"What is it you need?"

"I need baby stuff."

My eyebrow lurches up before I can control my reaction.

He waves a hand between us. "Nothing like that. No worries. It's for a friend of mine. She's taking in a foster baby. Kind of a sudden decision. A family thing. I thought the church could help out."

"Is she a member?" It doesn't matter, but curiosity is a vicious competitor, and it niggles with relentless pressure. In a town the size of Brownsburg, sometimes you find out your own business from your neighbor. That, I-wish-I-could-hide-under-the-covers feeling washes over me again. It takes hold every time I'm forced to the slightest admission that Izzy's situation will likely be uncovered.

"No. Not a member. I think she may have attended as a child, but not now."

I shake my head. "All right." Hitting a few keys, I save the document I've been staring at all morning, then come around my desk. "I'll show you where the baby closet is. She's free to take anything she needs. We just ask people to bring back items when they're done—if they're still in good condition, that is—so someone else can use them."

I lead him through the children's ministry office and open the storage closet at the back. Shelves are labeled by gender and size. Along the floor, a few items like bouncy seats and baby bathtubs are stacked. Every time I come in here, the sight steals my breath. I'll never know my first grandchild. When I've dreamed of that distant future, it's been tea parties and Christmas cookies, but I won't be able to hold her. These grandma memories will belong to someone else. What if her new grandma doesn't have time for books and snuggles?

"Wow. Now that I'm here, I know I don't belong." He picks up a breast pump, examining the long tube. "I don't have a clue what this is."

I coax a smile onto my face for his benefit. "And you don't want to." Taking it from his hands, I set it back in its place on the shelf.

"Hey, I can't believe I didn't think of this. You know the woman. It's Margaret Owens, Travis's mother." He rubs his forehead. "Where is my brain lately?"

Cold rushes down my arms, leaving my fingertips tingling. "Margaret is getting a baby? Whose baby?"

He shakes his head. "I have no idea. She didn't seem to want to talk about the details. I just thought I could help out and maybe it would bless her."

"Would you like me to put a few things together and take them to her? I'll make sure she knows it was your idea."

"No. I mean I would love it if you took the stuff, but please don't tell her it was me. I don't want her thinking I'm overstepping, which I probably am."

Something in his eyes tells me this is more than a cop being neighborly. All the years I've known him, I can't remember a woman catching his attention. So why would he pick someone like Margaret Owens? And what is that woman up to now?

"I'll put the box together today." I step out of the closet and suck in fresh, baby-free air.

Curt pulls the cap from his head, running fingers through thinning hair. "I'd better get back to work. Don't want to explain to the chief that I'm spending city money searching for baby clothes." His grin is so innocent, he's perfect prey for someone like Margaret.

The keys on his belt jingle as he saunters down the hallway and out the door.

I remember a court case where a set of grandparents sued for custody of a grandchild. New fears burn my brain. What if Izzy's baby is the one Margaret is planning for? No. This can't be happening. But how else would someone like her end up with a baby? They aren't just falling off trees.

I yank a collapsed box from beside the bookshelf, reshape it, and reinforce the bottom with packing tape. Then I fill it with all sorts of baby clothes . . . Every item for a boy.

Margaret

The streetlight flickers on and off. My foot splashes into the pothole in the diner's parking lot, cold water slopping over my institutional black shoe, and into my tights, chilling the bottom of my foot. I rub circles into the ache at the base of my back. Grease from the kitchen clings to my hair. Now that I've pulled out the hair band, my hair hangs heavy around my face. How am I supposed to keep up this schedule at work, build some kind of relationship with Deven, and take care of a baby? My body is screaming for sleep, and my feet feel like they've swollen up two sizes.

A light blue sedan is idling beside my car. Clouds from the muffler float away in the cool wind.

Its dome light turns on as a door opens. I snatch my keys from my pocket, threading one between my first two fingers.

Stepping out of her car and into the dim glow from the security lamp on the shop behind the parking lot, Jillian Cline looks ready to attack.

I pause, straining my eyes for a better look. Rage doesn't suit the church secretary. Her glare brings out wrinkles along her temple and mouth.

Jillian crosses her arms and steps in front of me.

"What?" I ask.

"I had a visit from someone at the church today."

"Good for you." I try to step around her, but Little Miss Perfect blocks my path.

"I have something for you." The sweet shift in her voice sends a shiver up my spine.

She crams her key into the lock on her trunk while her eyes stay targeted on me. The lid pops open and Jillian hefts a box out and thrusts it into my arms.

"What's this?"

"Baby things. I hear you're expecting a little one at your house."

"So?" I drop the box onto the wet hood of my dented and rust-covered car. "Why are you all bent out of shape?" My own rage brings warmth to my extremities. "Let me guess. You think I'm such a horrible mother, I have no right to care for anyone else's child? How is this any of your business?"

"When it affects my daughter, it's my business. She's placing the baby, and you're going to stay out of it. And you're going to keep your mouth shut. If you think you'll get your hands on that little girl, you're mistaken."

The shock comes only a second before impact. Izzy is giving Travis's baby away. How can she do that? How can she take the last and only remaining piece of my son and toss her away like outgrown clothes donated to Goodwill? My granddaughter. A girl.

I bite back the choking emotion, but the pressure is too much. "She's having a girl?"

Jillian takes a step back.

"And she's placing her for adoption?" I ask.

"Don't act dumb. You know she is."

I shake my head. "I didn't. I haven't really given it much thought. I just assumed Izzy would raise her. How can she give our grandchild away? Can't you stop her? Can she do that without your consent?"

"It's the right thing to do." Jillian's angry stance softens. "You didn't know? Really? Then what's all this about a baby coming to stay with you?"

"My sister's kid. She's in trouble and they needed somewhere for the baby to stay. It's only temporary." The way she looks at me makes me feel like a germ under a high-powered microscope. "It's none of your business anyway." My face grows numb with my body. Why won't my heart take the clue and stop throbbing?

"I misspoke." She eases away, climbs into her car, and pulls out of the parking space.

I can't move until her taillights fade into the fog. I've lost three sons, and now my first granddaughter. What is it about me that sends people running? I sink against the door of the car, wetness seeping through my clothes and sticking my uniform to my back. If God is real, if He isn't just a story from my brief childhood, why doesn't He show Himself? Why has He abandoned me?

Jillian

"Where have you been? I've been calling for two hours." Garrett climbs off the couch, leaving Zachary to finish the movie alone.

I dig in my purse and pull out my phone. "Sorry. The ringer was turned off."

He ushers me into the kitchen. "That doesn't answer my first question. I considered calling the police, you know."

"I had to drop off some things for the church. No big deal. Sorry I didn't call." Lie number . . . Who am I kidding? I lost track a long time ago. I hadn't called because I didn't want to tell him where I was going, and I silenced the phone because I didn't want him to stop me. A major mistake. There isn't much left to bring him back to me. I've just attacked a grieving mother, accused her of planning to steal my daughter's baby, and made sure she knew I think she's unfit. That's the kind of Christian love I'm spreading.

I swallow away the guilt and turn back to my husband. "Are you hungry? I can whip up some dinner."

"We ate. Food is not the issue or the solution."

"I hope it was something healthy." Raging acid burns my throat. I haven't had anything but coffee since I left the house this morning.

His fingers grip my upper arm and spin me around. "I can't keep this up. Who are you?"

"That's a ridiculous question. I'm your wife. I'm Izzy's and Zachary's mother." I'm a liar and a murderer and a bully.

"You don't seem to notice our marriage is in serious trouble. You know I won't divorce you, but that doesn't mean I have to live like this."

I yank my arm free. He's never been rough with me and I won't allow today to be any different. "Are you threatening me? Seriously? Our lives are crashing around us and you want to threaten me? This isn't my fault. I didn't make Izzy get pregnant, but I am the only one who seems to know what to do from here."

"This isn't about Izzy and the baby. This is about you and me. And all I ever get from you are denials and put-offs. I've learned to live with that, but then something happens, and you turn into a control monster. And I want to know why."

I cross my arms, digging my nails into my own flesh. "I'm not a control monster, I'm a mother. It's a lot different than being a father. My vision is on the future, and I don't have the luxury of playing games."

Zachary grips the edge of the counter with his good hand. "Stop it. Why are you always fighting? Is that why Izzy left?"

Garrett closes his eyes and takes a couple breaths then ruffles Zachary's hair. "It's not like that at all. We're under a lot of stress, and I think you deserve to know the truth. All of it." He eyes me.

I shoot a warning glare his way. He wouldn't. How can he even consider rupturing Zachary's world too?

"Izzy made a mistake. A big one. But she's doing the right thing and taking responsibility for her actions." His eyes are gentle in complete opposition to the bullet he's about to fire.

Zachary's eyes grow wide. "Is she in jail?"

Garrett tips his head back. "No. Izzy's at a special house where they help girls who are going to have babies."

Zachary's mouth falls open and his skin pales. His eyes narrow in question.

Sickness washes over me, filling my throat and weighing down my muscles. "I've got to take a shower." I turn away and rush toward the safety of my room. Shutting the door, I turn the lock. This can't be happening. How do I turn back the clock, and where would I start again if I even could?

It might as well be at the beginning. I'm as alone now as I've ever been. No more Izzy. And now the truth is starting to spill and there will be no more Zachary. My husband and my son will be the team they've always been. Izzy will never come fully back.

Crawling into bed, I curl my body into a ball and settle my head onto the pillow. The ache in my chest turns to a burning sting. Years of grief. When will I be punished enough? When can I leave it behind?

I'd started fresh. Met new people.

Everything I do is a sacrifice at the altar. I teach Sunday school, work in the church office, run the mission committee, serve meals to the sick. But it isn't enough. He demands more. He takes more.

They'd all be better off if I left. I wrap myself up tighter around the pain, pulling a pillow in and squeezing it to my stomach. Everyone I've loved slips through my fingers, and the harder I hold on, the faster I lose them.

Chapter 22

Izzy

Sierra and I stop at the bottom of the stairs. The other girls are getting ready for movie night, but I have a mission. If I can't help myself, I can at least help my roommate.

Sierra hesitates, but I pull her toward Irene's office. "We have some questions," I announce when Irene looks up from a stack of papers. The room isn't much bigger than some walk-in closets. Only the window looking into the living room keeps it from feeling like a cave.

"Of course. Come on in, ladies."

Irene shuts the door and shoves her papers aside as she settles back in her chair.

My knee bumps Sierra's as we slide into the cramped seating. I clasp my hands and look around the room at pictures of young mothers and babies. These must be girls who lived here before.

Irene stays quiet, just waiting for one of us to start. I nudge Sierra with my knee.

"I—" Sierra twists a strand of hair, takes a deep breath, and starts again. "I don't know how to pick a family for my baby."

Irene nods. "That's a hard decision. You've gotten a stack of books. Have you looked through them yet?"

"Yeah, but I don't know what's real and what they put in there to up their chances. Some of it sounds fake."

Outside the window Cate grins as she walks toward the front door. Someone must be here. Irene lifts her chin and sees Cate too, but she doesn't move to get up. Her face turns back to Sierra.

My mother would have gone to the door.

"You have a very valid concern." Irene twists her lips. "Have you thought about narrowing it down, then meeting with a few of the couples? Do you think that would help?"

"Maybe . . . ?" Sierra rubs the top of her belly.

"You know, this is completely your choice," Irene adds. "You have our support no matter what or who you decide is right for your child."

"I know." Sierra looks over at me. "Thanks."

The noise level outside the tiny room climbs. Stacey is here. Heavy plastic bags hang from her arms.

Irene taps her chin. "I have an idea. Would you mind if I brought Stacey in on this conversation?"

Sierra shrugs.

Opening the door, Irene gets Stacey's attention. "Do you have a moment?"

"Sure." Stacey drops her bags just inside the door and squeezes into the clearing against one wall.

"Do you mind if I share your news with these two?"

Stacey's head bobs up and down. "Absolutely. Yes. I mean, no. I don't mind, that is. Go right ahead. That's kind of why I'm here anyway."

"Stacey and her husband have been chosen to adopt a baby."

"It's a boy. We just found out." Her grin fills the room, and I can feel her happiness. I smile at her smiling.

"Sierra is going through that right now," Irene explains. "She has been looking at books, and she's having a hard time knowing which family to choose. With your experience on the other side of that decision, do you think you could help her?"

"I can't tell anyone how to choose, but I can offer my perspective."

I lean forward. "I'd like to hear that too. I bet most of us would, even if we're not planning to place our babies. Like me. I'm keeping my baby." The words tumble out like I'm assuring everyone I'm not doing anything wrong. I can't look at Sierra or Stacey now.

"Sierra, what do you think about letting Stacey talk to the house about her experience and then working with you individually too?"

"That'd be good, I think." She stares at Stacey's feet.

Bags crinkle as Stacey steps over them and kneels in front of Sierra. "I want you to understand. Even though I'm adopting, I don't want to sway your decision. You need to make a choice because it's the path that's right for you and your baby, not because you think it will please any of us. If I can help, I'd love to. You're an amazing young woman."

A tear slips down Sierra's face. And another slides down Irene's cheek. Why do these women care so deeply for us? What's in it for them?

I know my mother loves me. I love her too. But I don't always believe her choices are about me and what I need. It's like who I am and what I do defines her. I don't get it.

Travis cared about me for me.

Irene and Stacey, they just want to do the best they can for us, and they get absolutely nothing in return.

This time, I can't give my mother what she wants, because what she's asking me to do is give away the last little bit of Travis.

STACEY

Though the day isn't particularly cool, someone has turned on the gas fireplace. The flames heat my back and flush my skin, but I don't take another seat. When I came, I had just been bringing a donation, not preparing to share my story.

All eyes are on me. All mouths quiet, waiting to hear what I'm going to say.

I've never mentioned my own desire to have a child. It didn't seem right to lay my problems on them when they're in the midst of their own struggles. Like telling my story would somehow guilt them into a different choice, or maybe I'm afraid of seeing pity in their eyes. Maybe they'll see me as broken.

I clear my throat. "Hi."

Giggles start with Cate and move like a wave through the group, washing away some of my tension.

"So, I brought these bags with me today because I don't need what's inside them." I pull one of the sacks onto my lap and bring out a pink onesie and a princess dress.

Smiles are replaced by serious expressions. Concern.

"You see, I can't have a baby. My husband and I tried for a long time, but it's not in the plan for us. A few years ago, we decided we wanted to adopt. We did all the paperwork, the background checks, everything. Finally, we were matched with a birth mother. Britney became a member of our family. And she still is." Folding the tiny clothes, I lay them on my lap. Do I share the entire story, or skip the journey back in time?

Kaylee works the fabric at the edge of her skirt. "You don't have any children." It's a statement, not a question. They're paying attention.

"No, I don't. There was a problem, and we lost our son the day he was born."

"Children's Services?" Sierra's eyes are wide open, one of the first times I've seen this.

"No. He died. It was a rare complication. He didn't suffer, but it took me the last two years to heal enough to start over."

Erin pulls a throw blanket up to her neck. "So, you're here because you want one of our babies?"

I clutch my hands to my chest. "No." My heart thunders in my chest. I've been coming to the house for a couple months now, and I've gotten to know most of the girls, but I've never addressed them with authority. How can I regain their trust if they think I'm using them, if they think I've ever had the intention of adopting one of their babies? My heart splinters with the thought of any one of these girls feeling like I see them as luggage carrying the cargo I want. "No. My husband and I went to an agency. I specifically asked the caseworker not to match us with any of you." I hold up my hand. "Not that I don't love you girls, but I want my time here to be undiluted by my desire to be a mother. There's not a connection."

"Why *do* you help here?" Erin asked.

"I never intended to step foot in this house. When I was new in town, I met Irene at the grocery store, and she told me about A Child's Home. I didn't think I'd ever speak with her again. The thought of being around babies, it hurt too much. But after Irene and I met again at church, my husband convinced me to give it a try. As I got to know all you brave young women and with my husband's persistence, I finally knew it was time to open my heart again. Recently, we were matched with another birth mother. She's having a boy in a few months, and we're beyond excited. That's why I don't need these clothes. For some reason, when I found out we were going to have a baby, I assumed it would be a girl. I went right out and bought every pink thing I could get my hands on. A few days ago, I went with the birth mother to an ultrasound appointment, and well, he's a boy." Tingles run over my skin.

Sitting back, I take in the smiles. They don't hate me.

"I thought maybe some of you could use them."

Cate's eyes sparkle.

I pass the bags down the couch.

From the first sack, Cate pulls out a crocheted pink bonnet with beads worked into the edging. She lays it over Marianna's head. We all hear the baby coo and gurgle. "I think she likes it. She's all girl from the start. Nothing like new clothes."

Irene leans over the couch and smiles down at Marianna. "This is a precious child." She crinkles her face and blows air through her pursed lips, inches away from the baby. "Just like the rest of you." She looks from face to face. "Do any of you have questions for Stacey?"

Sierra raises a tentative hand. "Do you think you'll love the baby you adopt as much as you would if he'd been yours?"

"First of all, he will be mine. The means are different, but the love is just as full. I had the same question once myself. A friend connected me with a woman who had two biological children and two through adoption. After spending the day with them, I realized I couldn't tell the difference. The way her children came into her family wasn't as important as the fact they *did* come into her family."

"So, then you knew?"

"I'm not sure I was fully convinced until I held my son in my arms. He became part of me when he took a piece of my heart." I blink at the rush of tears. They never stop surprising me, but they're more welcome now. They're part of a memory, part of the love I've experienced in that one day of his life.

"Did you want a girl this time?" asked Kaylee.

I shrug. "I would have loved a girl, but I'm also thrilled he's a boy."

Cate looks up. "Will you keep helping out here once the baby is born?"

"Yes. Absolutely, if you'll still have me. I thought I could bring the little guy with me. What do you think?"

Cheers go up around the group.

"There's no better place for me to get the hang of being a mom than here."

Izzy

Learn how to be a mom?

I've never thought about that. Don't women just know what to do when their babies are born? Isn't there some kind of natural instinct or something?

I look myself up and down in the full-length mirror. My belly has rounded out like I have an expanding balloon under my shirt. Finally, I have breasts, but they look awkward, like they belong on someone else. My mass of curls has multiplied until I'm now forced to keep my hair tied back in a ponytail that draws attention to the pimples along my hairline.

Pregnant, yes.

Woman, not so much.

Six months ago, I thought I controlled my life. I knew what I was doing, and I knew I was doing it in the best possible way. Well, not everything, but most things. Now even thinking about this crazy responsibility makes me question all of it. Maybe my mom knows more than I give her credit for. All those rules I thought she enforced to steal my freedom and keep me under her control were, in fact, for my own good. If only I could go back in time and follow them.

I'd be different if I had the chance.

There must have been something about me early on. Some kind of clue this is how I'd end up. But now I'm here, and even if my mother knew what was best for me then, she doesn't know what's best for me or my baby now.

The wriggle who continually shoves her heel into my rib cage is the only thing left of Travis Owens. And I have the chore of being both mother and father to her, even if I still feel like I need to be cared for myself.

The tap at the door is classic Irene. Always steady. Always gentle.

"Come in."

Irene has the same kind of floppy curls that I have, but thinner and silver rather than dark. On Irene they look wise, tamed into soft submission. I tuck a loose strand behind my ear. I'll never have peace like she has.

"Izzy, you probably don't realize it, but you've already been a huge blessing here."

The way she smiles at me like she's proud or something makes me look away. "How is that?"

"You've made a difference in Sierra's life. Thank you for reaching out to her. She really needed a good friend."

"I feel the same about her."

"So, how are you doing? Any questions or concerns coming up?"

I cross my arms over my newly grown chest. "How do I learn to be a good mother?" Irene has a way of making questions rise to the surface and escape my mouth.

"That's a serious one. I'm sorry I wasn't here to meet your mom when she brought you. I understand she cares a great deal about you." She grins. "I know for a fact because she sends me emails every day to make sure you're safe and cared for."

I bury my face in my hands. "Oh no. Do any of the other mothers do that?"

"I'm afraid not."

Looking out between my fingers, I check out Irene. "You want to be harassed?"

She tips her head to one side then the other. "I don't know about *harassed*, but I'd love it if every mother cared as much as yours does. Most of the girls who come through here are from long lines of dysfunction. Hopefully, they can break those cycles. Sometimes miracles happen right before our eyes. You should get to know Cate. You'll be inspired by her story." Irene pulls me into a side hug. "But you want to know how to be a good mother. Well, we'll teach you the day-to-day things like changing diapers, nutrition, when to take the baby to the doctor. And we'll also teach you ways to bond with your baby. But the most important part is trusting God and walking with Him. I wish I had understood that when I was raising my daughter."

"I never thought about you having kids. Does she live around here?"

Irene's eyes grow dark. "She and I don't talk."

A weight settles on my heart. If this is how it worked out for Irene, how do I have a chance? Am I supposed to give up my whole life for a child who can walk away from me, never come back? I grasp my stomach. Nothing is ever for sure. Why didn't my mother explain how the world really is?

Irene tugs on one of my loose curls. "This isn't my story. This is yours."

"What if I do it wrong?"

I can tell her smile is forced. "All you can do is your best and trust God for the rest. You're going to be fine, Izzy. You have a huge heart and a generous spirit. That little girl is very lucky."

"But she would have been better off if I had waited. She could have had a mother and a father."

"There's no point looking back. That's already set. How can you change your thinking and start living from today forward?"

I sink onto the mattress. Pressing my elbows to my knees I hold my head in my hands. With a deep breath, I let the question settle in my mind. What can I do from here? "I can learn everything possible while I'm in this house, and I can be the best mom under this circumstance."

"I'm proud of you, Izzy. One more thing. I want you to start praying for your daughter. She'll need your prayers throughout her life. It's never too early to start."

"Do you pray for your daughter?"

"Every morning and every night."

Chapter 23

STACEY

Sipping my Diet Coke, I eye the Cinnabon stand in the food court. The scent of sweet cinnamon gooeyness floats in the air and makes my mouth water. I lick my lips and scan a hundred unfamiliar faces . . . again. Dropping my purse on one of the less sticky-looking tables, I unsnap the top and dive my hand through keys, receipts, and breath mint tins until my fingernails bite into the rubbery cover on my cell phone.

I check for a missed call or text, like I did three minutes earlier.

Nothing.

Swallowing my frustration—or is it fear?—I type out a text to Keith.

He responds within seconds. "Don't worry. She's always late."

That may be true, but every time my heart takes off like a racehorse. My fears gallop out of control with images of all the things that could and may go wrong. And each time Candice is a little later than the time before, like my emotions are a game for her.

That's not fair.

We're all under a mountain of stress, but in the end, I'll go home with a baby and be his mama. Where is my compassion?

Sinking into a cold plastic chair, I take another sip of my drink, more water than soda now. I wipe the condensation off my hands and onto my blue jeans, lace my fingers, and tip my head. Maybe Candice and I don't have to have an immediate connection, but I want to know her. After all, we share a very special interest. For the rest of our lives we will love the same person in a way no one else will ever understand.

My thoughts drift back to Britney. Maybe the bond we had was a once-in-a-lifetime kind of thing. Maybe I've set up expectations no other relationship can fulfill.

I sweep my gaze through the crowd again. This time it catches on the most vivid purple tresses. I'd never consider such an unusual color myself, but I can't help being drawn to the depth and brightness of the color. It's truly beautiful. Seconds pass before I'm aware the hair belongs to Candice. I swallow the brush of tingling anxiety that always seems to arrive with her.

The chair scrapes the floor as I push it back, take my bag, and make my journey through the crowd to Candice. Even though I'm only a couple feet away, she doesn't notice me. I tap her shoulder and she swings around, her hands lifted in front of her chest in a defensive posture.

"I'm sorry." I take a step back. "I didn't mean to startle you."

"You didn't." The pale wash of her face says something entirely different. "I was thinking."

"About what?"

Her eyebrows sink farther toward her eyes and she looks deep into me, leaving me chilled and wondering what she sees. "Nothing."

Another deep conversation.

"Can I get you something to eat or drink before we go shopping?" The plan is to pick out a couple outfits for the baby, and hopefully, something for Candice too. It's not that the sweatshirts she wears are a problem, I just want her to see I care for her as a person. It's a bonding kind of thing. I hope. Or an awkwardly desperate attempt to get her to like me.

Candice shakes her head and pulls out her cell phone, typing in a text. No doubt some comment about what a loser I am.

"All right. Let's get started. There's a maternity store around the corner. I thought we could stop in and find you something."

"I don't need any clothes."

"You might be more comfortable wearing something designed to fit."

"I don't need to be comfortable."

We walk past a group of yoga pants–wearing mothers pushing strollers.

"Maybe not, but every woman wants to look nice sometimes."

She slows her pace, turns aside, and acts as though she's entranced by the penny fountain.

Reaching my hand out, I lay it on Candice's shoulder.

She jumps and spins around. Her eyes are ablaze with a fuel of fear and pain.

I reach for her again, instinct outweighing common sense. The more she pulls away, the deeper my need to reach for her. Like somehow I must connect with her. My fingertips rest where Candice's elbow bends and the thick fabric of her coat forms a fold, a barrier between us.

With weary eyes she draws her gaze from my face to my hand. "I'm not like everyone else." Her words float above the splash of water like a feather on a gentle breeze. "I'm not pretty."

Letting my fingers slip from Candice's arm, I cup her elbow and guide her onto a bench close enough to the fountain to feel the occasional rogue droplet. "Candice, you're beautiful."

She combs her fingers through overgrown purple bangs, pulling them down to cover her eyes.

"What makes you think you're not?"

At our first meeting, she was distant but confident. Each meeting since then, she's further swallowed by an invisible force. By the time this baby is born, Candice will be in no shape to care for herself. Does she have anyone to help her?

Pressing my palms together, I sandwich them between my knees.

A child breaks away from his mother's grasp and speeds toward the fountain. Five feet from his goal, his stubby tennis shoe catches on some invisible barricade and he flies forward. Arms outstretched, he hits the polished floor and slides toward his destination. When he comes to a stop, he lifts his head and catches sight of his mother still rushing toward him. His mouth turns down and his eyes run over with silent tears.

I shift my gaze to Candice and curve my hand over her knee. "It's okay to cry."

Dark eyes, round like a frightened animal's, stare at me. They hold questions. Deep questions.

The emotions take hold of me, breaking off a chunk of my heart. Candice's face blurs through my own tears. The girl next to me is frustrating, closed, always late, just as valuable as anyone else. Something or someone has crushed her, and though she's tried to battle, she's raw behind her dented armor.

With the back of my hand, I wipe a tear across my cheek.

"Why are you crying?" Candice's voice is dry, lifeless. "I'm going to give you this baby."

"It's not the baby. Candice, you're more than a baby carrier. You are a child of God."

She shakes her head. "You don't get it."

"No, probably not. But I'd like to. Help me understand."

"And if I do, how will you be able to love this baby?" Her arms circle her baby belly. "You can't unknow stuff."

"You'll have to trust me then. I'm telling you: nothing you can say will ever make me stop loving the baby . . . or you." That moment, at the second the words slip over my lips, the truth in them becomes real. I love Candice without reservation. No matter what comes next, I will choose to love.

She stands, taking a moment to readjust her ill-fitting clothes. "Let's get what we came for."

And that's the end of our heart-to-heart.

◆　◆　◆

"What else can I do?"

Irene looks around the dining room, her face lit with satisfaction. "I think we're ready."

Warm sweetness softens the air. Along the center of the long table we've placed plates of cookies, cinnamon rolls, fruit, and pitchers of ice-cold milk. Balloons with metallic ribbons dangle from the ceiling. And the banner hangs just inside the door: Congratulations!

"I can't believe you do this all by yourself." I pull out a chair and rest, my legs straight. My arches throb, screaming for a foot massage.

"It's tradition." She waves a dismissive hand. "The same thing I did when my own little girl came home at the end of the school year."

"I bet she loved it."

Irene examines her hands. "She did. It was a special time. I never worked on the last day of school." She sighs. "Good times." But her eyes are holding back tears.

"You miss her."

She nods.

"Have you ever thought about looking for her? I'm sure she misses you too."

"Every time I move, I leave my new address so she can find me if she ever comes looking." Her eyes gaze out the front window. "She never has."

I step closer. This is the broken piece, the crack that runs through Irene's life. Knowing a sliver of her pain makes her real, touchable, but it hurts deeper than I would expect. It makes the work she does with the girls somehow more important.

"I see her in the girls. The way she was before our bad summer. Before her senior year when she stopped talking to me. One day, she just packed her bags and left." A pause, and then Irene shakes her head. "No. It wasn't like that. We fought. I told her to leave." Raising her hand, she splays her fingers over her eyes.

As I reach for her, my eye catches a glint of sunlight splashing off the van as it pulls into the driveway. "They're here." A moment too soon.

Irene turns away from the window. I think she's dabbing her eyes.

Seconds later the door bursts open and the girls rush into the living room.

As if the last few minutes never occurred, Irene's face is lit with a smile. "Congratulations!" She waves them all close. "I have something to say before we dive into the treats." She reaches out and takes Cate's hand.

Immediately the girl's eyes sparkle with tears. She blinks them away only to have them replaced.

"Cate has completed her high school requirements, and we all know she's been accepted to Oregon State University for the fall."

"Go, Beavers!" Kaylee lifts a fist in the air.

The room erupts with familiar laughter.

"Yes. But I have more news."

Izzy takes the car seat from Cate's shaking arm and unbuckles Marianna. She picks the squiggling little girl up and hands her to her mother.

"I received a call last week about our Cate. A family who has been very impressed by her perseverance has asked for permission to pay for her schooling. Full tuition. What do you say, Cate?"

The always present smile fades to a wavering line and her eyebrows furrow. "How could I ever repay—"

"Don't talk nonsense. God grants us all kinds of blessings in all kinds of ways. Just say thank you."

"But, to who? Who did this?"

Irene shakes her head. "I promised I'd never tell."

Cate lunges forward into Irene's arms. Her words are muffled so I can't make them out, but we're all brushing away tears now.

She steps back. "Thank you, all of you."

Irene runs a hand over Marianna's fuzzy head. "You are a joy, little one."

A tear slips from Cate's eye.

"What?" Irene asks.

"I'm—" She fans her eyes with her free hand. "I'm so happy. When I think of how this could have been. I almost aborted her. It seemed like the only answer."

Arms wrap around Cate and Marianna.

"Thank you. Without all of you—especially you, Irene—my life wouldn't be like this." She hands Marianna to Irene. "God is good."

"Amen." Holding Marianna up so they're face-to-face, Irene stares into the sweetness. A line of drool drips from the baby's mouth. She holds

Marianna to her chest and places a light kiss on her head. "Thank you for sharing this angel with us."

"Now?" asks Kaylee.

"Yes, dig in to all this food before I change my mind."

The girls chatter as they put cookies on napkins and pour glasses of milk, but Erin sinks into the corner of the couch, much more quiet than usual.

"You feeling okay?" I help her tuck a blanket over her shoulder.

"I think so. My head's been pounding all day and I'm a little dizzy." She closes her eyes and lays her head back on the sofa.

I lift one of her feet and lay it on the cushion. Her pant leg rides up and I'm shocked at her ankles. They're swollen like sausages. "Did the headaches start today?" I keep my voice quiet and calm, but inside my brain, alarms go off.

"Yes."

"And the swelling?" I tip my head toward her ankles.

She nods. "That's been getting worse all week. I had to take my rings off yesterday." She holds up her hand. "I have a doctor's appointment tomorrow. I figured I could ask about it then."

I pat her leg. She's closed her eyes again, her face flushed. With a wave of my hand I get Irene's attention. She kneels beside Erin, and I repeat everything the girl told me.

Erin sits halfway up, staring at us through glazed eyes. "Is there something wrong?"

"Shh." Irene touches her forehead. "We'll check in with the doctor."

"How can I help?" Cate asks.

"Get a cool rag for Erin's head, please. Stacey, will you call the doctor? The number is by the phone."

It doesn't take long for the nurse to order me to get Erin to the hospital. The emergency entrance.

Izzy has a hand settled on Erin's head, her lips moving in silent prayer. A beautiful moment, but it's time to go.

Chapter 24

JILLIAN

Zachary only looks back at me one time before he enters the school building. A piece of his innocence is gone, never to return. Nothing—not even a sudden answer to all our problems, not even reversing time itself—can undo this harm.

Isn't that the way these things always work? The boundaries blur around the tiny spaces in our lives where we hold the slightest bit of control. The mistakes, the bumps along the way, the moments in time we regret but can't change, they seep into the lives of those closest to us.

Is that what happened to my mother?

I pull away from the curb, giving my space to another mom who is waving frantically for me to move on. Doesn't she feel it? Doesn't the woman with the scowl on her face realize school drop-off, getting to the next place on time, these are the least of life's worries? We live in a world filled with pain and danger. If we turn our backs even for a moment, evil will pounce. It will take our comfort, our warm homes and family, everything we've built. Evil will come and leave us empty and alone. And this cycle will repeat until we give up, throwing out the flag of surrender.

I creep through the school-zone traffic, wait as children, weighed down with overfilled backpacks, race across the street and toward the school. I signal as if I'm heading home, but then I turn the other direction. Where did the time go when I savored my quiet mornings alone? Will I ever have those moments again, sipping tea and watching the world outside my window, or will fear always boss its way into my every thought?

The scenery shifts as I drive away from our small town and along the base of the arching mountain range. To my right the landscape climbs, its floor darkened by the overgrowth of Douglas firs. To my left, flat fields stretch out with white sheep dotting the green. Lambs bound around their mothers, exploring the world. I slow my car and open my window. The fresh scent of rain-cleaned earth mixes with soil warmed in the spring sun. My surroundings are new and familiar at the same time. It's like my life. I've known it to be safe, but then discovered I've walked into a trap.

A ewe bellows for her lamb, her eyes staring toward my stopped car, her body stiff with reservation. Even in the animal world a mother has to be on constant lookout. My breaths shorten as a sob chokes off my airway. I've failed to protect my children. All three of them. My failure is their suffering.

My body shudders as a high-pitched cry escapes my heart. When will it end? How can this be happening to my baby? All these years I've blamed my mother; now I sit in the same dirty puddle. Why hadn't I known how cold it was, how the breaking of a mother's heart absorbs every ounce of heat in her body, leaving her a frozen shell? A grieving symbol of what should have been if only she could have stopped time.

Maybe if I'd come clean, told Izzy the truth about the world and the evil waiting to attack. Maybe if Izzy had known about the darkness in my own life, she would have been prepared for the assault, taken a different route. Instead, the dirty part of life that pulls away innocence has her tight in its claws. And I'm to blame.

My face grows taut as salty tears dry on my cheeks.

I can't give up now, even if every cell and every feeling tells me to do just that. Izzy needs me. Like I needed my mother. At least one thing will be different in our stories. I will be there. Izzy will know I'm willing to do whatever it takes to help her through this, even if she can't see what I see now. There will come a time when she'll thank me for protecting her.

What if this is exactly what my mother thought? Did she think she was doing the best for me? Could she have possibly thought that driving me to an abortion clinic two hours away from our home was the answer that would save me?

The thought, the brief connection to a woman I haven't spoken to in years, makes my head pound.

I've never stood in my mother's shoes. I've avoided even the briefest thought of what it was like for her. Maybe it's guilt. Maybe I don't want to face what I did to her.

We were close at one time, only pulling apart when I was in high school and wanted independence, and she married a man who controlled our every move.

Our home had never been so tidy, so neat, so sterile. And the rules were suffocating. That's why I was drawn to Geoff. He lived outside the boundaries, made his own way, answered to no one. He smoked, he drank, and he loved me with a passion that made me feel like I'd grown wings.

I can still see my mother glaring out the front door as Geoff dropped me off at the sidewalk. Two worlds colliding. She'd said the same things about Geoff that I said about Travis. We're repeating history, with the exception of the abortion. But aren't I trying to tuck this baby away too?

No.

This is different. My mother only wanted to protect herself from ridicule and preserve her marriage. She didn't want her precious husband, a man who ridiculed and beat her, to be upset with the news that their daughter was a failure.

My desire is to protect my daughter. Or am I really trying to protect myself?

Izzy

Why didn't I know? Why didn't I see this coming? Until I noticed the sign in front of the hospital, I'd never imagined it, never even asked the name of the place I'd be having my baby. This is where they flew Travis. This is where he died.

In my mind it was always stark, with white walls, no pictures, no life. But the room we're in is completely different. Soft music, cushy chairs, and walls covered with pictures of babies and mothers. There are even fresh flowers in a vase in the corner. Did they take Mrs. Owens to a room like this? I wouldn't know. I haven't spoken to her since before the accident.

Pacing back and forth in the waiting room, I'm part of a group I never would have imagined; four girls near my age, three pregnant and one with a baby. We're the kind of group my mother would have thrown a fit about. But all of her *don't do thats* and *can you believe thems* didn't stop me from becoming my mother's worst nightmare. Fear never looked good on her. But pregnancy doesn't really look all that great on me.

A few months ago, I would have turned my nose up at these girls who are like a family to me now. That thought makes me cringe with shame. I see the looks from the "normal" kids at the new massive high school I'm attending. I'm nothing there. Not an athlete. Not a scholar. Not a leader. Nothing. If the leers of those strangers hurt so deep, how will I face the people who used to be my friends?

From complete silence, baby Marianna screams and nearly knocks me off my feet.

Cate lifts her from the car seat and yanks a bottle from the diaper bag. "I'll never get used to her sudden hunger." She snaps the lid off the bottle and slips it into the baby's gaping mouth. The screaming stops, replaced by loud slurps.

Stacey steps into the room. "Any word?"

We all shake our heads, tension pulling us into a single unit. The moment we arrived, the doctor ordered Erin back for surgery. An emergency C-section. Irene had gone along with her, and we were left behind to imagine the worst.

"I'm sure they'll be in soon."

Kaylee shakes her head, her eyes vacant as if she's teetering between here and somewhere else. "I heard the doctor say eclampsia. I read about that. It can kill the baby and the mother."

"Don't talk that way." Fear tingles across my skin and the room starts to spin a bit. I lean back into the arm of a stuffed chair. "Erin will be fine, and so will her baby." But what if I'm wrong? I'm no longer living in a world where nothing bad happens. Where people don't die, and we all have bright futures. That world shattered when Travis died. Tragedy is very possible. It's even likely. I try to swallow the sour taste in my mouth. Not again. I don't know Erin well, but I can't face losing someone else. Especially here.

Stacey walks to the woman sitting behind a tiny desk in the corner. I can't hear them, but I see the woman shake her head, her face grim.

"What? What happened?" I stand, my body trembling, my legs weak.

Stacey touches my arm, like my mother did after Travis died. "It's okay. She just said she can't tell us anything because we're not Erin's family. It doesn't mean there's a problem."

Kaylee starts to pace again. "We're the only family Erin has. Do you see anyone else here for her?" Her voice is loud enough the woman can't help but hear.

I don't care.

From around the corner Irene comes into view. Her hair is covered with a sky-blue paper cap, and she's dressed in matching scrubs.

We all go toward her, not willing to wait the half a minute for her to get to us.

Her tired features turn into a smile. "We have a healthy baby boy. He's a big one too. Almost ten pounds."

"What about Erin?" Kaylee's worry hasn't softened.

"She's doing great. They're still moving her to a room. Kaylee, why don't you be the first to visit her when she's ready?"

She shrugs. "I don't know."

"I'll go with you." I look around at all the other girls. Maybe it wasn't the right thing to say. My giant foot wedges into my mouth. "If it's okay, I mean."

"Sounds good to me," Irene says. "They want us to go back no more than two at a time today. He's such a beautiful blessing. He screamed as soon as he was out. Big and strong." She glows as if he were her very own grandbaby.

Irene genuinely loves us. I wish she was my mother, or that my mom was more like her. But my mom can't hear anything I'm saying over her own loud voice. I wonder if Irene held her daughter so tight the girl couldn't even breathe without permission. No. There's no way.

When the okay is given, Kaylee and I walk down the hall together toward room 2047. There's a scent here like my grandparents' house. Sanitized.

My skin buzzes with a thousand tiny currents, while my stomach is heavy, smashed, sick.

Kaylee opens the door.

A guy in jeans and an oversize T-shirt stands with his back to us. In the bed, Erin lies still. The strange guy lays a hand on the blue blanket bundled between Erin's side and her right arm. His head ducks and his shoulders fall. Erin's hand, the IV still attached, covers his.

I tap Kaylee on the arm and we back out of the room, unnoticed.

Margaret

Caleb's fingers wrap around strands of my hair. He pulls his fist toward his mouth with such force my scalp burns.

The caseworker drives away, splashing through potholes and leaving me in a situation I couldn't imagine and definitely didn't ask for.

I turn my head down to look at this baby I'm in charge of. Drool drips down his fingers and onto the front of his shirt, making the blue cotton as dark as night.

"What am I supposed to do with you?"

He looks up into my eyes as if he understood my question and doesn't have the answer any more than I do.

The DHS stipend is barely enough to pay for his childcare. For the time being, he'll need to come along when I clean houses. But how long can I make that work? He doesn't seem like a very sleepy kind of baby.

I've managed one day off from the diner, but I can't afford another.

Closing the door, I turn back into the quiet house. Just me and Caleb. If Deven were home, at least I wouldn't be alone with the baby. Some women make excellent single mothers, but not me. I may have nearly raised four boys on my own, but look at the outcome. One in prison, one stationed halfway around the world, one I'm struggling to connect with, and one . . . I bite my bottom lip hard, trying to stuff the bitter sob back into the place I store all thoughts of Travis.

The gentle fuzz of Caleb's baby-fine hair snuggles against my neck. Soft slurping sounds fill the emptiness. One hand in his mouth, the other opens and closes along the back of my arm, sending soft tingles across my skin. I ease onto the couch, allowing his body to conform to my curves.

Tears rush down my face and roll along my chin, dropping onto the baby whose breathing has slowed to the gentle, warm puffs of sleep. Holding him next to me pulls pain out of my heart, but not the kind that leaves me empty. It's a healing pain.

I cup his head in my palm. This is only temporary. He's here until the state finds a suitable home. One where he can grow up and belong, or go back to his mother.

My house is humble. We don't have extras. My boys have never been to special summer camps. We've never been on a family vacation. I've been tired, worn, and often short-tempered. But I did one thing right, I think. I protected my boys from their father's rage, choosing to raise them alone rather than hand them over to a drunk every other weekend and on holidays. The cost of that decision, no child support. His rights were cut off, and I'd given my approval. Every financial need fell on my back. Maybe it wasn't the smartest choice, but it was the best I could do.

If nothing else, I'm better than leaving a baby in a room with doped-up adults.

On instinct, I hug him closer.

The scent of baby shampoo and sweet infant breath curls around me.

Every cell in my brain shouts to put him down, quick. Make space between my heart and his. This won't end well. I can't survive loving him, then losing him too. How could I have known he would be so precious? So warm in my cold and lonely arms.

Tipping him back, I lay his spine along my legs. His tiny lips move in and out as though he's dreaming of a warm bottle, the way Travis used to.

If only I could hold my baby one more time. Kiss his chubby cheeks. Tell him I love him forever no matter what. Even if I didn't agree with his choices.

Will Izzy's baby have the same gentle curl of dark eyelashes?

My actions, my angry words that seemed like righteous protection at the time, they could keep me from ever knowing if Travis's baby carries a piece of the life he lost. I swallow the hard truth.

Chapter 25

Izzy

"But, where did he come from?" I keep my voice low even though the buzz from the living room is loud enough to cover our conversation in the kitchen. "I've never heard her talk about him."

Irene shrugs, putting the last bowl onto the dish rack. "Most dads fade away after the baby comes, some before, some . . . Not very many, but some actually show up when the baby is born and stay. I can't say what will happen with Erin, but we'll pray for the best."

"Travis would have stayed." I dry the bowl and slide it into place in the cupboard. "I'm just not sure I wanted him to." I can't look at her now that I've thrown the truth out into the room.

"There's nothing wrong with that. Getting pregnant makes us look at our relationships in a very different way. When it was only you and Travis, you could look past issues. But when life got real, suddenly all those bumps become mountains. Am I right?"

I nod. "It's my fault he's gone. I never should have argued with him. What's wrong with me? I used to think I loved him, but as soon as I saw the plus sign on the pregnancy test, it changed me."

Her warm arm wraps around my shoulders. "No. It's not your fault. What happened to Travis was an accident. A terrible accident. It's hard to say how things would have worked out between you. I'm sorry you won't have a chance to find out, and I'm really sorry your daughter will never meet him, but you have a father who loves you so much. And your mom loves you too. God will walk with you through whatever comes next."

I turn into her embrace. "I hurt all of them. My mom is a mess. Travis is gone. Dad, I know he loves me, but he can't even look at me now. My life is a total fail."

"And you're doing your best now." She kisses my head, like a grandma. "Come on. Tonight, we're going to learn when it's time to call your baby's doctor." She ushers me out the swinging door and into the living room.

She made it sound so easy, but it's not. No one understands. And I don't want to hear any more about God.

There on the couch, Erin's boyfriend sits leaning forward, ready for anything he can learn. He's sure brave to step into this house of relationship-burned girls. Travis would have done the same thing. He was a great guy. Someone I should have kept as a good *friend*. Then he would be safe and planning his college baseball career . . . Alive.

◆ ◆ ◆

The purple glove snaps my wrist as I tug it into place before plunging my hand into the cleaning bucket. I pulled bathroom cleaning as my weekly chore. Not a popular pick, but I don't mind. In fact I could enjoy the task if it weren't for the overinflated basketball shape of my stomach. I bend down to wipe the base of the sink and my balance is thrown off by my new center of gravity. Grasping for whatever will stop my fall, my hand grips the toilet seat. Yuck. This is why no one wants the job.

Plopping onto the floor, I yank off the gloves and toss them onto the side of the bucket. I swipe my palm across my damp forehead. How have I come to this? Only a few months ago I was an Olympic hopeful, at least in my mother's eyes. Now I can't wipe down a bathtub without breaking a sweat. I pull myself up to the edge of the tub and sit on the cold porcelain.

This house is like another universe. I wish I could walk out of here and pretend this was all a weird dream, but my daughter hooks me to reality. Everything I do from here until she's graduated high school will be for her.

Last night I listened to my mother go on for a solid thirty minutes about what I had to do. I wish I could. But she doesn't get it. She doesn't understand why I have to do this for Travis and how my dreams will never be the same. Anyway, how could I hand my daughter over to someone else, a stranger? Doesn't she understand her answer is only a cop-out?

Placing my baby into another family will not bring Travis back. It won't give him the chance to play baseball in college and have a career. It won't heal the scars or make the truth any nicer.

I'd give anything for Travis to still be breathing the stale air of our suffocating little town. It's the air I'll be breathing for the rest of my life. Brownsburg will be my prison. A fitting punishment for my sins. I didn't understand what Mrs. Owens's problem was. Now, I'm beginning to get it.

There's a knock at the door.

"Come in. I'm just cleaning." I brush at my maternity yoga pants like this will make me more presentable.

The door swings open, knocking into the wall. "I've found them." Sierra waves a spiral-bound notebook in the air. "These are the people. Stacey said I'd know when I found them, and I do." Her eyes are filled with tears and she holds the book out to me.

I take the two steps to get to her and wrap my arms around her. The book presses into my back and my shoulder trembles with her sobs. In the time I've been here, through all the conversations that lasted late into the night, this is the first I've heard Sierra cry out loud.

JILLIAN

"Mom, you just don't understand what I'm going through. You can't." Izzy's words reach through my cell phone and slap me across my already raw heart.

"You have no idea, Iz." A damp sweat prickles along my neck as I pace the church's asphalt parking lot.

"No, Mom. You really have no idea. I don't want to hurt you, but you've got to stop telling me what I have to do. This is my decision. It's my choice. Dad says he'll back me up. He said I can still live at home and finish high school. Why can't you put your precious pride away and really help me? People are going to find out. There's no way to hide me like a dirty little secret."

Izzy's words sting, infiltrating me like a burning injection. There's truth in what she's said. "It's not like that," I lie. "I want what's best for you. I love you." That, at least, is true. "Can't you understand I'm doing my best?"

"Only if you can understand that's exactly what I'm trying to do."

I lean into the meager shade of an oak tree planted last year. "I'll try."

"I have to go. We're walking down to the park. If you can stop hounding me, I'd like you to visit."

"What about coming home for the weekend?" I swallow. What if she says yes? There'll be no going back once she's seen.

"No. I can't be there yet. I can't face it. I've got to go. Bye." A beep, then silence.

My arms tingle and my legs are weak. I drop the phone into my pocket. I haven't felt this alone in years.

"There you are." Jasmine's high-pitched screech sends angry shivers down my spine. Why now? Why today? Why do I ever have to deal with this woman? Life is not fair.

I turn away, wiping my eyes. "What do you want, Jasmine?" My usual false sweetness can't be forced today.

"I need you to help me with the banquet setup. The computer won't let me start the video."

The banquet. I've managed to miss this event all five years Jasmine has held it in the church. Last year, I faked a migraine. Hours later Garrett returned home fired up to support the pro-life movement. He increased our yearly donation. Whenever I see that baby bottle coin bank on our counter, the one we drop our extra change into as an offering to the pregnancy center, I'm reminded that I'm a fraud. A liar.

"I'm sure there's someone more qualified to help you." I don't understand why she comes to me with her every problem. She doesn't think I'm capable of even reading a newspaper. I'm just a simple slave in her eyes.

"Seriously? You're the only one. And you can run the system better than anyone else. Honestly, Jillian, what is your problem? Don't you care about saving babies?" She cocks her head and looks me over like I'm . . . well, exactly what I am.

"All right." I make a direct line from the safety of the little oak sapling to the sanctuary. Behind me, Jasmine's heels click, making new accusations with each step.

I swing the door open and we dive into the chill of the air-conditioned foyer. Through another set of doors, and I step foot into the room where we gather to worship each Sunday. The rows of blue padded chairs have been unhooked. Round tables dot the room. On the tables sit centerpieces with pictures of unborn babies at various stages of development.

I swallow down my secret and reach for the nearest image. Below the baby, eleven weeks of gestation, there's a list of milestones he's already accomplished. His heart beats. Skin covers his tiny body. He measures two-inches, crown to rump.

Two inches.

I create the distance with my thumb and forefinger. Not a wad of cells. A tiny two-inch baby.

I set the display back in place and cover my heart with my hand.

"I can get the video to work now, but the audio won't go."

The large screen at the front of the room lights up. Soundless images of tiny toes, beating hearts, a fetus sucking her thumb.

I drop into a chair. My past is now my present, colliding in the one place I connect with safety. My church. But it's here the vulnerability flares up. Here where I've sought out God. Where I've begged for protection for my family.

Gripping my upper arms with fierce fingers, I pull back at my emotions with all my strength. Not now. Not with Jasmine standing only twenty feet away.

A hand touches my shoulder. I whip around, ready to attack or run. Why can't I get ahold of myself?

Jasmine stretches out her palm like a police officer might to a crazy hostage-holding criminal. "It's all right."

I wait for her next words. Her condemnation. But she's silent. Her eyes solid on mine.

No. I'm not going to spill my dark, mucky secret to Jasmine Monk. She'll spread it all over town. Then they'll all know. Garrett will know.

Just the thought of him, the image of his heart breaking with the truth of who he has married. The secrets I've kept for all these years. Tears rage over my face like a sudden winter storm with winds gusting across fields and whipping around houses that were silent only moments earlier. The past pounds on my chest and streams from my eyes.

"Can you keep a secret?" Jasmine's words seem odd when it's me who's obviously overrun with deception.

I nod.

"I was aborted."

I can't help it. I stare up into her eyes. Does she think this is some kind of joke?

"I'm not making this up. My mother went in to have an abortion. I was to be her third. She was homeless and alone. I wasn't . . . planned. A doctor agreed to do a late-term abortion because, really, who wants a junkie to reproduce?" She shrugs and looks over my shoulder. "The thing is, I didn't die. I would have, but a nurse wrapped me up and rushed me to a nearby hospital."

"I've met your mother."

Jasmine grins, her eyes sparkling. "My parents adopted me when I was two years old. I'd been in three foster homes by then."

My hands drop to my lap. "But you and your mother, you're so close." The two of them are more than mother-daughter. They're best friends.

Jasmine is a carbon copy of her mom. Had I just imagined the resemblance? I picture the two of them, all decked out for Easter last year. Their fashion flavors couldn't be more alike, but Jasmine's mother is easily six inches shorter. Her hair has turned gray, but must have been dark like her eyes. Jasmine's eyes are such a light blue even I have a hard time not staring. "Do you hate your real mom?" Heat rushes to my face as I realize the personal lines I've crossed with my question.

"My birth mother? No, I don't hate her. My mom helped me through my anger. Dori—that's my birth mother's name—she did what she knew to do. I pray for her."

My face tingles. Everything I know about Jasmine, or everything I've assumed over the years, is in question.

"So, if you had something you wanted to say. Something you didn't want anyone else to know. I could listen. It'd make us even in some way, don't you think?"

Would it? Jasmine was a victim. She didn't make the decision. She hadn't lied to her family. She hadn't left her mother behind, harboring bitterness in her heart toward the woman who'd given her life even if the intention had been death.

Jasmine pulls out a chair and positions it in front of me then settles in. She laces her fingers and rests them in her lap as if she's willing to wait for as long as it takes to get me to spill.

Before I can force my finger into the hole in the dam, twenty years of silence breaks free. "I had an abortion. I didn't want it. But I did it anyway. Now, Izzy is pregnant, and I don't know what to do. I can't help her because I can't tell her what I did. She'd be so ashamed. They all would be." Looking up, I'm ready to meet Jasmine's judgment and face the fire.

But her eyes are filled with compassion.

"I'm sorry that happened to you."

"What?"

Jasmine leans closer and pulls me into her arms. "I'm so sorry."

Chapter 26

STACEY

The grass in Oregon has a depth of green like nowhere I've ever been before. I push the sliding glass door open and step out onto my back patio. The warm air buzzes with the sound of my husband mowing our lawn. I inhale the sweet scent of our fresh-cut yard mixing with Oregon in bloom and the newly heated earth.

Blessed.

In everything, even the hardships, God has blessed me.

Keith is the picture of the husband I'd dreamed of. Maybe not perfect, but he loves me with a complete embrace. I've never felt as protected as I do in his presence. Watching him work, taking time to not miss the edges, I'm consumed with how much I love him.

I can't help but tip my head back and thank God for where I am at this very moment.

The engine cuts, and Keith runs a forearm over his sweaty brow. He blows out a long breath and turns, his gaze resting on me, a gentle smile playing a flirty game on his lips. "Hey there. Come to give me a big hug, right?" He stretches out both arms and moves toward me.

"No way." I hold my hands out as a weak barrier.

He makes contact, warm and damp, his heartbeat strong under my palm. Large fingers encircle my shoulders and pull me in.

"Yuck." Looking into his eyes, I contort my face in mock disgust.

"You love it." He winks.

"I love you. That's very different than loving you hugging me when you're all gross."

He dips his chin and a shiver runs across my skin. In an instant, he has my lips pinned by his, and I taste the saltiness of his skin. Pulling me closer, he lifts me off my toes.

My phone rings in my pocket.

"Ignore it." His voice is gruff, deep.

I run my tongue along my lips, wishing I could. "It may be Candice. We're getting close to her due date." I can't break the spell that glues my gaze to his. After all these years, Keith still has a way of holding me hostage with a look.

His arms loosen. "I doubt it's her, but you'll never forgive me if I'm wrong." His lips curve in a crooked smile that's almost more than I can bear.

Stepping back, the place where his body has just been turns cool in the summer breeze. I pull the phone out and look at the screen. Panic washes over me. It is Candice. "Hello?" She never calls. Not once in weeks. "Are you okay? Are you having contractions?"

"No. Nothing like that. I think we should talk. All of us."

"When?"

"Really soon. Adam is here with me. He wants to be there."

"Adam? Is that the father?" I signal Keith with my eyes. This is serious. Candice has never been willing to talk about the father before.

She ignores my question. "Can you meet us this afternoon?"

"Of course. Thirty minutes?"

"Great. How about Bryant Park, by the playground?"

"We'll be there."

The call disconnects.

The pink hue in Keith's cheeks has washed away, leaving fear exposed. "Is there a problem?"

I shrug. "I don't know. She wants to meet with us. She and Adam."

"The birth father?"

I twist my fingers with his. "She didn't say."

He wraps me into a hug that feels very different from the one he gave me only seconds ago.

I lay my head on his chest. Whatever happens, we'll be together. This time I really feel the comfort in the thought.

*   *   *

Across the open field, Candice sits shoulder to shoulder with a thin young man. Adam, I'm guessing. Even from this distance, with only their backs visible, I can't disregard their connection. They slant toward each other. Candice tilts her head and lays her cheek against his neck. Without hesitation, Adam smooths her purple hair.

Keith's cold hand surrounds mine, his unease mixing with his protection. If this goes wrong, there isn't anything he can do to stop the pain from coming. We've been there. We've felt the knife cut deep into our hearts.

He takes a step, pulling me along.

The sun has been harsh all week, but the earth still sinks under my feet. Lush and green, this park must be ignoring the current call to reduce water usage, like most of my neighbors.

In front of the picnic table, children swoop back and forth on extra-long swings. Others dig in sand. Two boys chase each other around a group of trees. Squeals and shouts fill the air. Each little face belongs to the heart of a mother. Each one completes someone else.

The hole in my heart grows wider. I touch my chest with my free hand and try to push away the ache. Instead of easing, the sensation, the memories, grow deeper.

Two steps from the table and Candice must sense us. She turns, mouth open but silent.

Adam stands and Keith drops my hand to extend his toward this new guy. "I'm Keith Frey."

"Adam Zaner. Good to meet you, sir." His gaze darts back to Candice.

She stands, but positions herself half behind Adam, his slender frame doing nothing to hide her wider one.

Keith motions to the table and we all slide onto benches, Candice sideways, straddling the seat and leaning forward on Adam's arm.

No one speaks for a long moment. The tension translates into shivers that scoot across my skin.

"Adam is my boyfriend." Candice looks down. "He's not the baby's father."

He rubs a hand up and down her arm. "I wish I were."

Keith's hand tightens on mine.

"We've been together for three years. I love Candice." His gaze is a direct shot at us, like a challenge for us to disagree with his statement.

"I'm sure you do," Keith says. "You must love her very much." He stops without saying the thing he must be thinking. The thing I'm thinking. How can he forgive her?

Candice looks back at him. "I broke up with Adam when I found out about the baby. I didn't want him to know what happened."

"I would have stood by her."

Candice flashes a sad smile his way. "I made a huge mistake."

Keith releases my hand and folds his together on the table. "Adam, are you saying you'd like to be the father of Candice's baby? Are you planning to raise this child?"

Their eyes meet again and unspoken words seem to pass between them.

"We still want you to adopt him." She drops a hand to her belly. "I don't think I can do it. Not knowing how he came to be. But Adam and I talked, and we think you need to know the circumstances, so there's no questions about his bio father down the road."

Two boys dart past us, lunging their bodies toward a water fountain. Within seconds they go from slurping to splashing. And just as quickly, I slip from mortal fear to deep, warm, soothing relief. I wrap my arm around Keith's and snuggle into his side. Our dreams are about to come true. And there's nothing Candice can say that will take them away. Not now that she's confirmed that she still wants us.

"Is the baby healthy?" Keith asks.

"Yes. Very. He's pounding away in there." Candice rubs her hand over her stomach. "I didn't cheat on Adam. I was raped." Like a weight flew away, Candice exhales. "I didn't want anyone to know. I thought . . . I guess I thought they'd think I deserved it. That I had it coming or I should have fought harder."

I stand and walk around the table. Kneeling in front of Candice, I rest my hands on her knees. "I'm so sorry."

"It's okay. I'm okay. But it's also not this baby's fault." Candice blinks, tears clinging to her lashes. "I tried to have an abortion, but I couldn't go through with it. This baby shouldn't be punished. Can you love him now?"

All the muscles in my body go simultaneously limp, my strength evaporating in the heat. How could I love either of them any less? My heart breaks into splinters. All I want is to protect them both. I take a minute to breathe in the sweet summer air and let the peace wash over me. Then I tip my chin up and make eye contact with Candice for maybe the first real time. "I love you both more because you trusted me enough to share your hurt. I'm so sorry."

Tears trace down Candice's cheeks.

Adam weaves his fingers between Candice's.

She reaches up with her free hand and brushes her fingers across his shoulder. "He said you'd feel that way, but I couldn't get myself to take the risk."

"I can tell you," Keith says, "that I have no doubt we will love this baby, but right now, I want to make sure you know you're loved."

Warmth spreads through my chest. My husband is a strong, brave, and mighty man, and he is mine. Even if something changes and we're never parents, I can't look past the gift beside me. Keith is more than the man I prayed for. More than any of my dreams. More than my heart can imagine.

I settle onto the bench.

"Adam's been taking me to see a counselor. I think it's helping." She shakes her head. "But sometimes, I'm still not sure what to believe. I don't want to be a victim."

"Candice, you are not a victim to God. And you're not a victim to us. I see you as a strong woman, a survivor."

"I think you're right." Adam looks from Keith to me. "I've been thinking about faith a lot lately. When Candice and I start a family, I want to do it right. I don't want our kids to go through the kinds of things Candice and I have been through. And I want to be a real dad, not like the one I have."

Keith reaches across the table and squeezes Adam's shoulder. "That's highly commendable."

But Candice only chews her bottom lip. Her forehead crinkles as she drops deeper into herself again.

MARGARET

The car seat handle cuts into the bend of my elbow while my bucket of cleaning supplies pulls hard on my other arm. "Caleb, I swear you're ten pounds heavier today than you were yesterday."

Looking up at me, the baby blows spit bubbles over his curled fist.

His smile breaks through my walls. Caleb has a way of doing that. He cracks the enamel surface of my grief. I've seen him have the same effect on Deven. How will I ever give him back? But really, how can I keep him?

On the top step, I set the car seat on the cement and rap on the siding. Inside I can hear Mrs. Donovan making her way to the entry. The security window swings open with a spine-chilling squawk. One eye locks on me. The window closes and the door opens.

"Margaret. I was expecting you half an hour ago." Her chin dimples as she scowls, deep wrinkles forming around her frown.

"I meant to be. Caleb"—I look down at the baby—"needed changing just as we were on the way out."

"Whose baby is this?" Mrs. Donovan steps out on the porch.

My chest tightens. I can't lose this job. Can't lose the income. "He's staying with me for a while."

"That doesn't answer my question. Whose baby is he?"

"A relative's. He was in foster care. The state asked me to take him." My heartbeat hammers in my chest. Why had I thought I could sneak Caleb in without an interrogation?

"Well, come on in." She steps back.

Gripping both handles, I enter the house. Her place is simple, yet every surface is covered in some sort of crocheted embellishment. On the tiny end tables are white doilies with miniature stitches, and across the backs of chairs and the sofa are blankets with varying stripes and colors. Beside Mrs. Donovan's recliner sets a basket filled with yarn and topped with a green and white pair of slippers, the metallic blue hook still dangling from one end.

We face each other. Mrs. Donovan's gaze studies me, making me concentrate on breathing and not looking away. In the five years I've cleaned this house, we've never had unkind words, but she isn't the type of woman who takes change well.

In the weeks after Travis . . . left, I avoided work. My clients understood, all except Mrs. Donovan. When I didn't show up on my normal schedule, she drove to my house and let herself in. The next day I cleaned for her. Like every week since.

That's why I didn't mention Caleb before showing up today. What would I have done if she'd said no? A babysitter would eat up every nickel I make. No, this has to work.

"He's a good baby. You won't even know he's here."

On cue, Caleb bursts out with an unbecoming rumble from below.

I cringe. Great timing. "I'm sorry. I'll take care of this right away and get to work." I pick up the car seat and look around.

"In the guest bedroom."

Ducking my head, I walk away before I have to see the judgment on her face. I shut the door and breathe in the cool freedom. Unbuckling the seat is a process, way more complicated than when my boys were small. Pulling out a diaper and a wipe from its storage compartment, I lay Caleb on a handmade quilt, then think better of the plan and tuck his blanket underneath him.

I've spent very little time in this room, only dusting the surfaces once a year. It's a shrine of some sort. On the dresser, next to a music box, sits a picture of Mrs. Donovan's daughter. Beside the bed, a Bible rests on another doily. I've seen the daughter's graduation gown hanging in the closet, covered in a thin plastic sheet. Why doesn't the girl ever visit?

Caleb gurgles, happy in his fresh diaper. His eyes dip, pop open, then settle closed again.

I glance at the clock on the wall. It's early for his nap, but this may be the break I've been hoping for. Pulling pillows from the top of the bed I build walls as a makeshift crib in the middle of the double mattress. Before leaving, I take one more look at his smooth, precious face.

With near-silent steps, I creep from the room and down the hallway to the bathroom. Back to normal. I start at the top and work my way down in the first real routine I've managed since Caleb was dropped off. There's comfort in the sameness. I still have to be diligent to keep my mind from wandering in the void of mindless labor and being hijacked by my memories.

But I lose my focus for a flash and there he is, Travis at Caleb's age. I drop back in time both physically and mentally. Why hadn't I held him more? Why hadn't I spent more time just cuddling all of my boys? What stopped me from giving myself fully to loving them?

Answers sometimes come simply now, as though the ripping of my heart made it possible to see the truth. I'd wanted to protect them from me, from being the same mess I knew I was. And I'd wanted to protect my own heart from the pain of losing someone else.

All that protection amounted to nothing.

I thread my hand into a purple rubber glove and reach the scouring stone into the toilet bowl.

We all ended up hurt. The older boys are vacant, searching for something or someone they can't even name. And I'm broken, lonely, scared, and empty.

Can I really form a family now with Deven? Is it too late?

I move on to the sink, the mirror, then the tub. My doubts grow stronger with the smell of the toxic cleaners.

Caleb's cries meet my ears. My heart thuds and panic crawls over my skin. How long has he been awake? Snapping the gloves off, I drop them into a bucket. Before I can reach the bedroom door, his cries begin to fade. I halt with my hand on the knob. Maybe he's put himself back to sleep. As I turn again toward the bathroom, I imagine him working his way through the pillows and tumbling to the hardwood floor.

I don't want to wake him, but I have to look, have to make sure he's safe. I crack the door open and peek in.

My mouth falls open, but I have no words.

Mrs. Donovan sits in a wicker chair near the foot of the bed. On her chest, Caleb lies slurping his fist, his eyes fluttering as he comes fully awake. She pats his back, her lips curled into a slight smile, then dips her chin and places a kiss on his baby-fine waves of hair.

I step the rest of the way into the room, breaking the magic, but needing my job.

"Well, there you are." Mrs. Donovan's mouth straightens into a rigid line. "Why was this baby all alone in here?"

"I'm sorry." Here it comes. I'll be fired for sure. Or I'll have to hire childcare, which is basically the same thing. "He was asleep. I thought it would be fine." I reach for Caleb, but she doesn't offer him up. "I'll keep him with me from now on. You won't even know he's here."

"Nonsense. A baby has no place around cleaning supplies." She looks down at Caleb. "He'll stay with me while you work."

It isn't a question.

Chapter 27

Jillian

The mirror reflects my washed-out tone and dark-circled eyes, but I run the brush through my hair again and fasten the buttons of my dress coat. I watch my image blow out a long breath as if the woman staring back at me is a stranger.

The bedroom door opens and Garrett leans against the frame. "You're going?"

"I thought I would. Wasn't that the plan?"

"Yes, but you always manage some sort of excuse. Honestly, I almost gave your ticket away today in anticipation of a headache, stomach bug, or whatever." His words don't have the edge of humor they used to. There's no compassion or curiosity. Only the cold syllables I should be accustomed to after weeks of hearing them.

What do I really have to fear now? I've already lost him in every way but as a roommate.

"You're right. I lied to you all those times." I swallow. My pulse throbs in my ears. The truth doesn't come out easy, but it isn't as sour as I expected.

"I figured." Still he doesn't move. His face registers no emotion.

"If you knew I was lying, why didn't you say so?"

He crosses his arms in front of his chest. "Would you have told me why? I doubt it. You never do."

My body shrinks under his words. They're heavy, harsh, and sharp, but I deserve every cut they make. This is the day I take my life back from the darkness, the moment I speak truth and let the consequences come. How much worse can losing my husband be? Have I ever had him?

I turn until we're face-to-face, only feet apart. Clasping my hands together, I force my gaze to hold tight to his eyes. "I don't talk about my mother because I've spent every year since I was seventeen punishing her."

He doesn't move, doesn't react, so I continue.

"I got pregnant. She told me there was only one answer. It was taken care of before I could even think about what I wanted, what was right for me, or what was best."

"She forced you?"

My skin goes cold. "No." There were never threats, no physical pushing. "I went along with it." The memories clear as years of anger-filled haze begin to lift. "She took me. And I went willingly."

"So you did make the decision."

My vision blurs. "I did. I'm fully responsible." A tear rolls down my cheek. Blaming my mother protected me all these years from the guilt of not making a decision. In the end, the choice to do nothing is really a choice just the same.

"And this is why you don't talk to your mother?"

I nod.

"So, the choice you made as a teenager, you let destroy your relationship with your mom, and allowed it to eat away at us?"

My stomach clenches into a ball. "Yes." Like I'm stepping outside of myself, everything is clear from this vantage point. What I've done. Why. And how much each step has led me further away from what I really wanted. I force my gaze up from my shoes to his eyes again.

His mouth opens and closes, hurt coloring his expression. All I want now is to crawl into his embrace, mold into his body, and grab hold of what we used to be. But his tight jaw binds my feet to their station on the carpet.

"I thought it would feel better when you finally told me. It's not like I didn't figure it out years ago. But, it doesn't feel better. I just . . . You didn't trust me. You didn't think I was strong enough to handle your youth. You didn't have the respect to tell me, your husband, the thing that changed your life and shut you down. I've spent twenty years with someone who doesn't trust me." Now he turns away from me, his shoulders sagging, but the rest of his body rigid, always the soldier.

"I'm sorry." I touch the sleeve of his royal blue dress shirt. "I didn't think. I was afraid."

"Afraid of me."

"Afraid of losing you."

"You've been pushing me away all along." Pulling his jacket from the back of a chair, he takes long strides out the door. "I'm going to the banquet. Come if you want, or stay here as usual. I don't really care which."

Shuffling my feet into my heels, I follow, grateful for the pinch of my toes that pulls some of my focus from the throbbing pain in my heart. Like a cut newly cleaned and bandaged, it hurts, but in a way that tells me it will get better from here. The object lodged in the wound has been removed. Whether there will be new cuts, I can't guess, but the ones that have been there most of my life can now begin to mend. There's something freeing in the realization. Something propels me forward from the shadows of years in secret. A part of me is still alive.

MARGARET

I arrive at Mrs. Donovan's house an hour before my shift starts, with Caleb and everything he owns, packed for the next eight hours.

Grief isn't holding back today. It's pounding on my heart and head as if Travis died just yesterday. I hate days when it takes over and clouds out the sun. I hate the way loss makes me feel as though I'm walking through knee-deep mud, but I have to keep going as if my son will be home waiting for me.

The door opens and Mrs. Donovan gives me a critical up and down.

My face flushes with heat. Mrs. Donovan offered to watch Caleb, I know that's what she said. Well, it was more like she ordered me to bring him here. Hobbs told me there was a space available at his church's daycare, but Mrs. Donovan said it was a baby institution. So, why is she looking at me like I wasn't expected?

"Well, what are you waiting for?"

My mouth opens, but I choose not to answer.

"You look horrible, you know that, right?"

I run a hand over my braid, checking for loose strands, then inspect my shoulders for spit-up. Nothing.

She shakes her head. "Not your looks, though a little rouge wouldn't hurt. Listen, losing a kid is bitter. It'll sneak up on you. You can't let it win."

I set the car seat next to her chair. "How?"

"How do you control it?"

"Yes." My eyes burn as though I spent last night in the middle of a forest fire.

"You give it just enough room. Go on now. Get out of here and have a good cry. Let it out. Then stand up straight and face the day with pride. You don't have to worry about the pain not coming back again. You'll get plenty of chances to mourn." Her face is deeply worn and wrinkled, etched by years of living what must have been a sorrow-filled life. I think about the room that never has any visitors.

A tear comes to her eye. Mrs. Donovan blinks it away. "Time to go." Her voice is stern.

I kiss Caleb's head and leave the house.

As if my beat-up car suddenly developed auto-pilot abilities, I find myself parking at the cemetery without remembering the route I took to get here.

I don't have to leave the car to see my son's grave. Though there is no headstone, the area is covered with flowers and high school memorabilia. His friends haven't forgotten him. At least not yet. Soon they'll be off to college and starting adult lives. Travis will fade into a memory of the one who died too young. It will be the loss they think of at reunions, not the life.

I step out of the car and approach the mound. Then I do as Mrs. Donovan ordered. I let my grief out. It rips free in gasping sobs that shake my body, in tears that flow like rivers down my cheeks. It weakens my muscles and leaves me empty and exhausted and aching for my son.

◆ ◆ ◆

"See you later, Charlie." I wave my bar towel in the air as a regular leaves the diner.

Before I can finish wiping the counter where Charlie sat, the door jingles. I look up and find Jillian standing near the register, a box in her arms.

"How many?" I dump the towel into the bin below the counter and reach for the menus as if she's any other customer.

"I'm not here to eat." She looks at the box. "I brought this for you."

My pulse beats behind my eardrums. "What is it?"

Jillian shifts the box lengthwise and slides it onto the counter. "It's baby stuff. Nice things. And diapers, wipes, the usual things."

I cock my head to the side.

She fiddles with the keys attached to the strap of her purse.

"You already gave me the baby box from your church."

"This one is from me, personally." Her gaze rolls toward the ceiling. "I messed up. I treated you badly, and I want to say I'm sorry." She shrugs her shoulders. "I thought it would be easier if I brought a gift."

"It doesn't hurt." I let my mouth curve into a smile.

She nods and gives a nervous laugh. "Can we start over? I promise I won't be such a jerk . . . most of the time."

I'm not practiced in the art of receiving an apology. This may be a first. I pull open the flaps of the box and hold up a blue and green bib with a hungry dinosaur on the front. "So cute."

"I know." She pulls out a sleeper that matches. "I couldn't resist these."

Together we sort through the box, gushing over the sweet baby things. I think this is what starting over must look like.

Chapter 28

Izzy

The baby rolls around, sending a wave across my stomach and desperation through my middle. Eight weeks. That's the best scenario. Eight weeks and my daughter, a child with no name and no father, will be born and depend on me for her survival and her future. If only she could stay inside, safe from my stupidity. But my huge belly won't even let me lean forward to brace my arms on the windowsill like I did a few weeks ago, and makes it very clear this can't go on forever. Soon we'll have to go home.

Sierra and Irene pull into the driveway. They've been at a meeting with the couple Sierra chose from the stack of want-to-be parents. Maybe now my roommate will come back to reality. It isn't that easy. She can't walk away as if nothing happened. If the stretch marks aren't enough, the looks on the faces of everyone we pass on the street is proof. Our sins enter a room before us.

But Sierra steps out of the van with a smile on her face that looks real. The grin lights up her eyes and her skin glows as she laughs at something Irene has said. Pulling a large shopping bag from the back seat, Irene joins her and they walk toward the house like a mother and daughter returning from a day at the mall. Not like a mentor and a pregnant teen coming back after interviewing a new family to take away Sierra's child.

The door opens and with the laughter comes the fresh scent of cut grass and warm air.

"Izzy." Irene tosses the bag on the couch. "You're going to love the plan we have for this afternoon."

I cross my arms in front of my breasts, a development I thought would be the one benefit of pregnancy, but they've turned out to be annoying and uncomfortable. "What?" I try to make my voice sound excited, but it comes out flat.

"Wait until we get everyone here, then I'll tell you," Irene says.

Sierra clasps her hands together and rocks back and forth on her feet.

Picking up the phone, Irene makes an announcement through the intercom system. Within minutes the living room fills with girls.

"We have a plan for today. It's been so hot, and I know you're all feeling cramped in the house. So . . . we're going swimming."

Blood flows away from my face. Not swimming. I picture my body shoved into a swimsuit. No, it will never fit. "Can't. I don't have a suit." I turn back toward the window.

"Yes, you do." The lilt in Irene's voice shakes me. "Come on over here."

I turn in time to see swimsuits pour out of the bag.

"They're not beautiful, but they'll cover what needs to be covered," Irene says.

The other girls dive in. Bright colored fabrics fly around as they search for one that will work. I stay planted.

"Hey." Irene walks up beside me. "What's on your mind?"

"Nothing."

"You've been pretty down lately for having nothing on your mind. Do you want to talk to the counselor again?"

"I don't think so. She means well, but she doesn't get who I am and what's going on."

Irene leans her hip into the window frame. "No worries. You're not the first girl to say that. But you do need to talk to someone. Keeping everything bottled up isn't doing you or your daughter any good."

Tears threaten me again, like a dark storm in the distance. I can't hold it back much longer. But what if it wins? The reality is too much. Too heavy. Even a second of thought steals my air and the light from the room.

"I can listen." She touches my arm. "Any time you need it."

I risk a glance at her. Lines reveal years of smiles and sad times too.

And a unique familiarity. Without sharing an ounce of her personal story, I know her.

"I'd like that, I think." But there's nothing left to say. She can't fix my world or restore what's lost.

"Glad to hear it." With a rough thumb, she pushes a curl away from my face. "You're beautiful. There's something so amazing about your face. Your eyes make me feel like I've known you forever."

I dip my chin. "Everyone says I look like my dad." What if my baby looks like Travis? How will I live with his eyes staring up at me day after day?

"Come on. Let's find you a suit. The water will do you good."

I nod. But I'll never enjoy swimming again. It's a piece of me I've forfeited.

◆　◆　◆

I ease onto the side of the pool. Moving my body is like positioning a boulder.

"You're finally getting in?" Sierra swishes through the water toward me. "It feels great." She smacks the water and droplets spray across my chest.

Dipping one foot through the reflective surface, shivers shake my body. Goose bumps dot my legs. And the summer heat is smashed. I swing my other leg in. Paradise. What could be better than this moment?

Like a flash, my mind turns, reminding me of my reality.

"Come on, Izzy." Sierra's face has grown serious. "Have some fun."

Have I become *that* girl? The one who mopes in the corner, wears dark colors, and eventually pushes everyone away? When did Sierra become the perkier roommate?

I pop into the pool all at once. Cold rushes up my body and takes away my breath. Dipping under the surface, I blow bubbles from my nose and feel the light tickle as each one climbs up my face. My hair floats above me, free, not confined in a cap. Crossing my legs, I slip down to the floor.

My arms relax and spread open in the willing water. I'm weightless here. If only I could stay here, in this fortress.

Burning spreads through my lungs as they scream for air, but I hold on a moment longer.

My daughter flutters hard within me. Like panic, she pounds me. My eyes shoot open. Pressing my feet to the rough cement, I lunge up, rocketing from the water and into the warmth. Heaving deep breaths, I suck in life. This isn't about me. It's about my still nameless child. The baby I owe life to.

Sierra stands still, her gaze staring hard at me, her mouth open.

But I shrug and turn away, gliding into the water, stretching my arms forward. My body takes over and does what's familiar. A piece of myself still exists in this new world. A tiny glimpse of me. How long before this piece disappears, and I become just another teen mom? A statistic with no individual identity. An outcast in the world I once owned.

Reaching my hands forward, I pull myself through the water, pushing myself on, kicking hard. At the wall, I pop up and gasp for breath. I fold my arms across the gutter. Blinking away the blur, my vision clears and a familiar figure comes into focus at the entry gate.

Stacey has become another member of the house. Sierra covets time with her. Some kind of adoption bond, I guess. Like if she gets to know Stacey well enough she'll know her own baby will be safe and loved in the home she's chosen.

Stacey drops her bag and towel on a chair. Her eyes turn my way, and she kicks off her sandals before walking toward me.

"Irene tells me you're quite the swimmer. It must be great to be back in the pool."

Tears rush into my eyes. I pinch my lips between my teeth and nod, but the water has become confining. There's no going back. Why pretend I can ever be normal again?

Stacey takes a seat on the edge and dangles her feet in the pool. "Want to talk about it?"

I bite down harder. Tipping my head back, I dip my head into the water. Being in the pool gave me a sense of weightlessness at first, but now the suspension has turned to weakness. I can't get away from the change.

I wipe my hands over my face and blink.

Stacey swishes her feet through the water in little figure eights. Her toenails are pink. "I know what it's like to lose someone."

"It's not the same."

"It's a very different circumstance. But I'm here to listen anytime you need."

"I—" I turn away. The other girls are circled around Cate, taking turns dipping Marianna into the water. Each time the baby squeals with delight. Maybe she'll be a swimmer. I turn back to Stacey. "I don't know what I'm doing."

She nods and twists a strand of blond hair around her finger, then looks me straight in the eyes. Isn't she going to say something? Give me some advice? Maybe an answer?

I bob up and down on my toes. Water flows in tiny ripples away from me. The only thing keeping me in the water is my ridiculous figure. "I don't know if I can do this."

Again she nods.

I bob higher, the waves growing. "I didn't love him. I knew that before I found out I was pregnant. I would have broken it off, eventually."

"That's difficult. It's never easy to end a relationship even if it's the right choice."

"But it cost him his life." I stop bobbing and turn my body toward Stacey. "Don't you see? He felt trapped. And it killed him. Literally, it killed him. And it wasn't even true. If Travis had lived, I know what I'd be doing right now. I'd be planning a life for my baby with a family who could love her and give her everything she needs to grow up strong, healthy, and okay."

"So, you'd like to place your baby?"

"No." I cover my middle with both palms.

Stacey's feet just hang in the water now, ankles crossed.

The silence is irritating like a rash I can't quite reach to scratch. "That's not what I'm saying. I'd never put her up for adoption now. I owe that much to his family. They have the right to watch the only piece of Travis left in this world grow up. I took him. I owe them this."

"Are you keeping your daughter out of guilt?"

The words settle down on me, pushing me deeper into the grabbing hands of the water. "It's not like that. Not anymore. Maybe it was in the beginning. But I love her now." My chest constricts. "I love her. I'll do whatever I have to do for her."

A smile spreads across Stacey's face. She slips into the water and wades toward me, putting a still-dry hand on my shoulder. "You're going to be a wonderful mother."

I drop my chin. Beneath the water is the mound that holds my future. And within me my daughter dips and dives as she swims in her own pool. She is a blessing. Not a curse.

Chapter 29

JILLIAN

Margaret forgives me. Jasmine looks past my mistakes. And, for maybe the first time in my life, I'm beginning to see what freedom really looks like . . .

But Garrett.

He's another story from another novel.

His gaze, the warmth that once bonded us together, in the rare moments when he looks my way, has cooled.

I place a water bottle in the sink and fill it with cold tap water. Four hours in the car with a man who can't get past my confession, my sin. Today is going to be a long day. But for Izzy, we'll pull it together. I hope.

"The car is running." Garrett fiddles with the stitching along his denim pockets. "We should get going." He looks past me and out the window.

Jasmine picked up Zachary half an hour ago. Before she left, she'd hugged me, giving me the only affection I've felt during the coldest weeks of my marriage. In five months, my life has pivoted and now points the opposite direction. Where I'd once prided myself on a solid relationship and children with bright futures, now the fragments of the home Garrett and I share slip through my fingers. My daughter faces uncertainty. The things that once seemed important, like swimming and competitions and academics, are now hazy memories I can only hope to revisit in my dreams.

And the women who'd made me crazy, Jasmine and Margaret, have become my strength.

Them and God.

For the first time in my life, God is truly real. I can feel Him. All I held between us is gone. He sent it into some dungeon. And I am free.

I've started going to the postabortion class Jasmine recommended. I'll always question my decision, but I accept it. I'm not a woman darkened for life with the stain of sin. I'm a daughter of the King. Even when I utter the words in my brain, they still sound unfamiliar . . . wrong in some way. But I'm learning. I'm growing.

Garrett clears his throat.

I swirl the lid on my water bottle and wipe the drips from the side.

Sweet morning sunshine warms my shoulders as I walk past the front yard still glistening with dew toward the car I'll be imprisoned in for the next two hours. *Lord, help us.* What more can I say? What more can I ask?

Before I can buckle my seat belt, Garrett pulls out of the driveway and toward the freeway, his hands clenched on the steering wheel, his jaw quivering at the corner.

I lay my forehead against the cold glass while pieces of our familiar life pass by in a blur.

Thirty minutes fade away without a word between us.

"I think we should talk." I turn to him, watching the slightest quake in his lower lip before it goes hard.

"What's there to talk about? You didn't trust me. Twenty years, Jillian. Twenty years and you never in all that time thought you could trust me."

"It's not like that."

Anger flushes his face. "Don't sugarcoat it with a bunch of junk about it not being about me. You kept this from me. What did you think I would do?" He turns his face my way for a second. Hurt and rage flash together in his deep eyes. "It's not the abortion. It's not the stuff about your family. It's the lies. All of them. You didn't even give me a chance to help you." He shakes his head. "I can't do this right now. I just want to see my daughter."

"We can't let Izzy know what's going on."

"Sure. Why not keep more secrets?"

"That's not what I mean. She has enough right now. Izzy doesn't need to know you sleep on the couch. Why would you want to lay it on her?"

"Enough, Jillian. I get what you're saying. I have no intention of hurting my daughter. I'm not the animal you seem to think I am."

"I never said you were an animal. Where's this even coming from? Garrett, I said I'm sorry. There's nothing else I can offer you."

He rakes a hand through his hair. "I know."

Silence falls on us. There truly is nothing more to be done.

Pulling a novel from my bag, I fan the pages with my thumb, but don't bother to open the cover. My mind speeds over the last twenty years, counting all the places I could have made different choices, taken another route. I could have told him in the beginning. Maybe he would have stayed. We were so in love then, connected in a way I'd not seen coming. He'd filled almost all my thoughts. He'd owned my heart.

And God had owned his.

Not that I minded. Garrett had enough love to share. For the first time since my dad died, I knew someone loved me.

How could I have taken the risk? Even now, with everything I stand to lose, I can't help thinking about all the times I may not have had. What if he'd walked away back then? There'd be no Izzy. No Zachary. No years of sleeping next to the man my heart loved.

No.

If he leaves me now, I'll be thankful for the time we had.

I can never take back the words that scorched him, and I don't want to. Even in our pain, I've found freedom. The time has come. Maybe if I'd been stronger and told Izzy the truth about my past, she wouldn't have repeated my mistakes.

Maybe.

Izzy

The toaster pops. I turn my head toward the back of the kitchen, wrinkling my nose against the smoky stink. Where have I been since I pushed the bread down into the slot? Time passes while my mind gets away from me. I pull the slices out and scrape them clean with a butter knife. Toast is an amazing food. Even burnt and ruined, it only takes a few quick swishes of a dull blade and it's fixed.

Maybe the baby and I can survive on toast.

I pull the five-pound tub of peanut butter from the cupboard and slather each piece with gooey yum. It melts and seeps into the holes.

Leaning a hip against the counter, I take a bite, letting the warm peanut butter stick to the roof of my mouth.

"I'm glad to see you're gaining an appetite."

I turn, finding Irene's lips twitching in an effort to hold back a laugh.

"That's for sure. I can't get enough." I run my tongue over sticky lips.

"No kidding. We just had lunch thirty minutes ago."

I cringe, looking down at my whale of a belly.

Irene's warm hand covers mine. "Don't worry about it. You can use a few pounds. You heard what the doctor said at your last appointment."

"I'm never going to be the same, am I?"

"Probably not." Irene tucks a curl behind my ear. "But you will be better. God will use this trial to strengthen you."

"I want that to be true. I'm so frustrated with myself. I can't get past the fact that I knew better. My daughter will never have a daddy. She won't grow up in a family with a mom and dad, brothers and sisters. I'll have to work to support her. I wish she could have all the things my parents gave me. All the things I threw out the window because I didn't want to say no again."

"What makes you think you've thrown it all away?"

I take another bite, chewing it slowly. The flavor is duller and the toast has become a clump in my mouth. I swallow it away with a gulp of water. "I felt so grown up. I thought I could handle anything. But that's because I had so little to handle on my own. Somehow I have to finish high school, get a job, support my daughter. I've never had a real job. My mom still did my laundry until I came here. Peanut butter toast is the extent of my cooking skills. What happens to children raised on peanut butter toast?"

Irene puts a hand on each of my shoulders. "All these things you can learn, but what your daughter needs more than fancy meals and clothes is love. Just love her. Give her your heart."

I bite my bottom lip until I can contain the shaking.

"You're not alone in this. We're here with you. We'll help in any way we can. And your parents will help too. Give them a chance."

Yanking my cell phone from my pocket, I gasp. "They'll be here soon." I blow out a heavy breath. "I have to tell them I'm keeping her. My dad will understand, but my mom, she thinks I'm ruining my life all over again. Maybe she's right, but I have to do this."

"I'm going to be praying for you."

"Won't you be here?" Alarms buzz through my limbs.

Irene shakes her head. "I'm sorry. I came in to tell you. I have to go to the prison. Nikki asked me to be there for her visit with Caleb. It's a start."

"You have to be there." This is one of the things I must get used to, the part where life is no longer about me. "I'll pray for you too." But will I really? The lie stings. I've put away my prayer life with my skinny jeans. No, I'll make the effort for Irene. After all, she always does anything she can for me.

"Stacey is here. She's helping Sierra write a letter to her baby, but I'm sure she'll be glad to sit with you if you want."

"Can you ask her for me?"

Irene cocks an eyebrow. "Let's talk to her together."

Jillian

Garrett comes around and opens my door, but he doesn't reach a hand in to help me out like he's always done before. Why hadn't I appreciated those small gestures? Now that they're gone, there's a painful hole left behind. I step into the blazing sun. Standing close enough to his side, I let my fingers hang loose near his in case he has the sudden desire to take my hand. He doesn't.

Instead, Garrett shoves both hands into his pockets and marches toward the front door, his shoulders rounded in an uncharacteristic stoop and his chin down. He's aged ten years in the past six months. Even from behind he seems vulnerable. Breakable.

We wait for someone to open the front door. I press my palm into the small of his back. Under my touch, he goes rigid, but I don't pull away. No. He'll have to learn to love me again, or walk away. There's no room in this marriage for middle ground.

The door swings open and Izzy meets us with a smile. She's grown. Her stomach, round and full, puts all chances of avoiding the scary subject out of the question. But she is smiling, and it lights up her eyes and warms me through to my heart.

Stepping in front of my husband, I wrap up my daughter, pulling our bodies together. How my arms have missed the feel of her. The ache of missing her is only fully clear now that she's in my embrace. The faint scent of chlorine lingers in her floral shampoo. Time ticks, but my arms hold tight. Life can change in an instant, and I don't want to waste this moment.

"My turn." Garrett's voice holds the hint of humor only I can recognize as fake.

Izzy steps back first, and I allow my arms to come together against my own chest. Izzy has changed over the last few months. Not only her body. There is something in her that seems harder.

Garrett threads his arm across Izzy's shoulder and pulls her to his side. "I've missed you, kid." He looks up into the cloudless sky, his jaw set firm.

"I've missed you too, Daddy."

A question assaults my heart. What if this wedge destroys our family? Is my freedom from the weight of my burden worth adding to the pain Izzy and Zachary already have to endure? A knot forms in my stomach. Too late now. I'll never have the choice back.

We step through the door and into the ornately designed living area. Intricate carvings along the woodwork give the feeling of richness to a home that seeks to give hope to those who don't have the extras in life. For the first time, I wonder what it's like for girls to step out of their lives and into this house. And for the first time, I can see the positive aspects this place provided Izzy. How could she ever have healed at home with the destruction of her parents' marriage cluttering our house?

"This is Stacey," Izzy says.

A blond woman steps forward, her face lit by her smile. I don't need to talk with her to know she's someone I would have liked under different circumstances.

"I want Stacey to sit with us while we talk about a few things." Izzy blows out a breath and moves to a long leather couch, but doesn't sit.

"I guess that's all right." I look to Garrett, but his face is unreadable. Are we really going to discuss private family matters with a stranger?

Stacey sits first. "It's great to meet you both. Izzy is such a wonderful young woman. It's been a pleasure getting to know her." She touches Izzy's knee in a way that speaks of reassurance. Like a mother would do.

The distance between the two couches lengthens and the air cools. I open my mouth to speak, to plead my case as Izzy's mother in some subtle way, but Izzy holds up a hand.

"There's something I really need to say before we talk about anything else. Do you mind?"

Garrett leans forward, his elbows on his knees and his hands clasped, all attention for his only daughter.

Looking Stacey's way, Izzy receives an encouraging smile.

"Go ahead, Izzy," I say. "We're here to listen." Why won't she make eye contact with me? She doesn't seem to have any trouble with Stacey.

Izzy cocks an eyebrow. "I'm going to keep my baby. I'd like to come home and raise her there with my family around. But, if that's not an option, it won't change my mind. This is something I have to do."

A soft smile takes a few years off Garrett's face. "Of course you can come home. We'll help any way we can."

He hasn't even looked to me for an opinion, hasn't cared what I think.

Or maybe he knows. I've been vocal about my desire for Izzy to place the baby. Looking at the rounded stomach and the tender look on Izzy's face now, I can't remember why I felt so sure. What makes me think I know what's best? Haven't I chosen all the paths of my own life?

"Mom?"

Garrett's eyes bear into me. No love. Only a lightly covered threat. Before I can contemplate the consequences, I nod. "Your dad is right. We'll do whatever we can."

Tipping her chin, Izzy's stare evaluates me until I drop my gaze to the toes of my shoes. Sweat dampens my chest, and I run my tongue across dry lips. Say no, and Garrett will be pushed further. Say yes, and Izzy faces a whole new world of hurts. I cross my arms and hold tight around my middle. The ache of my heart engulfs me. I'm a speck, watching the people I love live on, unable to do anything to help.

"Thanks. What do you think about my coming home for a few days? I think I'm ready to face my new life."

"No." I dart my gaze around the room. Izzy can't come home now. We need to have time, a chance to pull our own issues together. I see an image of the three of us traveling down the freeway in our heavy silence. How will we ever cover the distance now between us?

Garrett's palm grips my shoulder hard enough to demand my attention. "I think your mother wants a chance to get a few things ready. It won't take too long."

"Okay." Izzy's forehead crinkles. "If you're sure that's all right."

"It's your home, honey. We can't wait to have you back." Garrett stands and goes to her. She joins him, and he folds her up in his arms. Nuzzling her hair, he says sweet words I can't understand, yet I long to be a part of.

My body is a statue, part of the couch. The more my heart wants to reach for my family, the stiffer I become.

Chapter 30

Margaret

The door jingles and Curt steps in. "You ready to go?" One side of his mouth cocks in a crooked smile.

"Just about." I run a bar towel across the counter then toss it into the dirty bin. "Are you sure you want to do this? I really can handle it alone." I've already changed, checked my hair two or three times, and said goodbye to my coworkers. Yet I wish there was something keeping us from today's task.

He tucks his chin, sticking out his lower lip in a mock pout. "You're saying you don't need me?"

The obvious turn from friendly greeting to outright flirtation sends a jolt up my spine and draws the air from my lungs. "Officer Hobbs, you know that's not true." I pinch my lips together. What am I doing? I don't talk like this.

Before I can apologize his face breaks into a full grin, halting my explanation and bringing a smile to my own face.

"We'd better get to Mrs. Donovan's and pick up our little chaperone," he says. His gaze grows deeper, softer. Though the smile remains, it has mellowed into something rich and meaningful.

My face heats and my skin tingles. Quick, I look away while I still have a chance to break the spell. What is happening here? No way Officer Hobbs can see me as anything more than a charity case. He's Deven's mentor, that's all. But what does taking Caleb for a visit with his mother have to do with Deven? We've spent so many hours together in the last couple months. More time than I ever spent with my husband. Lifting my chin, I let my eyes drink him in.

He wipes a hand across his forehead.

"I'm ready."

His head snaps up. "Great. Right this way." He holds the door open as if I'm royalty, but his eyes don't mock. They don't even tease. Instead, he looks at me as though he's proud.

Thundering heartbeats rock my chest.

I reach for the handle on his Tahoe, but Curt jumps ahead of me and opens my door. With one foot in, our eyes meet. He holds me captive with only the tenderness of his gaze until my lungs cry out for air, and I realize I've stopped breathing, again. "Thank you."

He winks.

We don't speak on the five-minute trip from the diner to Mrs. Donovan's house, though my mind swirls with questions.

Before I can tell him to wait, he pops from the car and comes around to my side. This time, as he opens my door, tears form in my eyes. I blink them back, but a new wave takes their place. Only Travis has ever cared for me this much. The missing aches in my bones. Though I can now survive most days, when I least expect it, memories attack me and weaken my knees.

"You okay?" His hand touches my elbow.

I nod and wipe away a tear with my thumb. "Sorry."

He steps closer then takes two steps back. "We'd better get Caleb."

Has the air just chilled?

Mrs. Donovan meets us at the door, Caleb in her arms. His face glows with a drool-laced grin. "Now, you keep him safe, you hear?" Her gaze drills Curt.

"Yes, ma'am. I won't let the little guy out of my sight."

"I don't see what the point of this visit is. A baby has no place in there." Her eyebrows crinkle together and her lips form a tight circle.

I pull Caleb to my chest. "I love him too."

Mrs. Donovan's eyes pop open and she shoves the diaper bag into Curt's arms. "All right then. Get going." The door closes and Curt and I stand staring at each other on the porch step.

Curt shrugs his shoulders, places a warm palm on my back, and guides me toward the car.

With Caleb buckled in the car seat and the three of us driving toward the freeway, the reality of the day pours over me. I've never met my half sister. Maybe I shouldn't have let my father drift into a bad memory. From what I've heard, Nikki's life is a bunch of poor choices and sketchy men. What if she changes her mind and they let her have Caleb back? I'm weakened by the thought of losing him. I reach back and touch his warm belly. Caleb's tiny hand grips my finger.

"He's a blessing." Hobbs's eyes catch on me in the rearview mirror.

"He sure is. Caleb's restored our family in a lot of ways." My mind shifts to Deven. The boys have a bond. They've become brothers. "I'm scared."

Hobbs's right hand leaves the steering wheel. He reaches toward my face then pulls away. "I'm scared too."

"What are you scared of?"

"I'm scared that you and Deven will be hurt. I worry about Caleb, because I think he's in the best place he could possibly be right now, and I don't want anything to happen to him."

Looking away, I fold my hands together in my lap. "I couldn't keep him even if the state would let me."

"Why? You love him."

"It's not that. Look at all the lives I've messed up. I'm not any good at raising boys."

He doesn't respond.

◆ ◆ ◆

The images on television haven't prepared me for what a real women's prison visit is like, and Kane never bothered to put me on his visitor list. All around us metal clanks and voices echo. The caseworker meets us in the front office, and we are guided through security measures then placed in a secure playroom. Toys line one wall with chairs arranged along two others.

Curt drops into a lime-green seat, Caleb held out in his arms. The baby squeals with delight. It makes sense that Hobbs would be comfortable here. He is a police officer. I shudder. He's the one who put my son behind bars. What would Kane say if he knew we were here . . . together?

The reinforced glass door opens with a series of snaps and clicks. An officer leads a woman wearing an orange jumpsuit into the room.

As if sensing my need, Curt stands and places the baby in my arms.

Nikki looks everywhere but directly at me or Caleb. She's taller than I expected, even with the stoop of her shoulders. We have the same dark eyes, the same high cheekbones, but her skin is darker than mine. It's like whipped hot chocolate.

A woman who came in right behind Nikki settles into a chair in the corner without speaking. Her bright-blue eyes contrast with her soft silver curls. She seems to be keeping close tabs on Caleb.

The officer excuses herself, steps out the door, and stations her body where she can be seen through the glass.

I rock Caleb back and forth on my lap, my hold on him growing tighter until he squirms. Gratefulness swells and my heart opens up a place where I find compassion for the woman who's lost this little man.

"Would you like to hold him?" Funny thing, asking a baby's mother if she'd like to take her own son.

Turning her back to all of us, Nikki presses her palms against the glass. How can she move away from him? Doesn't she ache to smell the fresh scent of his baby-fine hair? Don't her arms hang useless without being filled with his wriggly weight? Doesn't she long for him when he's away the way I already miss every ounce of his goodness?

Flames burn my cheeks. How could she ever turn her back on him? Then conviction throws water on the fire. Hadn't I kept myself separated from my boys? Maybe the distance wasn't physical, but it was as real as an ocean between us. I'd built up walls to protect myself from rejection and to protect them from my curse.

I lean forward, tracing a curl along Caleb's temple with my index finger. A tear rolls down my cheek and into the crease of his neck. Curt's arm circles my shoulder and pulls me toward him. I tip my head onto his broad arm. With the back of one hand, I swipe away the tears and rise to my feet. "He's a wonderful boy. You should be very proud of him."

I sidle up next to the sister I've never met. "The doctor gave the go-ahead for vegetables. He loves sweet potatoes, but he spit out the peas all over Deven. Deven is my youngest boy. He's really taken to Caleb. Loves him like a brother." My voice catches on the last word. "The caseworker said you'll be out in another couple weeks. She thinks the judge would let you have him back when you get moved into the halfway house." I blow out a shaky breath. "We'd really like to stay in touch, with both of you."

Nikki's head turns and for the slightest fraction of a second, our eyes meet. Pain is etched across her face. She does love him. She has to. She must love him so much she can't bear to touch her own son. How can she raise him if she's afraid to let him near?

I shift Caleb to my other arm, and angle toward Nikki. "I've made a lot of mistakes in my life, especially as a mother. But I've learned the hard way. Please let me help you."

Silence hangs thick over the room. The drumming of my heart punctuates the wait for a response.

Nikki ducks her head. "I'm not feeling too well. I think I should leave."

Looking from Hobbs to the woman in the corner, I swallow stale air and hold Caleb so his cheek touches mine. "We're family."

"I don't have any family." Nikki raps on the door until the officer opens it. "They're ready to go."

Hobbs, the diaper bag already flung over his shoulder, puts an arm around my waist and nudges me out. The door slams, leaving the silent silver-haired woman and Nikki alone. And me with a fresh wave of grief ready to crash.

Caleb begins to fuss after the first set of heavy security doors slams behind us. His face shifts to a rosy color and the air fills with an unmistakable scent. "I'll need to change him before we head out."

Hobbs waves to the officer behind the glass wall.

He slides open the divider. "You're good to go."

"Do you have a place we can change the baby?"

I grab the corner of his flannel shirt. "No. I'd rather do this at the car." The sooner we leave the prison the better. Maybe I only have Caleb for another week or so. But for the time I have, I won't waste a second. Life and people slip away too quick, too easy. I have the now, and I plan to be very selfish with it.

"Sorry. I guess we've got it." Hobbs waves at the officer again.

A buzzer chimes as we take the last door to freedom. I inhale the outdoor air. "I couldn't stay in there. Not for another minute."

Hobbs pops open the back of the car and takes out the changing supplies, handing me each item as I need it. Caleb kicks his bare legs, happy to be clean and dry. I scoop him back into my arms.

Before I can evaluate what's happening, Curt pulls me into his chest, sandwiching Caleb safely between us. His breath blows warm across my ear. "I know. Me too."

I can't stop myself, can't resist the power he has to turn my walls into rubble. Resting my head on his chest, my heartbeat matches his.

The roughness of his palm cups my cheek, his thumb brushing across my lips. Tipping my head so our eyes meet, I soften further at the sight of the tears on his lashes. "I would do anything to protect you . . . and Deven and Caleb. Do you know that?"

My breath catches, and I know I do. I've known it for a while, but couldn't accept that someone so wonderful could love me. That Officer Curtis Hobbs could feel for me the way my heart feels for him.

He leans closer, his lips hovering above mine. Taking in the same air.

I blink. Is this real? Is this happening?

His eyes close, and I lift my chin.

"Mrs. Owens?"

Crack. We separate. The moment gone.

"Mrs. Owens?"

I peer around the corner of the car, my grip tight on Caleb, and my heart still pounding from the near-kiss. "Yes?"

The woman who sat in the corner, the one with the silver curls, steps closer. Her eyes are set on Caleb, her lips curved into a gentle smile. "Mrs. Owens, I'm Irene Smith." She holds out her hand to me.

Curt squeezes my shoulder, offering enough reassurance to help me take her hand, but when I look back at him his eyes are in investigation mode.

"What do you need?" I ask. "I was told no decisions would be made about Caleb until the judge ruled." I take a half step back.

"I'm not here to take the baby." Irene raises a hand. "I don't even work for the state."

"Then who are you?"

"I work at the maternity house where Nikki lived during the last few weeks of her pregnancy. I'm here as a kind of advocate, you could say."

"An advocate for Nikki?"

"For her, and for Caleb."

"I've taken real good care of him."

Curt runs his hand down my braid. "I'm Officer Hobbs of the Brownsburg Police Department. I can attest to what she said. Mrs. Owens has done an amazing job caring for this baby. She loves him very much."

"I have no doubt. And I think you're going to be happy with what I have to say. Nikki would like to sign over her parental rights to her sister. She's asked me to help her make the arrangements."

My face goes numb and my mouth falls open.

Curt pulls me into his side. "Will the state let her do that?"

"I've seen it done once before, and I plan to contact the same agency that facilitated that adoption. We've already talked to the caseworker. She believes the state will be in agreement."

My body wants to collapse into itself.

"Is this something you'd be open to?" Irene asks.

I look down into Caleb's round face. He reaches up and pulls my braid into his mouth. "I want him. Don't get me wrong. But . . ." I turn around, looking somewhere off in the distant mountains. "I'm not qualified."

"What do you mean?" Hobbs cups my jaw in his hand and turns my face to his. "You're a great mom. Caleb loves you and Deven, and you love them both back."

"Caleb deserves a family. Not a mom who barely makes ends meet and no dad. I was too selfish to see that with my boys. I won't do that to him too."

He pulls the baby from my arms and hands him to Irene.

Cold rushes over me even as the hot sun glares down on us.

He takes one of my hands and drops to one knee. "Margaret Owens, this isn't how I planned it, and the Lord knows this isn't where, but I've loved you since the first time you dripped hot coffee on my hand. I've waited for you while you figured out who God is, while you came to a place where I think maybe you can love me too. I hope you're at that place now because I'm tired of waiting. I promise to love all your boys as if they were my very own. I love you. Please, please be my wife."

My whole body begins to shake. "I can't ask you to do this."

He stands, taking my other hand. "I'm not doing you a favor. I'm asking you to do a huge one for me. I need you. I've spent every opportunity to be with you for years. I've drank thousands of gallons of coffee. I can't stand the stuff. But if I don't drink it, you don't come back to refill my cup. I'm really more of a cocoa guy." He winks.

His eyes are so generous, so true. Will I dull the shine? Will I regret my decision?

"Stop running crazy questions through your mind. You'll doubt me for a long time until I finally prove to you I'll never leave, but I can't wait for that to happen. I want to show you I love you. The real you. I want to show you for the rest of our lives. Are you in?"

I can't help it. The sweetness in his heart. The way he makes it sound like he's picking me first for his team. The way he leans forward as if he can't hold himself back. "Yes. Put me in the game, coach."

Before I can read his face, his arms are around me, and my feet are lifted off the ground.

Chapter 31

JILLIAN

Sinking down onto Izzy's soft mattress, I hug the teddy bear I've just laundered. The scent of baby detergent brings me back to the day I brought Izzy home from the hospital. That's when the guilt had really taken hold of my heart. When I held Izzy, and felt the intensity of love for my child, I couldn't help but let the what-ifs challenge the joy.

And some of the time the joy wasn't victorious.

The doctor and Garrett attributed the bursts of tears to postpartum depression. And I let them. How could I, with my daughter in my arms, explain that Izzy could never be my first?

"There you are." Garrett pushes a long thin box through the door and rests it against the wall. He pulls tools from his back pocket, leaving them in a pile on the floor. "You want to help?"

My heart ticks in my chest the way it used to when we first met. "Sure. What can I do?"

He rips the end from the box in one motion, sending cardboard dust swirling through the air. "Hold onto the crib pieces and I'll pull the box away." There's no inflection in his voice, but at least he's trying to include me.

Hardware falls loose and clanks onto my feet. "You picked a nice one."

"I felt like a fool in there. Grandfathers do not pick out this kind of thing."

I shrug. "Probably not, but you're special."

He stops, his eyes evaluating me.

"You're a great dad, and you'll be a wonderful grandpa."

His gaze drops to the disassembled crib. "Maybe so, but I'm not so good at being a husband, right?"

Tension torques my spine. "That's not what I said. You've been a wonderful husband to me. I take full responsibility for destroying our marriage."

"You think we're destroyed?"

"Don't you?" I rake my hands through my hair. "I can't imagine what's left for us. Why even pretend? Izzy will see through the act; everyone else does. You can't cover the fact that you don't love your wife."

Throwing a screwdriver down by his bent knee, his jaw clenches. "I didn't say I don't love you anymore. You said that."

"But it's true, isn't it?"

"Love isn't the issue here. Jillian, I don't know how to live with a woman who has so little respect for me that she lied and covered up parts of her life from me. Every time I look at you, I feel like you think I'm a joke."

I slip down, kneeling on the plush carpet. "I didn't tell you because I thought you were too good for me, too dependable. I didn't want you to see the dirt in my life. I didn't want to lose you, and that's exactly what I did. But I can't say I'd change things. The last twenty years have been so much more than I ever dreamed of. And if it's over now, well, I'm happy to have the memories and the two beautiful children. And I'll love you until the day I die."

The nasty ache in my chest constricts when I face this very real possibility. Heat flushes my cheeks and my throat swells with desperate emotion.

"It was my respect for you that became my excuse," I say.

He stands, looking around the room as if watching our lives go by. Then, extending his hand to me, he pulls me up. "Give me some help with the crib, okay?"

It isn't over, but the tiny snippet of normal, or a new normal, means there's still hope.

STACEY

Sun sparkles through the sheer pink curtains. I hold up a soft one-piece pajama with blue elephants. This is the one. I'll bring our baby boy home in this sweet outfit. Will he have a pile of hair, or should we bring the cap my mother crocheted? So many questions. So many uncertainties.

Three days have passed since Candice last answered one of our phone calls. But today, today we have an appointment. And today we should know for sure how close our son is to making his appearance into the world. Today is the due date.

I settle my hand on my chest, feeling the thunder of my heart. Sometime in the next two weeks this room will stop acting as a reminder of my heart's desire, and become the place where we will dream with and pray over our child.

A part of me can't wait a moment longer, but there's a bigger part that wants labor to hold off. Candice has come so far in the last weeks. She's become confident, like Adam claimed she'd been before. She stands taller, talks louder, and says more. She's becoming new. A new creation. Someone who I want so much for, and long to see blossom. When the baby comes, our relationship will make a sharp turn. I won't be able to guide her, to nurture or support her. My heart will need to be for my baby, and Candice will need space to adjust.

We'll all need time.

"There you are." Keith pulls my hair away from my neck and kisses me there, sending shivers across my skin. "What are you doing?"

"Just thinking."

"About the baby?" He takes the pajamas out of my hands and holds them up. "Are you sure he'll be this small?"

"I'm sure. That's not even a newborn size."

The phone in my pocket buzzes. I pull it out and show Keith the display. "It's Adam. Do you think?"

Wide eyes meet my gaze. "Answer it."

The phone shakes, and I swallow. "Hello."

"Hey. It's Adam."

"Is Candice in labor?"

The line is silent for too long. In the background, someone calls for Dr. Stevens. My heart speeds up.

"No. She's not in labor."

"But you're at the hospital. Is something wrong?" I hold one hand to my chest and Keith draws closer, listening with me.

"Everything is fine." The noise in the background grows muffled. "He was born last night."

Blood drains from my face. I lean into Keith, willing the tears to hold off enough to get the story. Long enough to understand what is happening.

Keith takes the phone from my trembling hand, pressing the speaker button. "Adam, it's Keith. What's going on?"

"I don't know, man. It happened so fast. And we . . . we just thought it would be good to do this on our own. You know, kind of have a chance to say goodbye."

Placing his hand behind my head, Keith pulls me into his chest. "We understand. This is a difficult situation. Can we come see him?"

There's too much silence.

Keith takes the phone off speaker and holds it to his ear. "Talk to me, Adam."

A moment later he hangs up.

Tears well in my eyes and constrict my chest. "Did she change her mind? Is she keeping the baby?"

"He didn't say that." He holds me out with both hands on my shoulders, his stare possessing my gaze. "He said we should come to the hospital."

Blood pulses behind my eardrums. "I don't know if I can see him if we can't bring him home."

"Don't jump to conclusions. We have to take this one step at a time."

I pick up the outfit where Keith left it on the changing table. "It doesn't hurt to be prepared." Testing a smile, the familiar sense of dread rises up my spine. Yes, it can hurt, but I'll go in ready for whatever we face. At least this little one is healthy. And Adam and Candice have come so far. My body quakes as I fold the material and lay it inside the diaper bag along with diapers, blankets, and the jeweler's box that holds the birthstone pendant we picked out for Candice.

◆　◆　◆

Gina meets us outside the hospital room. We haven't had reason to see the caseworker for several weeks. Her eyes are dipped with sympathy so deep words aren't needed. "We should talk." She ushers us toward a waiting room at the end of the hall.

Rabbits from Beatrix Potter–style illustrations weave a story in muted colors across the top of the soft-green walls. Keith takes my hand, and together we sink into the cushions of a love seat across from the chair Gina has pulled closer.

She leans forward, pressing her forearms into her legs and clasping her hands together. "Candice is rethinking her decision."

I bury my face in my hands, but I don't cry. Not because I'm not breaking apart, but because the weight of the emotion leaves me unable to do anything, including holding up my own body.

"This doesn't mean she's changed her mind. She's confused right now. This actually happens fairly frequently."

"This is normal?" Keith's voice is low, almost a whisper.

"I wouldn't go that far, but it happens. About half the time the birth mother decides to parent. The other half, she just needs more time to be sure." Gina touches my knee. The gesture feels too much like sympathy. "It's hard. But we want Candice to feel good about her choice. This is an important part of the process for her and for her baby."

She's right, but my mind is spinning, unable to settle on any thought for more than a split second.

"Would you like to see a picture?"

Keith covers my back with his arm.

"Yes." I reach out and take the cell phone as Gina offers it. The image melts into my heart. Not only is the baby beautiful, with full cheeks, long lashes, and the sweetest puckered lips, but Candice . . . There aren't words to describe the transformation. Her face glows as she looks down at the bundle in her arms. I slide the phone into Keith's hand. "Please, can you give Candice a message?"

"Of course."

"Tell her we'll be okay no matter what she chooses." I peer up into Keith's heartbroken eyes. His head bobs in agreement.

Gina's mouth opens and she looks back and forth between us. "Are you sure that's what you want me to tell them?"

Keith tightens his grip on my knee. "My wife is right. We support whatever Candice decides. Please tell her she'll be in our prayers."

It sounds like resignation. Maybe it is.

She stands, brushes at the front of her tan trousers, then leaves the room while we grip each other's hands.

"You okay?" Keith asks.

"I think I am. My heart is broken in two, but I can't blame them for wanting to keep him. And . . . I think she can do it."

"You're an amazing woman with such a huge heart. If we never have a child, I'll still be the luckiest, most blessed man on the earth because God gave me you."

I try to form a smile on my lips. "You're corny, you know."

He pulls me close and plants a warm kiss on my forehead.

"I was normal before we met."

Chapter 32

Izzy

The sound of the engine in the driveway draws my attention. *Lord, please let it be Cate or Irene.* I rock back and forth on the sofa as another wave of cramps makes my stomach tighten. I need someone who knows if this is it, if I'm really going into labor, or if I have a nasty virus. It's still three weeks until my due date. The muscles down my legs scream with a deep ache. Maybe this is what they mean by Braxton-Hicks. But if this isn't a true contraction, I'll never be able to live through the real ones.

I use the arm of the couch to heave myself up and waddle toward the door. Walking is difficult with a bowling ball wedged between my hips.

Before I reach the door, it opens and Stacey walks in, a brown bag dangling from her arm. She drops it by the door. I haven't seen her in a week, but right now, I don't care where she's been, or what she's been doing. I'm just so thrilled to see her.

"Hey there." Her tone is soft, but her eyes seem dark and her hair isn't as neat as usual. "How are you feeling?"

I look behind me to make sure that woman from the operating board hasn't come out of the office. "I'm not sure. I think I may be having some contractions. How am I supposed to know?"

Stacey's eyes go round as golf balls. She shrugs her shoulders. "Isn't Irene here?"

"No. And please don't tell that lady."

"Who?"

"The grumpy one from the board."

Stacey's face wrinkles. "Marian?"

"That's right." I rub a palm over my lower abdomen. "It could be a bug."

"Could be, but we'd better have you checked out just to be safe. Have you called your mama?"

I hold up a hand. "No. No way. We don't call Mom until we know for sure. She doesn't handle worry well." The thought of my mother pacing around, grilling the doctor, increases the sick feeling in my throat. "I don't want anyone thinking I'm a hysterical teenager who thinks every twinge is labor." At the word a tight band squeezes around my middle, taking my breath away and stopping my words.

"I don't think you're being hysterical. I really don't have much experience, but this looks like labor to me. We'd better call the doctor."

The office door swings open.

I grab Stacey's arm, pleading with my eyes for her not to tell.

"Stacey." Marian looks over the top of her reading glasses. "Did Irene let you know your driving application has been approved by the board?" No fluctuation in her voice, she seems uninterested in even her own comments.

"No. Thank you. That's handy." She winks at me.

I bite hard on my lip. No. Please.

"There seems to be a mix-up with Izzy's doctor's appointment. Now I can take her over myself."

Marian crosses her arms and looks me over. "You have an appointment scheduled this late in the afternoon?"

A contraction claws my belly. Forcing a smile, I nod.

"All right then. I guess you'd better be going. I don't know why Irene doesn't have it on the calendar."

Stacey shrugs, her smile a little too big. "I think it was a last-minute change."

Marian grumbles something about shoddy organization then disappears into the office again.

"Do you need your bag or anything?" Stacey asks.

I glare at the stairs, one hand on my tight basketball belly. "Those are getting longer every day." A drip of sweat trails down my cheek. Where did that come from?

"I'll get it."

"Thanks. It's on the desk by the door."

Stacey jogs up the steps, leaving me alone again. All I've wanted for the last week is a tiny bit of privacy. Well, now I have it. Now that the last thing I want is space from Irene, Sierra, and Cate. Stacey reappears, the hot pink and black diaper bag flung over her shoulder. God provided Stacey just in time.

I buckle under an intense contraction.

This is not my imagination.

STACEY

"Breathe, Izzy." We came right to the hospital, forgoing the doctor's office altogether when Izzy's contractions elevated to the point she couldn't talk through the pain.

She grips my hand. "Did you call?"

"Your parents?"

She nods.

The line on the monitor indicates the intensity of the last contraction is declining and Izzy's chest relaxes.

I wipe a cool rag over Izzy's sweat-glistened forehead. "I did. They're on the way and so is Irene."

Nodding, Izzy pulls my hand away from her head and holds it with both of hers. "Please don't leave me. This is harder than I thought."

"Do you want me to get the nurse and ask for the epidural?"

Izzy's pain filters through my body. It racks my gut and rubs against the rawness of my heart. Why isn't Irene here yet? What could possibly be taking her so long?

Tears pool in Izzy's eyes, and she shakes her head. Her face tightens and she squeezes my hand with the grip of a much larger person. Again the line rises on the monitor. Only a minute has passed. I can't be here when this baby comes. I can't see her tiny face. Not now.

I gasp for air as I realize I've been holding my breath too. "Breathe, Izzy." What if something is wrong? What if I can't hold it together for Izzy?

Leaning forward, Izzy's color turns from sick pale to red. Her cheeks extend.

"Wait, honey. The nurse said not to push until they said it was okay."

Her body relaxes again and she lies back on the bed, her eyes glazed as if she's left me here alone. "I'm sorry," she mumbles like a chastised child.

"It's okay. I'm getting the nurse."

"No. I don't want an epidural. I need to do this right."

"I know. I think she'll want to check you."

Hard sobs take Izzy's breath away. "I killed him. It's my fault. Travis will never see his daughter."

"No. It was an accident." I press the call button. "You've done a great job, Izzy. I'm so proud of you. And Travis would be too."

Our eyes meet. "Thank you for being here."

The nurse brushes through the door. "How are we doing?"

Deep grunts come from Izzy's throat.

"Sounds like we're moving right along. Breathe out short breaths and try not to push." The nurse does a quick check and smiles at me. "She's there. Let me get the doctor in here, and we'll have a baby."

How can she be so calm while Izzy works and suffers like she is? If I could take even a fraction of Izzy's agony, I realize I would do it. I'd pile it on top of my own pain gladly to give this girl a fresh breath of air.

Izzy grabs onto me and pulls herself up. We puff three breaths together then Izzy groans and pushes. There's no stopping her body from doing what it is designed to do.

Somehow the doctor appears at the end of the bed. He makes a few adjustments in the stool then places a hand on Izzy's stomach. The next contractions come with no rest in between. "Go ahead and push with this one."

"I already did," she says through clamped teeth.

The doctor smiles. "I can see that. Push hard, Isabella."

In an instant, before I think through my next step, I climb onto the bed behind Izzy and hold her body up as she pushes over and over again until a miracle fills the room with the lush, healthy cries of a newborn.

Izzy falls back into my arms.

Pure beauty rests in the gloved arms of the doctor.

"You did it. And she's beautiful," I say.

Tears run down Izzy's cheeks.

"She sure is." Irene's voice startles me. How long has she been here? Why didn't she take over? My body begins to shake. Squeezing out from behind Izzy, I settle her onto the pillows.

The nurse lays the infant on Izzy's chest.

"She looks like him. I prayed she would," Izzy says.

JILLIAN

The elevator doors swoosh open, and my heels click along the linoleum floor while Garrett's heavier thud follows at a slower rhythm.

"Can I help you?" The nurse drops a clipboard into a divider and turns her attention to us.

"My daughter is here, Isabella Cline."

"She's in delivery room twelve. Right over there." She points down the hall.

I speed toward the room, Garrett's thank-you fading behind me. At the door I halt, place my hand on the cold wood, and look back at him. "I'm not sure if I can stand seeing her in pain."

"You'll do fine." He pushes open the door just as a shock of a cry breaks through the hums and beeps of the hospital. I grab his hand.

The air is too thick to breathe. It holds me to the floor. She's here. We've missed it. Our only daughter has given birth to her first baby without her mother there to offer assurance and loving support. Isn't that the truth for her entire pregnancy? The guilt grows hands that grip my throat and squeeze.

Garrett doesn't urge me forward. His hand tightens over mine, his mouth silent.

A green curtain blocks the view of all but part of a doctor sitting on a stool.

"She's beautiful." The voice, familiar like someone I've once known, but yet with a different edge to it, both draws me forward and pushes me toward the hall.

I look to Garrett. "Who is that?" I whisper.

He shrugs, puts his arm across my shoulder, and steps forward, dragging me along beside him.

Around the corner, a blond woman, Stacey I think is her name, has tears in her eyes, her nose red and cheeks swollen. She sees us immediately. She taps Izzy and our daughter takes her gaze from her child and finds us.

Izzy doesn't speak. Only smiles in a genuine way I haven't seen in months. The kind of smile a mother feels all the way through to her heart when it pulses with the depth of love that takes her by surprise the first time she sees her baby.

Beside Izzy, along the side of her bed, someone else sits with her face turned toward the baby. Her long dress, in various colors, flows over her lap and down to the floor. Her hair, silver more than gray, curls in a soft bob at her slender shoulders. Even the intense love I have for my daughter and now my granddaughter can't keep my gaze from the familiar tilt of this stranger's head.

Stepping forward, I release Garrett's hand, my lungs squeeze, allowing only tiny breaths.

I come up behind her, close enough to touch her sleeve, but like it's a dream, I don't dare.

"Mom?" Izzy cocks her head, her eyes revealing her questions.

The woman turns, her face alight with the glow of happiness.

Then our eyes meet.

Any blood I still had in my face rushes away. My knees go weak, and I reach for the hospital bed for support. How can they do this to me? Is this some cruel joke?

I whip around, ready to run, ready to escape the laughter that will follow, but Garrett is right behind me. I slam into his chest. Before I can edge around him, I'm in his grasp. "Where are you going?"

"Mom? What's wrong?" Izzy's voice is edged with panic. Maybe she doesn't know.

I turn again. I'm stunned into silence, staring at the woman who echoes my expression, her hands over her heart.

"Jill?" She starts to rise.

Garrett keeps his hands on my arms. "You two know each other?"

My head bobs. "She's my mother."

Chapter 33

Izzy

In an instant, my life has taken another one of those sudden turns, leaving me grabbing for something to help me balance. One moment the doctor is handing me my daughter after what felt like an eternity of pain and suffering, only to have the horribleness of it disappear when I see her. I'm a mother. Her mother. Then, in another blink, I'm Irene's granddaughter. My arms tingle. The baby makes a soft coo, her tiny lips forming expressions without meaning.

Where are all these people now?

As soon as they settled me into this institutional room, everyone disappeared.

The baby fusses, her face glowing red, and she screams out. It's not like any cry I've ever heard before. It squeaky, almost muted, but desperate.

There's no one to help. I'm only seventeen. I'm a kid.

The baby's mouth opens wide and another shaky squawk lunges out of her.

I pat her back, rock her, then stare at the door again, but no one comes. With one hand, I grab the call button and press it over and over until a nurse rushes in.

"Is everything okay?"

"She's screaming."

The nurse's shoulders drop. She walks over and uses one finger to pull the blanket farther from the baby's face. "She's fine. That's not screaming. You'll know screaming when it happens, and it will happen." With a disgusted shake of her head, she leaves.

"Stop, please." I rock harder. "Please stop crying. I don't know what you want."

Someone taps on the door.

"Thank God. I don't care who you are, just please come in."

The door brushes open, putting me face-to-face with Mrs. Owens.

My heart finds a way to beat harder; the baby finds a way to cry louder.

"Can I still come in?" she asks over the noise.

"Yes. Do you know how to make her stop?"

Margaret Owens has never been the president of my fan club, but I'm desperate and my pride has long ago run out.

Mrs. Owens steps to the bedside. "May I?" She nods toward her granddaughter.

"Of course."

Scooping the baby into her arms, she nestles her close to her chest and pats her back. The screams die down until they're near-silent gasps for air. "She feels your tension." Mrs. Owens snaps her mouth shut as if she just cursed.

"It's okay, Mrs. Owens. You're right. I didn't expect to be alone with her so soon."

"I hope you can call me Margaret. If it's all right with you, I'd really like to be part of her life."

"You're her grandmother."

"So, we're family in a way." She tips the baby back and unwraps the blanket. Her gaze travels from the tiny toes to the little face. "She's so much like her daddy." Tears spill down her cheeks. "He'd be so proud of her. I know he would. Travis had a big heart." Her voice catches.

My chin shudders. Nodding, I try to get the words out. "I'm so sorry." The tears are like waterfalls pouring down my face and off my jaw. "It was my fault. If I could change things and bring Travis back, I would."

She steps back, turning toward the window, my daughter still in her arms. And I wonder if she's readying herself to let me have it. All the anger she must have toward me. All the hate.

"Hey, this shouldn't be a sad time. It wasn't your fault, Izzy. I should have told you. There isn't any excuse." She eases around, her gaze on the IV still in my hand. "Travis was at fault. Completely. Not you and not even me. He'd been drinking." Her voice trails off.

The smell of his breath comes back to me like something from a distant dream. Why hadn't I known? Again, it's my inexperience, my lack of knowing anything, that led me to this place. I press both hands over my mouth and let the guilty tears pour over my fingers.

"Please don't." Mrs. Owens is beside me, her hand on my arm. Her other holding my daughter with the confidence of experience I don't have. "Today isn't a day to grieve. It's a day to celebrate. I lost my son, and I'll miss him for the rest of my life, but we've been blessed with this sweet angel. What's her name?"

I pull in a breath that rattles in my throat. "I haven't named her." My voice still shudders with emotion. "I guess I couldn't really imagine her being here until she suddenly was."

"No ideas?" She pulls my blanket up higher on my chest, like a mother.

"Well, there's one. It's kind of odd for a girl, but I think it's cute."

Margaret runs a finger over the baby's cheek. "I'm sure I'll love it."

Where has the bitter, critical woman who hated me for the fact that I dated her son gone?

"I think I'd like to call her Carson."

A grin breaks across Margaret's face. "Travis's middle name. It's beautiful. You know that was my grandfather's name too. He was a preacher and a fine man. I always hoped Travis would grow up to be like him."

I wrap my fingers around Margaret's hand. "Thank you for coming. And thank you for loving Carson."

JILLIAN

"Mother?" I pace along the front of the chapel. Low lights and sun shine through the bright stained-glass windows, giving the room a dreamlike appearance.

A dream.

This could be a dream.

It makes more sense than my teenage daughter having given birth and finding my own estranged mother in the delivery room.

I put a hand on each side of my head and press. Part of me wants to lunge into her arms, but the other part is ready to scream.

Garrett has taken a walk down to the Starbucks on the corner to pick up some coffee and to give us a minute to talk. How can I straighten out twenty years of confusion in a moment's time?

Rather than jumping in with orders and demands the way I remember her, my mother sits on the carved wooden pew, waiting.

"How did you find Izzy?" It's the easiest place to start. Fire burns in my chest. How dare she establish any kind of relationship with my daughter without even a word?

"I didn't find her."

"She came looking for you?" Oddly, that seems somewhat fitting for Izzy.

"No."

I whirl around, hands pressed into my sides. "Someone came looking for someone. You didn't just bump into each other."

She cocks an eyebrow. "Actually, I think God did the work. It's only through Him that we're here together." She pats the pew beside her. "Come and sit, Jilly. We have a lot to talk about, and I have a lot to say."

She's grown older in the twenty years. Her silver hair frames a face with lines which could tell the stories of what I've missed. "How long have you been in Oregon?"

"I came back about ten years ago. After your father died, I married again." Her eyes sparkle and her lips tip up in a soft smile. "He was a retired pastor. A man with so much faith I couldn't help but seek after what he had. We were going to search for you. I promise. But we were also going to serve in Africa. None of that happened." Her eyes cloud over. "The cancer came on quick, and before I had time to really prepare, he was gone."

"I'm sorry."

"Thank you. You'd think I'd have learned not to let another day go by, but pride, it gets in the way. I did look for you, but I didn't know where to begin, and all I found were dead ends." She stands, wiping her hands on her skirt. "I found a new ministry when I came back to Oregon, and before I knew it, I was running A Child's Home. I'm the live-in house mother. Then Izzy moved in." She stops in front of me. Even four inches shorter, my mother has a power in her posture. "I didn't know who she was until today."

"How is that possible?"

She looks over at a window with a depiction of Jesus and Mary. "I don't know. It seems so obvious now, but she looks so much like her dad. I took to her right away. There was something special. Something familiar in her eyes. And her heart, she's such a deep and beautiful girl."

I warm inside. That she is. Izzy, even in the midst of this ordeal, is a woman I have always dreamed of being.

"God worked through a scary situation and brought about two miracles."

"Two?"

"He brought us back together, and He gave us a child."

I clutch my stomach, trying to put words to the hurt, but words aren't full enough. Is it even possible to mend this relationship? Isn't there an expiration date?

"I've carried the pain of what I did all these years. Jilly, I'm so sorry. It's not enough, but it's all I have to offer."

"I made the choice as much as you did. I could have refused. I could have done so many things in my life differently. Like not running away."

"Jilly, you've got to learn how to give up the guilt. It's only good when it helps you make wise decisions. You can't change the past."

"How do I stop hating myself?"

She laces her fingers into mine. "That's a question I've worked on for years."

Chapter 34

Izzy

I step back into my own home with my arms empty and my stomach somewhat shrunken. The living room is cool, nothing different. Nothing changed. The same quilt drapes the brown couch facing our well-used television. Peach curtains are pulled closed. Through the coffee table glass, I can see the same games still stacked below. In a way, I'm free again. The last nine months are gone, and I'm back in a time when life was shallow and easy.

Carson howls behind me as Dad makes his way from the car with her still buckled into the car seat. What are the neighbors thinking right now?

"She must be hungry or something." Dad's forehead is a mass of lines.

Mom steps around him. "I'll make up a bottle." She sets a brown bag on the counter and pulls out the cans of formula we stopped at the store to purchase.

Looking from my mom to the baby, I'm torn. Where should I be? What should I be doing? The ache in my muscles calls me to the couch, but the screams of my infant call louder.

The buckle doesn't want to give and Carson's cries become so intense while I'm working the strap that sound breaks off, leaving her in a silent agony edged with high-pitched gasps.

The clasp flies open, taking a chunk of my fingernail as payment. I lift Carson's tiny red body into my arms and hold her against my chest the way I've watched Irene, Grandma, do.

Reality is like a crazy dream. Irene, the woman who had become my support system through the toughest time of my life, is my grandmother.

Tears squeeze my throat and press from my eyes. How can I have enough tears to cry again? Shouldn't I have run dry by now? I'll wind up a shriveled mess soon.

Carson's cries soften against my neck.

"Here we go." Mom scoops the baby from my arms and cuddles her tight, rubbing the bottle against Carson's lips until she sucks it in. "Why don't you head into your room and get some rest?"

Mom settles into Dad's recliner. She wipes milk drool from Carson's chin with the corner of a receiving blanket.

I should be doing that. Even in the fog of sleepiness, I want to be the one to take care of my daughter. "You can't fix this for me by doing all the work."

Mom's gaze snaps up. "True. But, Izzy, you can't do this on your own."

"I can."

My dad's palm warms my shoulder. "Honey, your mom is right. You have school starting again in two weeks. You need to get your strength back. We'll work out the details of Carson's care."

I sink onto the couch. "I'm not a child anymore. You can't afford to have Mom home from work, and I can't take Carson with me to school. It isn't as easy as simple scheduling."

"My mom said she could come down one afternoon a week. That will help."

"Irene? Don't forget I lived with her for months. The girls up there need her. I can't take her away like that. Maybe Margaret can help out?"

Mom shifts Carson in her lap. She flashes a questioning look to my dad.

"I don't think that's going to work out either." He sits next to me, shifting my weight on the cushion and reminding me of what my body has been through.

"She's changed. I think we can trust her," I say.

Mom cocks her head. "It's not that. I'm sure we can trust her. I was so wrong about Margaret."

"Then why can't we ask her?"

"I didn't say you couldn't ask." Mom pulls the empty bottle from Carson's wet lips. Her little eyes are closed and her face relaxes. "She's coming to see Carson tomorrow. You can talk with her then." She exchanges a look with my dad that leaves me out as she tips the sleeping baby against her chest and pats her back.

"We should go to the Monks' and pick up Zach," Dad says, emphasizing the word *we*. "He's dying to see the baby."

"Do the Monks know?"

Mom settles Carson in my arms. "They do, and they're very supportive."

So much has changed. The way my parents look at each other. The way they speak about others. My mother. That's the real difference. Mom is not the same. What happened while I was gone and absorbed in my own problems?

JILLIAN

Holding Carson while looking at the calendar brings me back to the time when my own babies were tiny. I ached when I had to leave them and return to work. At the time, Garrett's income couldn't support our little family and pay off my student loans.

My dreams for Izzy were so different. I wanted her to have a choice. She could work if that's what she wanted, but she could also stay home with her children full-time. Too late for those dreams.

Four more days and I will return to my part-time job. Izzy will put off school for another couple weeks. Not even a daycare will take Carson before she's six weeks old.

The doorbell rings and Carson stiffens in my arms. I'll have to hang a sign.

Patting the baby on the back, I open the door and find Margaret chatting away with a giggling Caleb.

"I think he's grown in the last week," I say.

"I know he has. My arms ache." She makes a point of shaking out her muscles. "She's so beautiful, isn't she?"

I lean forward, placing Carson between us, her grandmothers. "Yes, she is."

Caleb puckers his lips and blows, sending a spray of slobber across both of our cheeks.

"Whoa there, buddy." Margaret steps back. "No showering the tiny one."

"Come on in. Izzy's asleep."

"No, I'm not." Izzy leans on the counter, her hair twisted in all directions, bags hanging from the dark area beneath her eyes. She yawns. "I'm up." She sounds like she's trying to convince herself.

I stand back, allowing Margaret room to come inside. "Good. Miss Carson has a couple visitors."

Izzy straightens. "Margaret. Mom said you were coming today. Who's that?" She comes closer and her eyes widen into perfect circles. "What are you doing with Caleb?"

Margaret splays her finger on the baby's back and pulls him closer. "How do you know his name?"

"He's Nikki's baby, isn't he? I mean the birthmark on his ear, it has to be Caleb."

Margaret runs a finger over the brown patch. "Yes. Nikki is my sister. And Caleb is my son now. Well." Her face breaks into a grin. "He'll be our son soon. We're adopting him."

"We?"

I sidle up next to Izzy, pulling her close around the waist. "Margaret and Officer Hobbs were married last week at the church. It was one of the most beautiful ceremonies I've ever seen. Simple and perfect."

With her bright new smile, Margaret still looks unfamiliar. "It's like a dream."

"Tell me about it." Izzy shakes her head. "I keep thinking I'll wake up and life will be back to normal."

"This is normal now." I go to the kitchen and turn on the burner under the teakettle. Returning, I hold an arm out toward Caleb. "Care to trade a minute?"

"Love to. Carson will give my arms a rest."

"I'll take him." Izzy pulls the boy into her body. "How've you been, little guy?"

He answers with the sound of a small airplane's motor and a spit shower.

"Sorry. Curt taught him that. He thinks it's hilarious." She shakes her head, but her face is glowing. "It's different raising kids with a good man in the house. I never really had that experience. Travis's dad was never there. He didn't interact with them at all, and then he was just gone. I'm not sure the boys even noticed the difference." She traces a finger along Carson's jawline. "Izzy, I hope you know I'll never question your decisions with Carson." Turning her attention away from the baby, her gaze lands on Izzy. "When the time comes, and the right man comes into your life, I hope you'll feel free to let him be Carson's daddy."

Izzy steps back.

"She's right, Iz." I tilt my head and make Izzy look me in the eyes. "Carson will need a father. Little girls need a daddy."

"No one will want me now. Anyway, Carson is fine. Babies need love more than anything else, and I have plenty of love."

Margaret's eyes darken. "I thought so too."

Chapter 35

STACEY

I pause in front of the changing table. Outside the nursery window, gold and red leaves swirl around the yard, the first to abandon their limbs. My heart mirrors the scene. Chaos twists my emotions into a storm both necessary and painful.

"Are you sure you want to do this?" Irene rests her chin on the back of my shoulder. "I believe with all my heart God will bring a baby into your life."

"Maybe so. Keith and I have prayed over this, and we both feel like we need to step back and let God work a miracle rather than trying to force one of our own. I'm not getting rid of everything. Just a few items that feel like Zane's."

The name still makes me cringe, Zane Zaner, but Adam and Candice are doing a fine job where it counts. They found a church and they're getting help from the members. They're set to be married on the first day of October. A happy ending . . . for them.

"Have you seen the baby yet?"

I nod. "Candice and I had lunch last week. He's gorgeous. And happy."

"You're an amazing woman. I'm proud of you."

I turn to her. "Coming from you that's a blessing to hear. But I don't think we'll see them again, and I couldn't have done it if I'd even held the baby once before they changed their minds." I let a smile warm my face. "I have a few things I'd like you to take to Izzy. Do you mind?"

"Of course not." Years have faded from Irene's face in a matter of two weeks. She's regained a youthfulness I hadn't realized was missing. And she wears earrings. When has she ever done that before? "Can you believe I'm a great-grandma?" Her face flushes. "I've missed so much with my grandkids, I don't want to miss anything with Carson."

The ache burns in my chest. How can I be so overjoyed for my friend and broken at the same time? "Please give Izzy my love. She's a special girl."

"Yes, she is, and I can say that with a clear conscience. I loved her before I knew she was my very own."

JILLIAN

News travels fast in a small town. It has a way of seeping under the doors like toxic smoke invading each home, one at a time, especially when the news is as smoldering as ours. The stares at the grocery store shouldn't surprise me. I duck behind a display of Oreo cookies to avoid a head-on confrontation with the associate pastor's wife.

My failure as a mother hangs like a thick chain around my neck whenever I leave home. But when I return, the links shatter and fall away. Carson sings love into everyone who sees her.

Emotions swirl in my chest. How can someone who never should have been conceived open up hearts to such deep love?

All the years of being and acting the way a Christian should present herself have cracked open and light shines in. He is a God of mercy and grace, both of which I've seen with my own eyes in the weeks since Carson's birth.

Maybe it's the lack of sleep. Carson screams every two hours from nine at night until five in the morning, but I've never felt so free and alive.

Until I leave home.

I shake my head. Carson is no one to be ashamed of, and Izzy may have made mistakes, but she's taking responsibility. She could have had an abortion. She could have kept the loss as an icy secret tucked into her heart for years. Instead, she's taken another very hard path. And my heart is so full of pride.

Standing with my spine straight, I walk around the aisle toward two women who have kids in the high school. "Good morning." I force my lips into a smile and walk on, willing my neck not to turn for a glimpse of their shocked expressions. Just to answer any questions other shoppers may have, I dump the largest box of diapers I can find into my cart.

My cell phone buzzes. "Hello?"

"Hey, it's Jasmine. I need your help. It's an emergency."

"What?"

"The baby who's supposed to be on the new brochure is sick. We can't afford to bring the photographer in again. Can you and Izzy please get Carson to the church in an hour? It's really important. I need you to do this."

My gut takes a tumble. Carson hasn't been out of the house since we walked her in the first day. Actually, neither has Izzy. But maybe this is just what they need. "Okay. We'll be there."

Izzy

"No way, Mom!"

"I already told her we'd do it."

My face burns. How can she treat me like a child when I'm someone else's mother? "Don't you think you should have asked me what I thought?"

"Iz, you don't understand. Jasmine has done so much for me."

I cock my hip. "Jasmine Monk? Are you serious?"

"More than you will ever be able to understand." My mom licks her lips in the way she does when she has something to say but isn't sure how to push the words out.

"What?"

Her face ages. "We'll talk soon. I promise. Can we do this for Jasmine?" It's like she's begging.

"Okay. I'll get her ready."

Carson is still asleep in the crib in my room. Waking her seems like the worst idea I've heard in . . . well, forever.

I catch my reflection in the mirror beside my door. I'm old. When will I ever get to sleep all night again? What will we do for money? How long can I let my parents support us? How can I ever handle school and a job, when I can only dream of a day when I'll be able to keep my eyes open for thirty minutes straight?

There's no point in asking the questions. There are no answers.

I pull the pink dress with the lamb on the front from the basket of baby clothes next to the dresser. She'll look so peaceful in this. Maybe it will trick Carson into acting the part.

I'm struck by how much I love her. The love is so deep I hadn't known I had it in me. I would literally lay my life down for this eight-pound bundle. The need to protect her from the world is intense. I'm beginning to understand why my mother suffocates me.

Slipping my hand under the baby, I cringe at the warm wetness. How can she sleep in a puddle with the sounds of voices calling through the house and traffic outside the open window, but in the middle of the night, with the lights off, the house still, and her diaper dry, she can only fuss?

I lay her on the changing pad, still on top of my bed from the last time. My pillow calls me to sink in and drift off into old, silly teenage dreams. Standing there, my arms hang heavy, the balance tipping to the side of sleepless haze.

"I've got a fresh bottle in the diaper bag, but there don't seem to be any wipes." My mom holds a zipper sandwich bag in one hand. "I thought we could put a few in this just in case we need them."

"It's only an hour, right?"

"That's what she said, but if you leave the house with a baby and no wipes, she'll need them for sure." She comes up next to me. Shoulder to shoulder we both look down on Carson as she stretches, her face wrinkling into a sour expression that will crack into a scream in a moment. "She's precious."

"I know." I tip my head onto my mother's shoulder. "Thanks for loving me so much."

"What are you talking about?"

"I mean, I'm starting to get why you do all the things you do. You love me as much as I love Carson. And, even though you really thought I should place her, here you are, doing everything you can to help me. I love you, Mom."

She sniffs. I've gotten to her.

"I love you too. Now let me finish changing my grandbaby while you get yourself together."

I run a hand over my crazy hair. It's like I've given up on myself. When did I become so content to look like this? Lack of sleep makes answering my own question impossible.

JILLIAN

The numbers on the dashboard clock constrict my throat. I've never been good at handling lateness, but today, being late puts extra pressure on nerves already burdened by worries. What will people say to Izzy when they see her with the baby? Will they be cruel? Will they turn away? We will surely run into someone at the church on a Saturday afternoon.

As I pull into the parking lot my fears are confirmed. There are more than a handful of cars. It's a particularly busy Saturday. I've been out of the office since Carson's birth, but I can't remember placing an event for today on the calendar.

Izzy slides open the van door and fiddles with the car seat. "I can't get this loose." Frustration laces her words.

Coming around the van, I take over, pressing the seat back down into the base and clicking the handle into position. I give a good heft upward and the seat releases. "You'll get the hang of it. At least you know she's secure." I smile at my daughter, hoping the expression will translate into reassurance.

Izzy's mouth tips in a sarcastic response. "Sure, Mom. Thanks." She reaches for the car seat.

"Do you want me to carry that? You look exhausted."

She cocks her head. "And thanks for that too."

I grin. "Your spirit seems to be coming back with a force."

"Ha ha ha. I have to learn to manage this on my own, so I'll carry the seat. What I'm really wondering is how moms lift these things with those huge kids in them."

We walk to the church's front doors. "Your muscles grow as they do."

"I'll look like the Hulk before she can walk."

I throw the door open.

"Surprise!" A rush of voices fills the foyer.

Jasmine comes forward from a group of twenty or more women. "Surprise," she says again. "We didn't think you'd had a baby shower, and we wanted to welcome Carson."

Izzy's mouth hangs open, her eyes wide and shiny.

My vision blurs, making it impossible to see who has come out to bless us in such a tangible way. "I can't believe you did this."

Jasmine hugs me. "We're proud of Izzy for making a hard decision. And we're here to say we'll support and encourage her in any way we can."

Izzy has taken Carson out of the car seat and holds her high against her cheek. Her mouth is open and her eyes are fixed on a sign hung on the far wall.

Placing a hand over my heart, I read the words. *Every child is a blessing from God. Welcome, Carson.* I touch my palm to Carson's soft back. "Thank you, Lord," I whisper.

Blinking away the tears, I take in each woman one at a time. All ages are represented, from a couple of Izzy's youth group friends to a woman who just celebrated her ninety-fourth birthday. Family.

And there in the back, her reading glasses hanging from a chain around her neck, is my own mother. I have no idea how Jasmine contacted her, but I'm shocked at how happy I am to see her.

But the real surprise is Margaret, who is nowhere in sight. There are days she seems to be moving forward, and so many where grief takes her down. The joy and sorrow all at the same time would be more than my heart could take.

My daughter tips her head onto my shoulder.

I put an arm around Izzy and hold the other out to my mother, and she steps into my embrace. Two generations have become four.

Izzy

"Mom?" my mother says to Irene. The word still sounds funny coming from my own mother's lips. "Can you stay for dinner?" We've returned from the baby shower, unloaded the van, and now sit in the living room in awe of the hill of baby supplies lying in front of us.

Irene kisses Carson's chubby cheek and hands her back to me. "That would be great. Now that I'm sharing responsibilities with the intern, and we have Stacey, I feel like I have all the freedom I need, while still getting to be the home-mom. The board was right. I was overwhelmed." She twirls a silver curl around her finger. "Stacey already said she could stay late."

I'm instantly struck with a not-so-flattering comparison. "She must be settling into motherhood better than me. She's already back at the house?"

Grandma Irene's lips curl down. "Things didn't work out how they expected."

I tip Carson onto my shoulder and pat her diaper. "What do you mean?"

"Candice and her boyfriend decided to parent the baby." She doesn't look up from her lap.

"What?" I pull Carson away and look at her cheeks, which grow rounder by the day. "Is Stacey okay?"

"She will be. In fact, she sent a few things for you to have for Carson." She walks to the door and picks up a handled brown bag. Setting it on the counter, she pulls out tiny yellow pajamas. "Isn't this precious?"

"Sure, but tell me more about Stacey." No one would make a better mother than Stacey Frey. Why does God keep taking babies away from her? "Is there another baby?"

Irene shakes her head. "It's not that easy. Stacey and Keith need some time to grieve before they start the process again."

"I feel just horrible."

Mom comes closer, putting her arm around my shoulder. "There's nothing we can do. Sometimes hard things happen."

"I know." I hold up Carson. "Trust me, I know. But it just hurts me to know."

Irene nods. "Me too."

◆　◆　◆

Moonlight casts shadows through the thin curtains and across my bedroom wall. I roll over toward the clock. Five hours of sleep in a row. That's a first. Yawning, I look toward the crib near the door. A tingle of fear runs over my skin. Carson's old record is a measly three hours. What if something is wrong? What if she stopped breathing?

Pressing my toes into the carpet, I rub circles over my eyes to clear the blur. At the edge of the baby bed, I reach in to feel Carson's tiny breaths, but my palm only makes contact with the cool cotton sheet.

I blink again. The light from my window is bright enough I can see that Carson is gone.

My heart thumps hard. I pull the door open and step into the hall. A voice, deep and familiar, floats over me. Following the sounds, I inch around the corner.

His back toward me, his head dipped, my dad is in the recliner, rocking back and forth. "You know, little Carson girl, you're a precious gift from a gracious God. You are a princess. A child of God. And as much as your mommy and grandmas and grandpa love you, God loves you even more."

He's said those same words to me over and over as I grew up. And I'd never been one of those people who questioned their value. I didn't sleep with Travis because I was looking for love. I didn't compromise because of a lack of self-respect. I just made a bad choice.

Unfortunately, the circumstance around that choice cost Travis his life and took so much from Carson. Things she'll never know are missing. Little pieces of the life she should have had down the line.

The greatest gift, until Carson, that God has given me is the blessing of a dad who truly and fully loves me. It's the gift I can't give to Carson. Only two weeks old and already there are so many things, so many memories, I can never give my daughter.

My cheeks burn and my chest tightens. Love hurts so deep. It hurts from the middle of my body, from the center of my heart. Carson is the reason for every breath I take, and the depth of love, that full commitment, isn't enough to give her the security I was given.

Maybe if I didn't know, if I hadn't been so fully blessed. Maybe then I could go on and not see the places I'll fall short.

But I do know.

And I will always see the holes.

There's a time when Carson and I will need to move out on our own. There'll be a time when Grandpa and Grandma become just that, her loving grandparents, not an extension of me. Not a replacement for Travis. There's no guarantee that I'll ever find a Christian guy willing to marry a ready-made family.

My body shivers with realization. As I sniff, the magic is broken and my father turns. The pain is still real.

Chapter 36

Margaret

Two dresses lie across my bed. One black, the other sky blue.

I bite the inside of my cheek and swish my newly cut hair around. My heart shifts every few minutes. Is today more like a wedding, or a funeral? Is it a day to grieve or a day to rejoice?

Curt closes in on me, Caleb clinging to his other side. "Having trouble?"

"You wouldn't believe."

"Try me."

I look up into his gentle yet wise and knowing eyes, and my heart softens.

Deven bursts through the door. "Dad, will you help me?"

Curt's eyes sparkle. He hasn't said anything, but it's obvious the new title means the world to him. "What's the problem, son?" They're a pair, airtight.

I pull Caleb from Curt.

He flaps both arms like a baby bird trying to fly.

"It's this tie." Deven pulls it off his neck and wads it between his hands.

He's never had a reason, aside from Travis's funeral, to wear a tie. Had he worn one that day? Those days are a blur of sadness. A time that only exists in a bad dream. The counselor who brought Curt and me through our brief premarital counseling showed me I can hold on to the good times I had with Travis. That it's okay to have rough days, and it's just as okay to have happy ones.

Joy does not mean I have abandoned my son.

I hook my finger through Curt's belt loop and rest my forehead on his back.

Curt threads Deven's tie around his own neck, flips one side over the other, and quickly arranges it in a perfect knot. "There you go." He pulls it over his head and drops it over Deven's, tugs it to fit Deven's neck.

"That looked easy when you did it. Can you show me how sometime?"

"Of course. That's what I'm here for." He musses Deven's hair. "You still need shoes."

Deven looks down at his socks then jogs out of the room.

"I think you're here for more than tie lessons." I twist around his waist. "God gave you to us, and we're going to suck everything we can out of you." I wink.

Curt palms Caleb's chubby belly and wiggles his fingers in a gentle tickle. "Your mommy thinks she's really funny, huh?"

Caleb's body jumps with giggles.

Curt takes him back into his arms. "Wear the blue." He kisses me, warm and soft, on the forehead.

Today is a day to celebrate, even in the pain. Today we will rejoice.

Jillian

Ladies from the women's ministry arrange finger foods on platters in the church kitchen. Never before has this task been done in such complete silence. Their quiet punctuates the fear swelling in my chest.

Is this my fault? It's the question that's hammered at me this past week. Did I push Izzy to this? Because from here I can see how wrong I was, and there's no end to my regret.

I throw open the back door and rush out into the icy wind of another harsh fall. Summer was too short, and yet it seemed to stretch on forever. Cold rain pelts my face.

How can I bear this? How can I keep breathing?

"I hope you don't mind." My mother steps up beside me. "I saw you come out here, and I thought you might need to talk."

I whip around. "I have to make this stop. Please, go tell everyone to go home. This can't happen. I can't . . ." Tears bite my cheeks and constrict my throat. "I don't want this."

"I know." She combs her fingers into my hair and pulls me close. "I know."

Pain-filled sobs rack my body. "I thought nothing could hurt like the mistakes I've made, but this . . . it's going to kill me."

"It won't kill you. I promise." She pushes my head back and wipes away tears with the calloused edge of her thumb. "This isn't yours to fix."

The words sound out of place in the moment, until they seep in. I can't fix this. I can't manipulate reality until it becomes something I can stomach, something I can pretend is genuine. Today and every day before and after are out of my control. "How do I live with that?"

"When you came to me and told me you were pregnant all those years ago, I wanted to fix it for you. I wanted to make everything okay again. But I only messed up all our lives. I pushed you into a decision you didn't want to make, and the consequences were brutal for both of us. Not a day goes by that I don't ache for the grandbaby I'm missing. I was wrong, in so many ways."

I shake my head. "I blamed you for a long time, but now, I think I may have done the same thing, even if you fought me on it."

"Maybe so, but mother's guilt is a nasty companion. No matter what may have happened, I live with what did happen, and my responsibility in that."

I blink at more tears. "I forgive you."

A weak smile creases her cheeks. "That means more to me than you'll ever know."

I lace my fingers into my mother's. "Will you go with me?"

"I wouldn't be anywhere else."

IZZY

Soft music fills the prayer room. I sit on the couch with Carson lying on my legs.

Her face has filled out and her body expanded. Only a few weeks old, but Carson barely resembles the wrinkled pink bundle we brought home from the hospital. What will she look like in a year? A month?

Will she continue to look like Travis?

Will the tiny wisps of dark curls make her look more like me?

Will she be tall and strong, short and thin?

Will she like sports?

Will she be an artist or an engineer?

The world is open for Carson. She is at the very beginning, and I am going to give my daughter all she needs.

Even if it rips my heart out of my chest.

My hands shake. I place one on each side of Carson's head. "I want you to know I love you. I love you so much. And Travis would have loved you too. But most of all, God loves you. Every day of my life, I will pray for you. And every day of my life, I will ask God to watch over you."

A tear drips from my nose and onto Carson's face.

She blinks her little eyes and bunches up her lips.

There's a soft tap at the door.

"Come in."

The door opens and my mother and grandmother come near. Both women look down at Carson. My mother's eyes are dry, but her skin glows pink under a freshly applied layer of makeup.

Grandma Irene lays a hand on my neck. "It's time, sweetheart. Are you ready?"

I take in a deep shuddering breath. "I'm ready." A sob shakes my shoulders. I stand, holding Carson to my chest.

Four generations meld into a hug.

The only thing protecting my heart from breaking.

◆ ◆ ◆

I stand in the back of the low-lit sanctuary. Piano music, the song I specifically chose, softens the tension.

The pianist finishes her song and the vocalist walks to the microphone. Exhaling, she glides her gaze over the small group seated in the first three rows on either side of the middle aisle. Then she pulls the microphone free of the stand.

The piano begins again. Carson is deep asleep, lulled by the music. The woman's angelic voice floats over me.

Carson's fist rubs across her face.

Every eye is on us.

The warm assurance of my parents and my grandmother behind me is as real as the cross on the wall.

We walk slowly to the front, me fully aware of keeping my shoulders straight and my head held high. I'm doing the right thing for my daughter, finally. The right thing for both of us.

At the end of the aisle, I stop.

The singer finishes her song and leaves the stage.

Our pastor comes forward. "Isabella, will you please come up here along with Carson and your family?"

I climb the stairs and turn. My eyes stay away from the people in the front row, but I focus on Margaret and motion for her to join us.

She hands Caleb to Officer Hobbs and comes forward.

"Carson is a very special baby," the pastor begins. "She is loved by so many." He goes on to lead us in prayer, asking God to bless Carson and watch over her all the days of her life.

I hear tissues being pulled from the box in the front row, but I still don't look. Not yet.

"Deven and Zach, will you join us now?"

The two middle schoolers, dressed in button-up shirts and ties, stand by Pastor Gordon. Between them they hold the box I decorated. Zach pulls off the lid and Deven holds the bottom.

"Each of these people love Carson and each of them have a special gift for her." Pastor Gordon motions them forward.

The boys bring the box to Margaret.

She blinks fast. "My name is Margaret Hobbs. Carson is my granddaughter. I love her very much. I represent Travis and the rest of our family. My son never got to hold his daughter. He was never able to smell her sweet baby smell, or see her beautiful smile. But he would have fallen madly in love with her. Just like I have." She blows out a breath. "What I want for Carson is belonging. I pray she will always know she belongs, she is cherished, and she is part of something big." From a bag, Margaret pulls a picture. "I'm giving Carson a picture of her father. She'll see the resemblance when she's older, but more than that, I want her to know he was a great kid." Her voice catches. "He loved fully."

Margaret lays the photo along with a baseball medal into the box.

I step up to her and hand my daughter into her arms.

Tears streak Margaret's face. She holds the baby close, rubbing her cheek against Carson's hair.

The boys move to my mom and dad.

Dad tucks Mom into his side in a way that gives me more comfort than a hug of my own. "This is a tough day for us." His voice shakes. "There are no words to tell you how much we love this little girl. Our prayer for Carson is that she feels how much she is valued. Not only because we love her, but because God loves her."

Mom looks up at him. She starts to speak, then shakes her head.

"We're giving Carson the Beginner's Bible we read to Izzy and Zach when they were little. May it start her toward a lifelong relationship with her Savior." He slips the well-worn book into the box.

Deven and Zach again step to the side.

Margaret turns to my mom, says something I can't hear, and transfers Carson into her embrace.

"I'm Carson's great-grandmother," Irene starts. "I'm Izzy's and Zach's grandmother, and I'm Jillian's mother. I'm a blessed woman, and I'm honored to be included in today's ceremony." She tips her head to Carson. "I want you to know, Carson, that love often requires sacrifice. That this life God gives us is not about ourselves. I pray that you always have a heart open to giving love and receiving love." She leans down and pulls a folding picture frame from a bag at her feet. Opening it up, she holds it out for all to see. "In these four frames are four newborn babies. The first is me, the second is Jillian, the third, Izzy, and the last picture is of Carson. But this is just the beginning. Our family is growing. But I'm not strong enough to hold the frame with every woman who will touch Carson's life and whose she will touch." She places the pictures in the box.

Mom wipes her cheeks and places Carson into Grandma Irene's arms.

It's my turn. My legs wobble and my arms seem useless without Carson in them. "I've already put my gift in the box. When Carson is older, she'll understand." Grandma hands my baby back to me.

Margaret and Mom lace arms.

I look down at my daughter, still asleep. "Carson, I love you more than I thought was possible. I love you so much that I'm doing what I feel is best for you."

Now is the time.

My eyes pin on Stacey.

Keith squeezes her hand, and they stand and come forward.

"Stacey and Keith have been waiting a long time for a baby, but that's not why I'm placing Carson with them. It's the love I've seen and felt from Stacey, and the fact that they can give my daughter all the things she needs. Most of all they can give her love and a family. This is the hardest thing I've ever had to do, but I want Carson to have a mommy and a daddy, just like I had." I look back at my dad.

His eyes are wet with tears, but his nod shows me he's proud. Coming closer, he whispers reassurance in my ear.

The tears come fast now, running down my face.

Carson exhales a soft baby coo.

"Stacey and Keith, God brought you into my life, and I believe it was for this moment." I lean down and kiss my sweet baby's cheek. "This is your daughter." With shaking arms I hand the bundle into Stacey's waiting embrace.

STACEY

All the times in the past when I've said the word *bittersweet*, those times were wasted, because until this very moment, I didn't really understand the meaning of the word.

Torn between Izzy's sacrifice, the sound of sniffling noses, and the feeling of completion that having Carson in my arms gives me, my heart wavers between utter joy and solid sadness.

Can we really walk out of the church with this perfect little girl and start our family? Can I survive the agony of Izzy's pain?

I study Carson's pucker of a mouth, so precious, so gentle.

When I look up, I find Izzy smiling at me.

"How does it feel?" Izzy asks.

The question is too big, too full, too wide. How does it feel to be in this moment where my joy cuts into so many people's hearts? I can't put words to the truth of the emotion. "Bittersweet. It's bittersweet."

Jillian peers over my shoulder. "My daughter is a very smart woman. Listen to her. You're going to be a great mom."

Without warning, the silent tears that prickle my eyes turn into a torrent. I lean my face closer to my daughter. "Thank you. I can't tell you how honored we are." I slip one hand away from Carson and wipe at my face. "Thank you."

Warmth surrounds me with the arms of all the women who love Carson, and who I now love for their sacrifice.

"Thank you." Jillian brushes hair off my face. "Thank you for letting us pass Carson into your arms and for giving us this special moment."

Her husband reaches out to shake Keith's hand, then draws him into a masculine hug.

There's so much more here. We've become parents, and at the same time, we've received another extended family.

Chapter 37

JILLIAN

TWO MONTHS LATER

The scent of turkey already fills the air in the entire house. Did I put it in too soon? What if it's dry?

I wipe my wet hands on a kitchen towel then pull open the oven door. Hot steam slaps me in the face, burning my eyes. Brown crackling covers the surface, but the little red indicator hasn't popped yet. It could be wrong though. I close the door.

"Don't worry." Garrett's deep voice comes from behind me.

I turn.

He leans on the counter that divides the kitchen from the family room, fingers laced, elbows bent.

"I should have waited to put the turkey in."

"That's not what I'm talking about."

I cock my hip.

"You're worried about Izzy."

How does he see into me like that? "Aren't you?"

"Sure. But I'm excited too." One side of his mouth tips up into an awkward smile.

The days after the placement ceremony were hard. Izzy cried at any mention of Carson or any other baby. I found her in the middle of the night curled up on the couch with one of the blankets that hadn't gone with Carson. Over time Izzy has settled into her new life. She's gone back to school and become very close with a girl from church. And last week, she started filling out college applications.

Garrett comes around the counter. "She's going to be fine. And so are we." Taking each of my hands, he lifts one and kisses my knuckles. "Didn't you commit to giving up control?"

I want to be angry at his statement. I want to throw the words of our counselor back in his face. But Garrett is right. And I can't deny my marriage is better now than it ever was.

"I hear a car." Garrett steps away.

My middle bubbles with nerves. I peek out the kitchen window toward the road. The same place I once saw Travis's car now holds a minivan filled with the Hobbs family. Zach runs through the yard and disappears with Deven. A year ago, I'd never heard my son mention his name. Now they are best friends. How the year has changed us all.

Margaret steps out. She looks different, happy but still with a hint of sadness about her eyes. I toss the towel in the sink and rush out to join Garrett. And to get my turn with Caleb.

Before I can get there, another car pulls up.

We're all silent as Keith parks.

My hand warms when Margaret takes hold. "I can't believe this."

I turn and look her in the eyes. "Me either. I don't know what's wrong with me. We're blessed. We have family." I follow Margaret's gaze back to the house.

Izzy stands on the front porch, her arms crossed in front of her chest, her mouth a straight line.

The back door opens and Stacey steps out, Carson in her arms.

Izzy's face breaks into a smile, and she jogs across the lawn, hugging Stacey first then taking Carson.

Garrett leads us all inside.

The tables, borrowed from the church, fill the family room. I've covered them with deep-orange cloths and set fall-themed dishes out. Steam billows as potatoes boil on the stove. Bowls of cranberry relish sit with plates of butter and dishes of olives.

I open the oven. The indicator has popped. Covering my hands with oven mitts, I lift the twenty-pound bird onto the cutting board and inhale the rich scent of turkey cooked with butter and rosemary.

"Can I help?" My mom's voice is eager. It's been tough at times, putting the past away and moving forward with her, but something is growing where the void used to be. She comes down regularly, now that she shares the responsibilities of the house with another woman. I think we'll make it.

I lean against the stove, my back warmed by the heat of the oven. There, at the edge of my kitchen, is Mom, and Margaret, and Stacey, and Izzy, and Carson.

Beautiful women.

Made in the image of God.

Brought together in tragedy.

Connected by blessing.

Family.

Acknowledgments

Writing stories is an honor. I hope you've enjoyed the look into these women's lives as much as I enjoyed committing it to the page.

This story has a special place in my heart, not because this is my story, but because I've been blessed by adoption in different ways.

Family is not formed by biology but by love. I learned this as a very young child. My grandparents, not by blood but by choice, loved me with a depth and width that changed the course of my life and the generations to come after me. Their decision to step in and love me, no matter what they had to give up, will forever be one of my greatest blessings.

Little did I know that, many years later, adoption would again touch my heart. I don't want to miss this opportunity to thank the birth mothers who gave me the blessings of motherhood. I'm in awe of your strength, love, and determination.

Children and families deserve the best chance possible. People such as those involved in Every Child Oregon dedicate their time to serve vulnerable children and families in our communities. As I went through these pages, considering the role Irene played in the lives of Izzy, Sierra, and Nikki, I found myself thinking of women like Tyan, Kim, Claudette, and Andrea, as well as many others who invest their love freely. Thank you!

A book is the compilation of effort and support given by many people. I could not do this without my husband, Jason. He is my opposite and my perfect match. And my kids, they're the right kind of weird. Thank you for making me smile, supporting my crazy ideas, and making life fun.

I loved getting to work with Dawn Anderson again. She is such a great editor and teacher. Thanks, Dawn.

Kregel Publications blesses me over and over. Thanks to everyone there who puts up with my emails, my questions, and my mistakes. There's not enough chocolate in the world to properly thank you all.

Thank you to my former agent, Karen Ball, for representing this project and giving me a chance at this incredible job.

Thank you to my agent, Cynthia Ruchti. You push me to be better, and I love you for that! It's an honor to be represented by such an amazing author and person.

Thanks to Jodie Bailey, who prays for me, challenges me, and holds me accountable. I would never get to the end without you.

Thanks Karen Barnett, Heidi Gaul, and Marilyn Rhoads, who make up my critique group and who are wonderful friends. You are all such great writers, and I love that I get to share this with you!

I've been given so much more than I deserve, and I thank the Lord that He saw fit to bless me so richly.

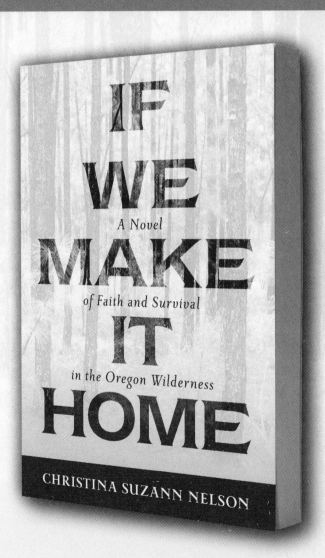